**'I am looking forward to Elizabeth's ball,' Sarah said, gazing up at him.**

'You have not forgotten your promise to me, sir?'

'How could I?' John asked, his eyes intent on her face. He realised that he wanted very much to dance with her, to hold her close, hear her laughter and inhale the intoxicating perfume of her skin. Surely there was no sin in letting himself admit the feelings he had for her? 'I am looking forward to it, Sarah—and I hope you will keep two dances for me.'

Sarah glowed in the warmth of his smile. Her heart had begun to race wildly and she was sure that he felt something for her.

'No matter who asks, I shall not give your dances away,' said Sarah.

'Good.' He reached for her hand, holding it with a firm, gentle grip. His touch sent a tingle winging down her spine, making her want to melt into his arms. 'We are friends, are we not, Sarah? We have always liked one another?'

'Yes, of course.' Sarah hesitated, then, 'It might perhaps have been more once, had I not been such a foolish child…' She caught her breath as she saw the look in his eyes.

## Author Note

In the late eighteenth and early nineteenth century there was a passion for gothic novels. When huge old houses were lit by candlelight and there were none of today's modern conveniences, it must have been gorgeously frightening for society ladies to read of young girls cruelly locked away and at the mercy of evil men. How much more terrifying would it be for a young girl stolen from the bosom of a loving family to be forced to take part in a satanic ritual? And think of how her family must have suffered when she could not be found! But in the age of Romance there were at least three brave men willing to walk through hellfire for the sake of the women they loved.

This trilogy deals with the abduction of Miss Sarah Hunter and the search for her by her brother Charles, the Earl of Cavendish and Mr John Elworthy. It began with Elizabeth Travers and the Earl of Cavendish, and continued with Charles Hunter and Lady Arabella Marshall, ending in this last book with Sarah's own story.

The element of darkness is balanced by the thrill of romance, and I hope you will love reading it as much as I enjoyed writing it for you.

# A WORTHY GENTLEMAN

Anne Herries

MILLS & BOON®

First published in Great Britain 2007
Large Print edition 2007
Harlequin Mills & Boon Limited,
Eton House, 18-24 Paradise Road, Richmond, Surrey TW9 1SR

© Anne Herries 2007


ISBN: 978 0 263 19401 2

Set in Times Roman 15¼ on 17¾ pt.
42-0807-88806


Printed and bound in Great Britain
by Antony Rowe Ltd, Chippenham, Wiltshire

**Anne Herries**, winner of the Romantic Novelists' Association ROMANCE PRIZE 2004, lives in Cambridgeshire. She is fond of watching wildlife, and spoils the birds and squirrels that are frequent visitors to her garden. Anne loves to write about the beauty of nature, and sometimes puts a little into her books, although they are mostly about love and romance. She writes for her own enjoyment, and to give pleasure to her readers.

**Recent novels by the same author:**

THE ABDUCTED BRIDE
CAPTIVE OF THE HAREM
THE SHEIKH
A DAMNABLE ROGUE*
RANSOM BRIDE

*Winner of the Romantic Novelists' Association ROMANCE PRIZE*

**and in the Regency series *The Steepwood Scandal*:**

LORD RAVENSDEN'S MARRIAGE
COUNTERFEIT EARL

**and in *The Elizabethan Season*:**

LADY IN WAITING
THE ADVENTURER'S WIFE

**and in *The Banewulf Dynasty*:**

A PERFECT KNIGHT
A KNIGHT OF HONOUR
HER KNIGHT PROTECTOR

**and in *The Hellfire Mysteries*:**

AN IMPROPER COMPANION
A WEALTHY WIDOW

# *Prologue*

The man bent to lay a single yellow rose on the freshly turned soil. For a moment he stared at the inscription on the simple wooden cross, reading the words aloud, as if he wanted to hear them. As if only by saying them out loud could he believe that it was true.

'Here lies Andrea, wife of John and mother of Nathaniel. May God keep and love her for all time.'

Tears trickled unashamedly down his cheeks so that he tasted their salt on his lips. He was weeping for the waste of it, for the loss of a young life and the bitterness of despair.

'Forgive me,' he said. 'I failed you. You asked me to save you and I couldn't. I am sorry…so sorry. I should have done more…I am so sorry, Andrea.'

His mind was tortured with regret, with the sense of failure and guilt. He thought of the empty house awaiting him, the shadows that gathered in its dark corners and taunted him in the watching hours.

Turning away at last after a long, cold vigil, his heart heavy with regret, he did not notice that hostile eyes had been watching him from a distance. Because he did not look back as he walked away, he did not witness the figure that took his place by the side of the lonely grave—lonely because it had not been permitted on sacred ground. Andrea Elworthy had taken her own life and was therefore buried outside the churchyard, on a hillside and sheltered beneath the protective arms of an ancient oak tree. It was the best John Elworthy could do for his late wife, but it did not please the one who now wept bitter, angry tears at her grave.

Perhaps it was as well for his peace of mind that John did not know his rose had been snatched from the grave and torn to pieces. He was unaware that he had an enemy…an enemy bent on revenge.

'I am sorry that you are leaving, Signorina,' the man said, giving the lovely girl at his side a soulful look. He was tall, dark haired and his smile was very attractive. 'Is there nothing I can do to persuade you to stay here in Italy?'

Sarah Hunter smiled. It was so warm and peaceful here in this beautiful garden that she was tempted to stay. Conte Vittorio Vincenzo di Ceasares had been a constant friend to them since they had first taken this villa in the hills of Tuscany. He had asked her to marry him twice and she had refused in such a way that she had kept him her friend. Her gentle dignity and her smile had enchanted him, bringing him back to her again and again like a moth to the flame.

'We must return, sir,' she said. 'Mama wishes to see her grandson. She misses her friends in England, even though we have made so many new ones here. It will be hard to part with them, of course, but Mama longs to be home by the summer.'

'I shall miss you,' he said, his dark eyes intense as they dwelled on her lovely face. There was something unforgettable about her, something that made him want to cherish her and keep her safe. 'But perhaps you will return to us one day?'

'Perhaps.'

Sarah stopped to pick a rose, holding it to her nose to inhale its fragrance. The sunshine of Italy had healed her spirit. She was no longer the sad, nervous girl she had been when they arrived. She was a woman, much admired and sought after. Vittorio had not been the only gentleman to offer her marriage during her stay in Italy.

Sarah believed that her fear of marriage had gone.

The nightmares caused by her abduction from the gardens of her home over three years ago were a distant memory. Yet she had never felt any inclination to marry any of the wealthy, titled and, in Vittorio's case, handsome men who had proposed to her. Perhaps if one particular English gentleman had travelled to Italy as she had hoped he might…if John had asked her to marry him or written to her…but she knew that he had taken a wife six months after she'd left England.

It was more than two years now since they had come to Italy. Sarah had forgotten most of the things that had hurt her—but she could not forget John Elworthy. She had believed that he loved her, but he had married so soon after they parted. If his feelings for her had been real, he would not have done that, and it was foolish to think of him. She had tried to put the memory of his smile from her mind, and sometimes she thought that she had succeeded.

She smiled and handed her rose to the handsome man hovering attentively at her side. 'Perhaps we shall meet again one day,' she said. 'Keep that in memory of me, Vittorio.'

He took the rose, placing it inside his coat, next to his heart. 'I shall never forget you,' he told her with a wistful look. 'But I think that you will soon forget me when you are home.'

## Chapter One

'Oh, Sarah, it is so good to see you again,' Arabella said to her sister-in-law. They hugged each other in mutual delight. 'We were so pleased when your mama's letter came telling us that you were returning to England. As you know, Charles intended that we should come out and visit you this year but...I am afraid something changed our plans.' She laid a gentle hand on her stomach. She was hardly showing yet, though into the fourth month of her second pregnancy. Her son Harry was now a year old, a sturdy little child already able to stand and take a few steps about his nursery without help.

'You look blooming,' Sarah said. 'You are even lovelier than I remembered, Belle. Motherhood and marriage must suit you.'

'Yes, indeed it does,' Arabella agreed. 'I never knew life could be so wonderful, Sarah. Charles is all that I could ask of a husband, and I believe he is happy too.'

'I am sure he is,' Sarah agreed. She glanced around the sitting room. Arabella had made some changes since she had last seen it, which Sarah liked and approved, though she was not sure that her mother did. However, Arabella was the mistress here now, and by rights Mrs Hunter should be living in the Dower House elsewhere on the estate. 'I love this duck egg blue, Belle. It is such a soft, restful colour. I remember this room was a rather dull shade of green before. I think that light colours like this bring peace and elegance to a room.'

'The green was perhaps a little too dark for my taste,' Arabella said. 'But what about you, dearest? You look very well. I think Italy must have been good for you?'

'Yes, it was,' Sarah said. 'We were lucky enough to take a lovely villa in the hills of Tuscany. It is owned by the Conte di Ceasares and he lives in a larger house quite near by. He visited often and invited us to meet all his acquaintances. We made lots of wonderful new friends because of his kindness. He was sorry to see us leave.'

'Yes, I expect he was.' Arabella's eyebrows went up, a little smile on her lips. 'Your mama told me she thought he was in love with you—was he?'

'Yes, I think so, just a little,' Sarah said, a faint blush in her cheeks. 'He is rich, handsome and generous, Belle. Mama was cross because I did not encourage him. She does not know that he asked me to marry him and I would prefer that she did not. She is a little impatient over the subject of marriage. She says it is impossible that I remain unwed for ever—and she thinks I should have forgotten all that nonsense of the abduction by now.'

'Have you forgotten it?' Arabella asked, looking at her with warm affection. They had become so close in the months after Sarah's abduction, perhaps because the girl had been very ill after she'd escaped from her captors. For a long time she had not even known her own name. It would not be surprising if she still carried mental scars. 'Has time erased the fear from your mind?'

'Yes, I believe it has,' Sarah told her, wrinkling her brow. It all seemed so long ago now; in the warmth of Italy's sunshine, she had forgotten the dark depressing days of her illness. 'I did consider marrying Vittorio after I heard that John was married. He is kind, generous and very charming, Belle. I like him better than most of the others…'

'There were others?'

'Oh, yes, several…' Sarah laughed at her sister-in-law's teasing look. 'One of them was Captain

Hernshaw. We met him when we were in Rome for a visit. He didn't actually ask me to marry him, but he seemed to enjoy my company and I think he might have had I given him some encouragement. At times he was a little sad and I believe I reminded him of home.'

'Captain Hernshaw?' Arabella nodded, remembering the gentleman for his kindness. 'He may have saved my life the day Sir Courtney tried to kill us both, Sarah. I always liked him. He might be a good choice if you wished to marry…' She hesitated for a moment, and then, 'Have you heard about John?'

'John Elworthy?' Sarah's heart caught a beat. She looked at Arabella intently. 'What about John?'

'You said that you knew he was married?'

'Yes, I had Charles's letter.'

'His wife gave birth to a son seven months after they were married. I heard that she fell down the stairs and that was why the baby was born early…' Arabella paused, feeling uncertain. Sarah's eyes were shadowed with some painful emotion and she almost wished she had not begun this, and yet it might be best if it came from her. 'Andrea killed herself six months after her son was born. John tried to convince everyone that she was ill and didn't know what she was doing, but the church refused to allow him to have her buried in consecrated ground.'

'Oh, no!' Sarah cried, looking shocked. Her own pain was forgotten as she thought of what he must have suffered. 'That is awful for poor John. He must have felt wretched. Why did she kill herself, Belle? What can have made her do such a terrible thing?'

'No one knows for certain. I don't think John understands it—though I know he blames himself for her death. He says that the birth of the child had pulled her down, upset the balance of her mind…that she must have walked into the river in some frantic fit of despair.' Arabella also sensed that there were thoughts that John did not share with his friends, for she had seen the shadows that lurked in his eyes and knew that he was tormented by his wife's suicide.

'That is such a terrible thing to happen,' Sarah said and tears stung her eyes as she pictured John's distress. 'He must have been so distressed. He could only have been married a short time.'

'Just over a year in all,' Arabella said. 'I know how it feels to lose someone you love, Sarah—but my first husband died a hero. John bears the burden of his wife's shame and her illness. I have seen him only once since the funeral, but Charles has visited with him for a few days. He says that John blames himself for her death and I am sure he is right. It is hardly surprising that he should feel it so deeply. You know how gentle and caring John has always been, Sarah.'

'Yes, I do,' Sarah agreed and her throat was tight with emotion. 'But I am certain that he has no reason to blame himself. His wife must surely have been ill?'

'That is what Elizabeth and Daniel both say,' Arabella said. 'I am not sure if you know the Earl and Countess of Cavendish? They live quite close to John and knew his wife a little, though she did not go out often. I only met her twice. That reminds me, Daniel and Elizabeth are coming to stay with us in a few days so you will meet them then.'

'I remember the earl,' Sarah said. 'He and Charles were friends before I was abducted. It was the earl who first discovered what had happened to me, wasn't it?' She nodded as Arabella confirmed it. 'Yes, I thought so. I don't believe I have met his wife, though.'

'You will like Elizabeth,' Arabella said confidently. 'She is one of my best friends now. We visit each other often. Elizabeth has twin sons of about Harry's age. She would like a daughter, but as yet it has not happened for her.'

'She is lucky to have her sons,' Sarah said, a slightly wistful look in her eyes. She had held her nephew Harry and the feel of his soft, warm body in her arms had made her feel decidedly broody. 'As you are to have yours, Belle. Do you want another boy or a girl this time?'

'I really do not mind,' Arabella said, a look of serenity on her face. 'We are quite happy to have whatever God sends us, Sarah. Another boy or a girl will be equally loved.'

'Yes, of course,' Sarah said and held back a sigh. She could not help envying her sister-in-law her obvious contentment with life. Such happiness would be denied to her, unless she married. 'Mama keeps telling me I should marry, Belle. I think it would be all right. I am not afraid of being touched by a man now, as long as I truly cared for him, that is—but I haven't found anyone I can love. Is it foolish of me to hope for it? I want to be loved and happy the way you and my brother are. Or should I marry for position and comfort as Mama seems to think I ought?' She frowned, for it seemed to her that she was unlikely to fall in love again. She had met several attractive and charming gentlemen in Italy, but none of them had touched her heart.

'I think you should wait until you are certain,' Arabella told her. 'You have a month here with us before the Season starts. Just relax and enjoy yourself, dearest. Charles will be on your side whatever you want, you know that, Sarah. He wouldn't let your mama push you into an unwise marriage.'

'Thank you, dearest Belle,' Sarah said and laughed. 'I dare say Mama is right. I ought to marry one day, but I do not want to marry anyone I cannot love.' She sighed and a wistful look came to her pretty face. 'Oh, I don't know…' It was foolish to look back. She had to move on, to leave the nightmare of the past behind.

Arabella kept her thoughts to herself. She had not forgotten that time before Sarah left for Italy. She had sensed there was something special between the girl and John Elworthy. In fact, she had been quite shocked when John married so soon afterwards. She had gone to his wedding, thinking that the slight, pale girl he had taken for his bride was not the equal of Sarah in either looks or intelligence. She had seemed desperately shy of all her husband's friends, even nervous. Arabella had wondered why John had married the girl, because she had sensed that he was not in love with her. Oh, he had been gentle and kind, constantly attentive to her—but it was the kindness that a man might show to his young sister rather than the woman he loved.

Arabella felt a little guilty that she had not told Sarah that John was also to be one of their guests. Equally, John had no idea that Sarah and Mrs Hunter were staying. She was hoping that the shock of seeing one another without warning might start spark off some reaction, making them realise that the feelings they had had for each other more than two years ago were still there.

* * *

'I am looking forward to seeing Lady Tate and Tilda when we go up to London,' Mrs Hunter said as she sat in the front parlour with her daughter-in-law some days later. 'How is dear Hester? She left us as soon as she heard you were with child, because she wanted to be of use to you in your confinement. And of course Tilda accompanied her home. I understand she is living with your aunt now. That attack of smallpox laid her very low and she thought she would rather be in England. Sarah and I missed them—though of course we had already made so many friends in Italy that we were never alone. Did Sarah tell you how sorry the Conte was to see us leave?'

'Yes, she did mention it. Tilda divides her time between Aunt Hester and us these days, which suits us all,' Arabella said. She had heard of the Conte di Ceasares several times from Mrs Hunter, and knew that her mother-in-law was suffering from frustration at Sarah's apparent lack of interest in finding a suitable husband. She smiled at her mother-in-law and showed her the exquisite smocking she was working on a gown for the new baby. 'How was it that Sarah nursed Tilda when she was ill? I am surprised that you allowed it, Mama.'

'Sarah seems to be immune to the disease,' her mother said. 'Some friends of ours had it years ago.

Sarah had been playing with their children, but she did not take it from them. Nor did she seem affected in Italy. She nursed Tilda, as you know—but did she tell you that she insisted on caring for the children of one of our friends there?' Arabella shook her head. 'They had gone down with it too and Sarah suspected that their nurse was not looking after them as she should. She took over the nursery and happily both recovered. I think it was that act of courage that made the Conte fall in love with her. He said that she was as brave as she was lovely and gave her a beautiful gold brooch to thank her.'

'Yes, she is brave. I have always thought so.'

'Brave, but very stubborn,' Mrs Hunter said. 'I am sure she might have married him if she had given him the least encouragement. One would think that she did not wish to be married—but I know that she adores children. The children in Italy were always hanging round her neck, especially the street urchins. She gave them coins whenever we visited the markets.'

'Where is Sarah this morning?'

'Oh, she went for a walk as far as the lake,' Mrs Hunter said, frowning slightly. 'In Italy she walked a great deal. I think she is determined that she will not be influenced by what happened before…'

'Yes, that is very sensible of her,' Arabella said

and sighed, easing her back, which had begun to ache. 'I wanted to tell her that the latest monthly journals arrived earlier. I believe there are some fashion plates that might be of use to her when she is planning her new wardrobe.'

'Oh, I am sure she will be pleased to see them,' Mrs Hunter said, looking at her anxiously. 'Are you quite well, my dear? You look a little strained.'

'I have a backache,' Arabella said. 'I do not regard it, Mama. It will pass in time. Indeed, I think I shall take a little stroll in the gardens to ease it. I might meet Sarah as she returns from her walk.'

'Oh, I wonder if you ought to go so far?' Mrs Hunter said. 'You must take care of yourself, Arabella. It is so easy to miscarry a child. I lost two and it was a great sadness to me.'

'I shall not overdo things,' Arabella replied and gave her a patient smile. Her mother-in-law did tend to fuss a little too much, which could be irritating if one allowed it to be. However, she had decided that she would take it as well-meaning concern, and would not allow there to be friction between them. 'Please do not worry, Mama. I am quite well.'

She got up and left the room, glad to escape into the fresh air of the garden for a while. It was quite warm that morning, the chill air of the past weeks seeming to have gone for the moment. However, her intention to walk as far as the lake to meet Sarah was curtailed as she saw a carriage arrive and knew that it was her guests.

She went to greet Elizabeth as one of the grooms handed her down. They kissed and greeted each other with pleasure, the earl waiting until they had finished before taking his turn.

'It is so good to have you here,' Arabella said, linking arms with Elizabeth as they moved towards the house. 'But is John not with you? I thought you might all travel together?'

'John drove himself,' Daniel Cavendish told her. 'He cannot be far behind us, though he intended to stop at the blacksmith in the village to have one of his horse's shoes looked at. He thought it might be coming loose.'

'Ah, I see,' Arabella said. 'Well, come in, my dear friends. Charles had some business this morning, but he will be back at any moment. Mrs Hunter is sitting with me in the parlour, and Sarah has gone for a walk. I dare say she will be back quite soon.'

Sarah stood watching the swans gliding effortlessly on the lake. They had kept to the far side and she had not been able to entice them nearer because they were fiercely guarding their very small cygnets. However, she had collected a crowd of rather noisy ducks about her, and she laughed as they squabbled over the last scraps of bread she had begged from the kitchens.

It was peaceful here and the scenery was beautiful, less wild than the rugged country she had been used to in the past couple of years. The hills of Tuscany had their own charm, and the gardens of the villas owned by Conte di Ceasares were very beautiful. Just before Sarah had left Italy, the villa garden had been a riot of colour, flowers spilling over from large terracotta pots, and the overpowering scent of their blooms heavy in the air. She thought that she would miss Italy and the people she had counted as friends.

She ought to be returning to the house. She had made her escape earlier because she was aware of her mama's silent disapproval. Mrs Hunter had been cross with her daughter because she believed that she had discouraged the Conte di Ceasares from making her an offer—she would be very annoyed indeed if she knew that Sarah had twice refused him. Sighing, Sarah turned away from the lake and began to walk slowly across the grass. She had liked the Conte very well, and perhaps she ought to have obliged her mama…

Walking with her head down, lost in thought, Sarah was not immediately aware of the man standing quite still a short distance ahead of her. He was on foot and had come through the woods to the left of the lake from the direction of the village. It was not until she drew near to him that he spoke to her, making her start.

'Sarah? Miss Hunter…'

Sarah felt a thrill of fear, which was gone in a moment. Just for a few seconds she had been back in the old nightmare, but it faded as she stared at the man standing a few feet away. Her heart raced and she felt a dizzy sensation as she knew him. He was much as he had always been and yet there was an air of sadness about him that she had not remembered. Because of his wife, she realised, as she recalled what Arabella had told her a few days earlier.

'John? Mr Elworthy…it is you, isn't it?'

'Yes.' John stood frozen to the spot, as if he was held by some spell and could not move. 'I am sorry if I startled you. I thought as I saw you coming this way that it was you, Miss Hunter—but I did not know that you had returned from Italy and wondered if I was mistaken.'

'We arrived just two weeks ago and have spent most of that time here with Charles and Arabella. We go up to London in about three weeks from now. Mama and I will stay with Lady Tate, though Arabella does not intend to accompany us. She is expecting her second child and prefers to stay quietly at home until her confinement. I believe Charles has some business and may come up for a few days.' She was talking too much, but did not know how to stop. 'I was not aware that you were to be a guest here, sir.'

'I hope it does not displease you?'

'No, of course not. Why should it?'

Sarah came up to him, offering her hand. He took it for a moment, holding it loosely, as if he thought she might break.

'Forgive me. I cannot help remembering…' His eyes were intent on her face. He smiled and shook his head. 'That seems a lifetime ago. You look wonderful—such a difference…not that you were ever less than lovely. What a mess I am making of this, Miss Hunter. You look beautiful, of course.'

'Thank you.' Sarah laughed as she saw his confusion. She had been paid many more effusive compliments during her stay in Italy, but she was warmed by John's stumbling offering. 'I know that I look different, Mr Elworthy. Arabella remarked on it when she saw me for the first time. I think perhaps I have grown up, become a woman. I was a lost and rather foolish girl when you last saw me.'

'A girl perhaps,' John said and let go of her hand, which he had retained until now, 'but never foolish. You had been through a traumatic experience, Miss Hunter. I hope that you have recovered now? You seem very well.'

'Yes, I am,' Sarah said. 'Italy did me a great deal of good, sir. I think it was because no one knew anything about me and I was able to make friends without being asked about what happened during that time. Those dark days are a distant memory to me now. I no longer suffer from nightmares.'

'I am glad to hear it,' John said. His eyes were serious, dark shadowed, but in every other way he was much as he had always been. John Elworthy was not a striking man, but he had a quiet air about him that was pleasing and his smile touched hearts. 'You have perhaps been told that I am a widower?'

'Yes, Arabella told me your news. I am very sorry, sir. It must be a great loss to you.'

'The loss of a young life is always sad,' John replied. 'There is a child—a boy. I have left him with his nurse, but I fear that he will feel the loss of his mother as he grows to understand what has happened.'

'Yes, of course,' Sarah agreed. 'But he has his father and that will sustain him.'

'Perhaps…' John was silent for a moment, apparently lost in thought. They had fallen into step with one another. 'You are planning a season in town, Miss Hunter? I had thought perhaps you might be betrothed, but I see that is not so…' He glanced at her ringless left hand. 'Or perhaps there is someone in Italy?'

'I might have married had I chosen,' Sarah said for

pride's sake. 'I have not yet decided what I wish to do in the future, sir. Mama wishes me to marry soon, but I do not know what I want…'

'You must take your time,' John said. 'You are still quite young…'

'I shall be one and twenty this year,' Sarah said. 'I dare say it is not too late should I wish to marry—though I believe I look older than my years.' She put up a hand to touch the wings of white at her temples. Her hair was in general a beautiful pale golden colour; shining and thick, it had grown in the past two years, though was nowhere near as long as it had been before her illness. She wore it twisted up at the back in double knot. Her gown was a simple muslin with a turquoise blue sash caught high at the waist, its colour almost a match for her eyes. 'Mama hoped that these would grow out as I recovered my health, but they have not.'

'I think the wings of white are distinctive,' John told her. 'You have an air about you, Miss Hunter—a quiet dignity that sets well with your hair.'

'Conte di Ceasares thought I was older,' Sarah replied with a hint of mischief in her eyes. 'Not that he heeded it, for we were great friends. I made many friends in Italy. Have you ever been there, sir?'

'Yes, I visited that country when I was young,' John told her. 'My father considered it a part of my education. It was a wonderful experience. I spent more time in France and Spain when I was with the army—but I have not travelled overseas since my return home after the war.'

'You did not go abroad for your honeymoon?' Sarah asked and then blushed. 'Forgive me—that was an insensitive question. I had no right to ask it. Indeed, I should not!'

'You meant no harm by it,' John said. 'Andrea was not particularly strong even then. She did not wish to go away. She was quite happy at home with her dogs and her books...' It was not entirely true, but John could not tell anyone about the strange haunting sadness that had come upon Andrea after their marriage.

'I see,' Sarah said, but wondered at the strange expression in his eyes. Clearly it pained him to speak of his wife; she thought that he must have loved her very much. She decided to be careful not to ask such clumsy questions again. 'Tell me, sir—what part of Italy did you like most? We visited the lakes and many of the beauty spots, but settled in Tuscany.'

'Yes, Arabella told me,' John said. 'I believe I like Florence very well—and Venice, of course. Did you get as far as Venice?'

'Yes, indeed, we visited Venice almost as soon as we arrived,' Sarah said. 'Tilda particularly wanted to take a trip in a gondola…' She smiled up at him, feeling on safer ground now. It was easy to talk of things and places they had both seen. Much easier than talking of personal feelings. She felt that John had suffered much since their last meeting and something inside her made her want to reach out and heal that hurt—but there was a distance in him. She sensed that he had built a barrier between himself and the rest of the world. He was happy to converse on almost any subject, but that of his wife—and that, she suspected, was taboo.

However, they had sufficient to discuss about the wonderful old buildings and treasures of Italy, and continued their walk up to the house in harmony. So much so that, when Arabella looked out of the parlour window and saw them coming, she was able to smile and consider that her plan had worked out very nicely.

Sarah had dressed in a gown of pale green silk for dinner that evening. She wore a single strand of pearls around her throat, and her maid had dressed her hair so that one smooth ringlet fell on her shoulders. Her skin still had a golden sheen to it, and she looked very beautiful as she came down to join the others in the drawing room.

She was the last to arrive, perhaps because she

had taken particular trouble over her appearance that evening. It had taken her half an hour to make up her mind which gown she wished to wear, and even now she was not sure whether she had chosen the right one. She was not certain why she felt it was so important, except, of course, that she wanted John to think that she looked nice. She was trying to be sensible, to stop herself hoping that he might find her attractive. His manner earlier had convinced her that he was still in love with his late wife, still grieving for her—and yet he had cared for Sarah once. If she had let him, he would have asked her to be his wife before she left for Italy.

Sarah had often wondered if she had made a big mistake by telling him that she did not think she would ever wish to marry. It was true that she had felt like that for a while, but the feeling had passed. She was still not certain that she wished to marry— but for very different reasons. Once she had thought that she could not be any man's wife, but now she knew that there was only one man she wished to wed.

She had realised it after parting from John and going up to her room to tidy herself for lunch. Meeting him again so unexpectedly had made her heart race wildly and she understood why she had refused the Conte when he had asked her to be his wife. She had liked him. She had liked Captain Hernshaw when they met in Rome, but neither of them had touched her heart the way John Elworthy did when he looked at her. His smile made her breathless and she was certain that she could be happy as his wife—but she was not sure that he would ask her. Perhaps he would not wish to marry again. It was obvious that his heart had been broken by Andrea's death. However, he had mentioned that his son would miss having a mother, so perhaps it was possible that he would take another wife for the sake of his son. Sarah did not know whether she was prepared to accept a man who needed a wife for his son's sake. It might prove too painful to know that one could only ever be second-best.

'You look lovely, Sarah dear,' Arabella said as she took a seat by her on the sofa. 'But that was a pensive expression on your face just now. Serious thoughts?'

Sarah laughed and shook her head. 'Not at all, Belle. I was just wondering what was for dinner. I am feeling hungry.'

It was a lie, of course, but it covered any awkwardness. John had glanced at her once when she entered, but his face remained impassive. She had no idea whether he thought she looked well or not. He seemed intent on his conversation with Charles and did not look her way again until dinner was announced. He came to her then, a polite smile on his lips.

'I believe I have the honour of taking you in, Miss Hunter?'

'Oh, do you?' Sarah said. She felt her stomach clench as she laid her hand on his arm and felt proud of herself because it did not tremble. It was difficult to know how to behave with him. He had called her Sarah when they were all staying at Arabella's manor two years previously, and she had felt that he truly cared for her at that time. Yet now she was unsure. He was polite, and of course, John Elworthy would never be less than attentive or kind to any lady, but there was a new reserve in him. She was sure it had never been there in the past—either before her abduction or after. 'That will be very nice, sir. We may continue our conversation about Italy.'

'Yes, of course,' John said. 'Did you attend many balls in Italy, Miss Hunter? I dare say you will be invited everywhere when you go up to town.'

'We shall give a small dance of our own,' Sarah said. 'But Lady Tate has told all her friends, so I imagine we shall be invited out quite often.'

'I am sure you will,' John said. 'Elizabeth and Daniel are going up at the same time. They have told me that they are giving a ball. Daniel made me promise that I would attend. It is some time since I danced with anyone…and I am not sure that it is convenient, but perhaps…'

'Oh, you must,' Sarah said. 'I shall know hardly anyone, Mr Elworthy. I hope that you will attend and that you will dance with me.'

'Well, perhaps,' John said and gave her the gentle, sweet smile she remembered so well. For a moment the air of sadness that hung over him had vanished and he was just as she had known him when she was a young girl. 'But I am sure that you will soon have many admirers, Miss Hunter.'

'Admirers are one thing, friends are another.' The look she gave him was so direct that John caught his breath. She was the girl he had remembered, but so much more! Italy had changed her, making her the woman she had been destined to become.

'Yes, very true.' John's eyes focused on her face and she thought she could read regret and a faint wistfulness in their depths. 'Yes, I think we might be friends, Miss Hunter. At least, I see no reason why we should not…'

'No, of course there is no reason why we should not be friends. We always were, John. You did so much for me—and for Arabella too. I thought we were friends before I left for Italy?'

'Yes…' John hesitated as if he wished to say more, but then stopped. They had reached the dining room and he drew her chair for her, seeing that she was comfortably settled before seating himself. Discovering that Elizabeth Cavendish was on his other side, he turned to exchange a word or two with her, leaving Sarah to speak to her brother on her other side.

It was not until the first course had been served that he spoke to Sarah again. 'This is very good wine, is it not? I must ask Charles who his wine merchant is and where I may find him. I should like to lay a stock of this down in my own cellar.'

'It is Italian, I think,' Sarah replied. 'The Conte di Ceasares was an important winegrower in the district and he taught me many things about wines. I believe I am not wrong about this, though it was not grown in Tuscany—perhaps it comes more from the north of the country.'

'You seem to have known the Conte very well?'

'Yes, he was our close neighbour. We actually stayed in a small villa he owned. It belonged to his family and he sometimes allows others to hire it for a while. We were very lucky to stay there. It was beautiful, though not as magnificent as the Conte's own villa.'

'He is, one imagines, quite wealthy?'

'Yes, indeed,' Sarah agreed. 'And very kind and a good friend to us.'

'You were fortunate,' John said. 'One hears of travellers who return less than satisfied with the conditions they discover on their travels, but you seem to have been well served.'

'Yes, we were,' Sarah said. 'I do not think Mama would have stayed so long otherwise. She came home to visit Arabella and Charles, of course, and to see her grandson. We shall stay for the birth of their second child, but I think Mama might wish to return to Italy for the winter sometimes. She likes Italy very well.'

'And you—will you return?'

'I am not sure,' Sarah said. 'I have many friends there, of course—but it depends on…' She shook her head because she simply could not answer his question without giving too much away. 'I confess that I like the climate. England can be very cold in winter.'

'Ah, yes,' John agreed. 'Their winters are far less harsh than our own, of course, especially in the south, I believe.'

'Oh, yes, considerably better.'

Sarah was aware of a slight restraint on his part. He lapsed into silence and then turned to speak to Elizabeth again. After a few moments he laughed, and Sarah was a little envious of his ease of manner with the countess. It was obvious that they were good friends. She wished that she might have been as easy with him, but they exchanged only a few words throughout the rest of the meal, discussing the various dishes and complimenting Arabella on her chef.

Sarah was a little relieved when the ladies left the gentlemen to their port. John was clearly not entirely comfortable in her company and she thought it a shame—she had hoped for something more.

'How do you find it here in England?' Elizabeth Cavendish took a seat next to Sarah and smiled at her. 'I expect you will miss Italy. It is very beautiful. Daniel took me there on our honeymoon. I loved it. We talk of going back again one day, but I should like to have a daughter first. Once our family is complete, then we may travel more.'

'Yes,' Sarah agreed. 'Arabella is taking great care. She would have liked to come to London with us, but has decided against it because the doctor warned that she ought to take things easily. Being shaken for hours in a carriage is not exactly a good idea when a lady is with child.'

'No, you are right,' Elizabeth said. 'We are coming up at the same time as you go to town, Sarah. We have decided to give a ball for our friends. My brother was married last year and this is the first time we shall all be together again. We decided to make the most of it—in case I cannot go up to London next year.'

'It will be nice to have some acquaintance there,' Sarah said. 'I have been used to having friends in Italy and I shall feel a little awkward at first, I think.'

'Oh, I dare say you will soon make many acquaintances,' Elizabeth told her. 'But we must meet often, Sarah. I shall be delighted to take you into my circle, though we are rather inclined to be bluestockings. I hope you like to read?'

'Yes, indeed I do,' Sarah replied, her face lighting up. 'I love poetry, though I do not mind novels—but poetry is my first love, and music, of course.'

'Do you play the pianoforte?'

'Yes, a little,' Sarah replied. 'I play the harp as well, but I think I prefer the pianoforte.'

'Then we shall be good company,' Elizabeth said. She wrinkled her smooth brow. 'Tell me, was John in spirits at dinner? I have been concerned for him recently. It was difficult to persuade him to come with us on this visit. He spends too much time alone these days. Daniel and he are such friends, but even he sees less of John than he would like. Before he married he visited us almost every week.'

'I dare say he has been grieving,' Sarah said. 'He has had an unfortunate loss.'

'Yes, though I am not sure if…' Elizabeth shook her head as if she had said too much. 'I know that he has been grieving, but it is more than a year since

Andrea died. He cannot keep himself shut up from the world for ever. He blames himself, of course, but it was not his fault.'

Sarah would have liked to ask more, but at that moment the gentlemen came into the room and she did not like to push for more information. Now was not the time. She would ask Elizabeth what she meant another day.

Arabella was beckoning to her. Sarah got up and went to her, agreeing to a request to play for them. Sitting down at the pianoforte, she began to play a sonata by Mozart that she was very fond of, her face assuming a dreamy expression as she was carried far away. Sarah was smiling as she thought of an evening in Italy when she had played this piece. It was the night when Conte di Ceasares had first proposed to her.

'What are you thinking?' a voice asked and she discovered that John had come to stand by her side. 'You look as if you are lost in the music.'

'Yes, I was,' she said and stopped playing, for she had reached the end of the piece. 'Do you not love Mozart's work? I think he was so wonderful, but his own people did not appreciate him until it was too late.'

'Too often the case,' John said and reached over her to play a few notes himself. Sarah smiled and let him play for a moment before joining in again.

'You enjoy music, sir. Do you often play?'

'Sometimes,' John said. 'Perhaps we may perform a duet one evening, Miss Hunter?'

'Yes, why not?' she said. 'We must practise together before we play for others, I think.'

'Oh, yes,' he said and smiled oddly. 'But I have interrupted you. Please continue.'

'I think Arabella has sent for the tea tray,' Sarah replied and stood up. 'Another time, perhaps.'

'Yes, perhaps,' he said. 'Excuse me. I am promised to Charles for a game of billiards. I shall hope to see you in the morning, Miss Hunter.'

'Yes, of course,' Sarah said. 'Goodnight, Mr Elworthy.'

She watched as he, Charles and Daniel left the room, before taking her seat close to Arabella so that she could help to pass round the tea.

'John plays the pianoforte very well,' Arabella said to her. 'I have not seen him take an interest for a long time, but he certainly enjoyed your playing, Sarah.'

'Oh, I am not as proficient as many ladies are,' Sarah said. 'But I like to play sometimes.'

'So does John,' Arabella said. 'It is a pleasure you share, Sarah.'

She looked very happy about something, which made Sarah wonder exactly what was on her mind.

## Chapter Two

Sarah was sitting in the rose arbour reading a book of poetry when John came upon her the next morning. He paused as if fearing to intrude, smiling hesitantly when she looked up and saw him.

'I did not wish to disturb you, Miss Hunter. Forgive me. I shall go.'

'I hope that you will not,' Sarah replied and closed her book. 'It is very peaceful here. I sometimes sneak away to read for a while, but I am not averse to your company, Mr Elworthy.'

'Are you escaping from someone?' John asked and smiled as he sat down on the wooden bench next to her, being careful not to crush her gown.

'From my mama,' Sarah confided with a naughty look. 'It is very wicked of me, but I could not resist. Poor Mama is in a cross mood this morning. She had a letter from one of her friends in Italy and something in it upset her. I do not know what. She has been scolding me for not making more of my chances while we were there.'

'Your mama would perhaps like you to be married?' John's eyes were steady on her face.

'Yes…' Sarah felt her cheeks getting warm. 'She thinks it is time that I put the past behind me. Indeed, I think I have done so, but…' She shook her head. 'It is not that I do not wish to oblige my mama, but she is too impatient and I need time.'

'Perhaps you still think that you would rather not marry?'

Sarah was silent for a moment, her head bent, cheeks pink. 'No, it is not quite that, sir. Just that, as yet, no one that I would wish to wed has asked me.' She turned her head as she felt his eyes on her, afraid that she might betray herself and pretending interest in a rose that was still in a tightly formed bud.

The silence stretched between them for a few moments, and then John spoke words that sent a chill of ice into her heart. 'I dare say you will meet someone in London. A gentleman of good birth and fortune who has a whole heart and will fall in love with you the moment he sees you.'

'Yes, perhaps,' Sarah said. She felt that the tears were very close and got quickly to her feet. 'Excuse me, I must see if Mama has come down yet. I believe she has arranged for us to have a fitting with

Arabella's seamstress this morning. Some of the gowns we ordered in York were not well finished.'

'Sarah…' John spoke to her retreating back, silently cursing himself. He thought that perhaps he had hurt her, which was the last thing he had intended. Once he would have responded very differently to such an invitation, for he believed it had been a gentle hint that he might find favour in her eyes. 'Damn! Damn it! Why did I not just walk away? Forgive me, Sarah. I am not worthy…not worthy of you…'

John turned away from the house, striding out towards the woods. It was his intention to fetch his curricle and horses, which had been stabled at the inn in the village. The blacksmith would have done his work by now, and John meant to take his leave of Arabella and the others as soon as he decently could. If it were possible he would leave now, make some excuse, but it would offend his friends. He could bear it for a day or so longer, though it almost wrenched the heart out of him when Sarah looked his way and he saw hurt mirrored in her lovely eyes. Would that he could turn back the past two years! He ought to have followed Sarah to Italy as had been his intention, but he had lingered, uncertain of his reception, and then it had been too late.

If only he had walked away from Andrea that

day…if he had not listened to her pleas for help…but it was useless to look back. He had married her, given his name to her child, stood by her—and all to no avail. She had taken her own life while in a fit of despair and the sight of her lifeless body as it was taken from the river had nearly destroyed him. He had failed her. Andrea had begged for his help, but he had failed her. And now his guilt haunted him like a dark shadow at his elbow. He had nightmares, which woke him sweating with fear, and he had begun to imagine things; sometimes he wondered if his mind was playing tricks on him—it was as if his late wife were haunting him.

He had ordered that her personal belongings be packed and taken to the attics, but small things kept reappearing, tucked in amongst his own clothes as if placed there on purpose to remind him. A kerchief had been under his pillow when he went to bed the night before he left Elworthy House, and a few days earlier he had discovered her prayer book in his dressing chest; another time he had smelled her perfume in his room. It had been so strong that he had almost believed she was there.

He did not believe that he had placed any of the items where he found them. He had questioned his housekeeper about them, but the woman denied all knowledge of Andrea's things, except to say that they had been taken to the attics. Indeed, she had gone so far as to say she was certain the prayer book had not been in the dressing chest the previous evening when she had placed some clean linen there herself, and she had looked at John curiously as if suspecting that he had put it there. But John was certain that he had not done anything of the kind. Yet how could it have come there...unless Andrea's unquiet spirit was haunting him?

Surely not! John did not truly believe that such a thing was possible. He knew that he had failed Andrea, but he had not been deliberately cruel—so why was he being punished for her death? She had taken her own life by walking into the river. It was true that he had been a little irritated with her earlier that day, but he had apologised almost at once for his brusque manner. Had it really been a few cross words that had driven her to take her life? Or was it something more? Perhaps she had guessed that his feelings for her could never be more than kindness?

They had known each other since they were children, their parents friends and neighbours. After John's father died, Sir Andrew Walton had offered to help John put his estate in order. He had not needed his help, but he had remembered the kindness given and when Andrea had turned to him in her distress, he had done what any decent gentleman would do. Rather than let her face the shame that a wicked rape had brought upon her, he had asked her to marry him, and she had gratefully accepted. Indeed, he knew that she had hoped for it when she came to him.

After he had married Andrea, John had tried hard to put Sarah out of his mind, but he was afraid that his wife had sensed his heart was not hers to command—that he would never love her as a man ought to love the woman he had married. John had been kind, but she had been suffering from the sickness brought on by her condition when they wed, and he had left her to sleep alone that night. After the birth, when she recovered, she had told him that he might join her in her bed, but he had told her that she was not yet well enough and she had not asked again. Somehow they had drawn apart as the days and weeks passed, and Andrea had retreated into a silent world of her own.

They did not quarrel. Perhaps it might have been better if they had, but each treated the other with unfailing politeness, speaking when they met but never really talking. After the harsh words that morning, John had realised that this situation could not go on. Either he must make Andrea his wife in all ways, or they must live apart. He had made up his mind that he would talk to her that evening—but by then they had taken her lifeless body from the river.

Was it his fault? John had told himself that he had done nothing to harm Andrea, and yet his conscience would not let him rest. Had he made Andrea so unhappy that she had taken her own life? It was a hard cross to bear, and the reason why he had begun to wonder if he actually had placed those items amongst his things. Was he trying to punish himself without knowing he did so?

No, this was ridiculous! John shook his head. There must be another reason for what had happened, something that ought to be apparent but was not. He had no reason to torture himself in this way. Andrea had known he did not love her when they married. Surely she must have known? But she had not understood that his heart was irrevocably given to another woman.

He had tried to forget Sarah. He had believed that she would never return to England, and for months he had succeeded in dulling the sense of loss that lived with him. Now, seeing her, being close to her, the scent of her perfume teasing his senses, he knew that he had never ceased to think of her. Staying here in this house was exquisite torture, making him achingly aware of a need within himself. Yet how could he ask her to marry him?

John knew that Andrea's death had set off some whispering. People had wondered why a young woman delivered of a fine son would take her own life…no one had said it to his face, but John believed that some suspected that she might not have gone willingly into the river.

He had no idea who had begun the rumours, but they had been brought to his attention a few weeks earlier by Andrea's father.

'I know it is all nonsense,' Sir Andrew said when he rode over that morning to show John the letter he had received. 'Had there been any truth in this wretched insinuation, this would surely have been signed. It is a damned lie and I do not believe it for a moment, but I thought you should see it.'

John had read the accusation, his lips white with anger. He handed the letter back to his father-in-law. 'I swear to you that there is no truth in this, sir. Andrea was a little unwell after the birth of…our son, that is all.'

'No, no, John, let us be straight with one another,' Sir Andrew said. 'We both know that the child was not yours. Andrea told me the truth after she had spoken to you. She wanted me to know that you had not shamed her.'

'I never knew that,' John said. 'She need not have told you. I promised her that no one would hear of it from my lips—and, as far as I am concerned, the boy is mine.'

'You are a good man,' Sir Andrew said, 'and that is why I know this is a lie. I shall destroy the letter, but it may not be the end of it, John.'

And it had not ended there. John had received a vicious letter himself a few days before he left home for this visit. The writer said that he or she knew the truth and that John would pay the price of his evil. It was again unsigned and John had destroyed it at once, but the shadow had lingered. Sir Andrew had refused to believe him capable of murder—but others might not be so convinced of his innocence.

John knew that he could not think of marriage while such a shadow hung over him. He shivered, feeling the chill creep down his spine. If he married again so soon, the rumours would increase and might be difficult to disprove. How could he marry anyone until he could clear his name of any wrongdoing?

Indeed, if Sarah heard the spiteful whispers, she might wonder if there was some truth in them. She would certainly not wish to be the wife of a man who might be accused of murdering his first wife. He must put all thought of it from his mind!

Sarah spent the rest of the morning being fitted for a new walking gown and two afternoon dresses. Although Mrs Hunter intended to order several new gowns in town, she thought highly enough of her daughter-in-law's seamstress to trust her with a part of Sarah's new wardrobe.

Her mother's fussing over details enabled Sarah to put the incident with John out of her mind. She was aware that she might have revealed her feelings too plainly, but when they met again before dinner, he greeted her as always with his gentle smile. He was sitting opposite her this time, for Daniel had taken her into dinner and she felt some relief that she was not obliged to make polite conversation with John.

'How do you like being back in England?' Daniel asked. 'Do you find it very different, Miss Hunter?'

'Yes, it is different,' Sarah agreed. 'But I am very happy here, sir. And of course we go to London in almost three weeks.'

'Ah, yes, you will be thrust into the social whirl,' he said, smiling at her kindly. 'Elizabeth tells me you share her interest in books. I warn you that she will expect you to attend all her afternoon meetings. You must say if you have other engagements. My wife likes to manage us all.'

The smile and the wicked look in his eyes were enough to tell Sarah that he was amused and there was no malice in his words. He was clearly very much in love with Elizabeth, and Sarah felt a pang of envy as she saw the way they looked at each other. If only she could find that sort of love!

Glancing across the table, she discovered that John was watching her. He looked serious, although he smiled and inclined his head as their eyes met. Sarah sensed that he was concerned about something, and wondered at the signs of tiredness in his face. John was always gentle, unfailingly kind and caring, and yet there was something about him that inspired confidence. She knew that he was to be relied upon in a crisis and she sensed an inner strength that was perhaps not immediately obvious to a casual onlooker.

He must still be grieving for his wife, of course. It was only a year since Andrea Elworthy had died. No doubt he had loved her very much and could not be expected to think of marrying again just yet.

John had turned to Elizabeth, who was sitting to his left. They were laughing at something now and Sarah wished that she might feel the ease of an old friendship such as they obviously shared. John had been her friend once. He had cared for her, but she had walked away from him and he'd fallen in love with Andrea.

Why did that hurt so much? Sarah knew that she had only herself to blame. With a little encouragement John would have asked her to marry him more than two years previously—but that was then and things had changed.

Sarah realised that, since learning of his wife's

death, she had been secretly wishing that he might turn to her, might ask her to marry him. His behaviour in the rose arbour that morning had destroyed her dreams. John was not ready to marry again just yet.

Would he ever be? Sarah frowned at her own thoughts. She would be foolish to hope for something that might never happen. Had John felt anything for her, he would surely not have answered her as he had. By telling her that she would meet a gentleman with a whole heart, who would love her, he could not have been clearer.

John was still in love with his late wife. Sarah must not embarrass him by showing her feelings for him. In future she would take great care not to be alone with him.

Sarah's ordeal lasted for just two days more. On the morning of the third day, Arabella told her that John was leaving them.

'He has some business that will not wait,' Arabella said. 'I am sorry he cannot stay longer, but he seems anxious to keep his appointment and I am afraid we must allow him to go, Sarah.'

Sarah was torn between regret and relief. It would be easier when she did not have to meet John at every meal, but a part of her wanted him to stay. She knew that he was grieving, but sometimes when they spoke she felt that something flowed between them.

She was sitting in the downstairs parlour when John came to take his leave of Arabella. Looking up, Sarah's heart jerked as she saw how elegant he looked in his buckskin breeches and a blue coat that fitted him to perfection. He was of a slighter build than either Charles or Daniel, but Sarah thought him the most attractive of any gentleman she had met thus far. More than that, she felt a warmth inside every time he smiled at her.

'Are you sure your business will not wait?' Arabella asked as he said his farewells. 'We had hoped you would stay at least a week.'

'It was my hope too,' John replied in his easy, gentle way. 'Perhaps another time?'

'Yes, of course. You know that you will always be welcome here, John.'

'Thank you. I shall remember,' he promised. Sarah thought there was a hint of regret in his face as he turned to her. 'It was good to see you again, Miss Hunter.'

'Yes,' Sarah replied. She got up from her chair and walked to meet him, offering her hand. John hesitated briefly before taking it in his. Sarah tingled at his touch. There was a clean fresh scent about him that she found appealing and she wished that he might take her in his arms, but he had let go of her hand and was about to turn away. He must not go like this! Before she could prevent the words they leapt from her tongue, 'Perhaps we shall meet in town, sir?'

'I am not sure,' John said with a vague look in his eyes.

'But you promised to dance with me at Elizabeth's ball!' Sarah knew that she ought not to press him, but something inside told her that if she did not speak now it might be too late. 'Surely you will not disappoint Elizabeth—and me?'

John was caught as he saw the appeal in her eyes. She had never looked prettier than she did now in her jonquil-yellow morning gown and it hurt to refuse her anything. He hesitated for a moment before inclining his head. 'It seems as if I gave my word and must therefore keep it, Miss Hunter. I shall come up for the ball.'

Sarah's heart beat wildly. He was grieving for his wife, but he still liked her. She was sure in that instant that John felt something. Perhaps it was not yet love, but that might come in time.

'I shall save two dances for you, sir. Do not leave me standing alone.'

'I never lightly break my word,' John said. 'Excuse me, ladies. I must say goodbye to Charles and Daniel. I have spoken to Elizabeth.'

Sarah was silent after he left the room, but there was a look of such longing on her face that Arabella guessed what was in her mind.

'John is a man whose thoughts and emotions run deeply,' Arabella said, looking pensive. 'You must be patient, Sarah. I think he has much on his mind, but I am sure that he will find a solution to his problems.'

Arabella wondered if she ought to explain that John was being threatened. He had confided to Charles that someone had begun spreading rumours about the nature of Andrea's death. Charles had, of course, dismissed it as spiteful nonsense. He was very angry that letters and whispers were circulating.

'How anyone could think it for one moment!' Charles had burst into furious speech when they were alone the previous night. 'John is the last man on this earth I would suspect of having killed his wife.'

'Why would anyone wish to spread such a rumour?' Arabella had asked him. 'It is scandalous and cruel. Someone must hate him to do such a thing.' She frowned as a thought occurred to her. 'Could it have anything to do with that other business?'

'You mean because of the part John played in thwarting Sir Courtney's attempt to abduct you and force you to marry him?'

'Yes,' Arabella replied, looking anxious. 'John risked his life for our sakes, but why should he be the one to suffer now? And Captain Hernshaw fired the shot that killed Sir Courtney when he tried to kill Sarah and I…'

'As well us as John if someone wanted revenge for that affair,' Charles agreed. 'No, I think this has more to do with John. There is something else…something that runs deeper.' He explained that John had found some of Andrea's possessions in his room. 'Someone must have put that stocking on his bed. It did not get there of its own accord.'

'Is that so surprising? I dare say the maids found it tucked away somewhere. My things often get left in your room. It could have been caught under the bed or some such thing.'

Charles shook his head. 'I do not think John's marriage was like ours, Belle. He would never speak of his intimate situation but…I have never thought it a love match.'

'Nor I,' Arabella agreed. 'He was attentive and kind to her—but not as a man in love might be.'

'John thought it right to inform me of the rumours and mentioned that he was under a strain. However, he said nothing of their relationship. What I have told you is merely my opinion.'

'I had already formed my own,' Arabella said. 'It seems that John has an enemy, Charles.'

'Yes, that was the conclusion I formed. I made him promise to seek out Tobbold—you may recall that both Daniel and I have found him a useful man?' She nodded. 'John needs someone to help him now. He must discover who is spreading malicious lies. Meanwhile, this remains a secret between us. Mama is not to be told, though both Elizabeth and Daniel have been informed. John wanted them to know because of the ball.'

'You don't think…' Arabella was dismayed. 'I imagined the gossip was confined to John's village and home. It will be uncomfortable for him if it becomes generally known and believed.'

'It will not be known from any of us!'

'No, certainly not,' she agreed.

Seeing the sadness in Sarah's eyes after John had left them, Arabella was tempted to confide in the girl. However, on further reflection, she decided against speaking. It was not truly her affair. John might resent it if he knew that his secret had been betrayed. After all, had he wished Sarah to know, he would no doubt have told her himself.

'I should not have rejected him before I left for Italy,' Sarah said, breaking the silence between them. 'He would have spoken then had I allowed it. I thought for a while that I should never wish to marry anyone.'

'And now?' Arabella asked, but before Sarah could

answer, the door opened and both Elizabeth and Mrs Hunter came in. 'Ah, there you are. Did you see John just now? He has been taking his leave of us. He has important business elsewhere but has promised to come up to town for your ball, Elizabeth.'

'Has he?' Elizabeth was surprised. 'He must have changed his mind, for he seemed to think he would not manage it. I am glad that he will come. He looks tired and drained, and I am sure that it is no wonder. He needs to be with friends.'

'Yes, that is what Charles thinks,' Arabella agreed. She glanced at Mrs Hunter, who was clutching some letters. 'Did those just arrive?'

'Your housekeeper gave them to me,' Mrs Hunter said. 'One is for you, Arabella—and one for you, Sarah.'

Sarah took the letter from her mother. She walked over to a small table by the window and sat down on an elegant parlour chair, breaking the seal. She knew who had sent it—it carried the wax impression of the Conte di Ceasares' seal. She scanned the few lines swiftly.

'This is from the Conte,' she told her mother. 'It is just to say that he hopes we had a good journey.'

Mrs Hunter looked disappointed. 'I had thought he might have written to say he intended to visit London.'

'No, Mama. It is simply a polite letter to inquire after our health.'

'Did you wish to see him again, Mrs Hunter?' Elizabeth said with a teasing look, for she had no idea of who the Conte was or what age he might be. 'Or perhaps Sarah…'

'He was very taken with Sarah in Italy,' Mrs Hunter said and looked thoughtful. 'Had she been more sensible, she might have been married to him by now.' She gave her daughter a straight look.

'Mama!' Sarah cried, blushing bright pink. 'I pray you will not say such things.'

'And why should you pray that, miss?' Her mother looked at her in some annoyance. 'The Conte is rich, attractive and charming—and not so very much older. You are foolish not to have taken him when he asked, Sarah.' She nodded as Sarah stared at her. 'I am aware that you refused him without reference to me. Had you asked, I should have advised you to take him.'

'Please, Mama, do not,' Sarah begged, feeling as if she could sink. It was so very embarrassing.

Elizabeth had realised her mistake. She sent Sarah an apologetic look. 'Tell me, Mrs Hunter, where do you intend to take Sarah for her new clothes when you are in town? Have you heard that we have a new and very talented modiste? Her name is Madame Henriette Deloir and she made a wonderful gown for me this spring. Everyone thought that it must have come from Paris.'

'You mean your green gown,' Arabella said. 'It is exquisite, Elizabeth. The lace she used to trim the sleeves is finer than anything I have. I shall ask her to make something for me once the baby is born.'

The conversation was successfully turned as Mrs Hunter asked for the modiste's address. Sarah stood looking out of the parlour window, her back turned to the others. She had not realised that her mother knew she had refused the Conte's offer and it was a shock to learn it so publicly.

Tears stung her eyes as she thought of how different it might have been had John asked her to marry him.

Staying here with Arabella, watching as she and Elizabeth held their children in their arms, holding the babies herself, Sarah had come to realise that she wanted a home and children of her own. Her heart belonged to John, but if he no longer cared for her…

Sarah sighed. She was not sure that she could marry just for the sake of a home and children, though she knew that it happened. In Italy most marriages were arranged and many of them turned out well. Some of the ladies she had counted her friends were completely happy with the husbands their families had chosen for them. She suspected that two of the ladies had secret lovers, but it was never spoken of.

It was not what Sarah wanted! She knew that if she married John she would never look at another man, but what if she were forced to take a husband for other reasons? Arabella had said that Charles would not allow Sarah to be pushed into an unwelcome marriage. However, he did not have to live with Mama! Mrs Hunter could be very disagreeable if thwarted too often.

Sarah knew that by giving her this London Season, her mother was offering her one last chance. Mrs Hunter expected her daughter to make a good marriage. If at the end of the season Sarah was not at least promised to someone, her mama would be most annoyed, for she might never have a better chance to find a husband.

Sarah was not afraid of her mother, but she did not wish to be at odds with her. Nor did she wish to remain at home with Mrs Hunter for the rest of her life. She envied Elizabeth and Arabella their freedom.

Sarah's heart lifted. John had promised to attend Elizabeth's ball. Perhaps when they danced together he would fall in love with her again.

John drove his horses hard for some minutes. He was determined to put some distance between himself and Sarah, determined that he would not give into the voices in his head telling him to turn back.

He had been a fool to weaken over Elizabeth's ball. Seeing Sarah again was bound to bring him pain. Besides, if Charles was right, he had an enemy. Someone who was bent on ruining him and perhaps worse.

John was not certain he could prove his innocence if it came to a trial at law. He had spent some time with his agent the morning that Andrea had killed herself. Afterwards, he had gone for a long walk alone, needing to sort out his thoughts. His path had taken him to the far side of the estate. At no time had he been anywhere near the river, but could it be proven? He had some ideas that might be foolish nonsense, and yet he could not help thinking that he might know the writer of the letter. The hand had been disguised, of course, and yet he had his suspicions.

If he were forced to prove his innocence, it might be only his word against another's. He believed that a man had written the unsigned letter. John might be acquitted by reasonable doubt, for if he could not prove his innocence no one could prove his guilt. However, the mud would stick. People would say that there was no smoke without fire. Even if he were merely called before the local Justice of the Peace, some would think him a murderer. John had told his friends of the threat, believing that they ought to be aware that he might be disgraced at any time.

'You might prefer that I did not attend Elizabeth's ball, Daniel.'

'Damn it, John! Do not dare to say such a thing to me again. None of us would believe such a wicked lie.' Daniel had been outraged.

'But others will,' John had pointed out with a wry smile. 'Some will cut me, I make no doubt. You could be tarred with some of the filth they may throw at me.'

'Anyone stupid enough to think you a murderer will no longer be welcome in my house,' Daniel said, looking grim.

Charles had said much the same. Neither of his friends was prepared to think the worse of him. John had thanked them for their loyalty, but he knew that he would find a rather different attitude in others should the rumours become common knowledge.

'Speak to Tobbold,' Daniel had advised him. 'He will get to the bottom of this if anyone can, John. It is a pity that you did not keep the letter. If you should receive another, make sure you retain it as evidence. Someone is out to ruin you. You have an enemy, my friend, and you must fight back. He must not be allowed to get away with this, whoever he may be.' Daniel frowned. 'I suppose you have no idea who it might be?'

'No, none at all,' John said, though it wasn't quite true. He had wondered, but his suspicions seemed so ridiculous that he could not bring himself to voice them aloud. 'I have racked my brains to no avail. I thought that perhaps Andrea's father might blame me, but he was disgusted by the letter sent to him, and the first to bring this matter to my attention.'

'I am at your service,' Charles told him. 'If there is anything I may do to help, John, you have only to send word.'

'The same goes for me,' Daniel agreed. 'I am certain we can sort this out between us, John. I shall make inquiries myself, because there is more to this than we yet know—but you must speak to Tobbold. Your enemy is a dangerous man and may not be satisfied with your ruin.'

John was feeling better for having confided in his friends. Both had declared him perfectly sound of mind, which meant that he might be dealing with more than one enemy. And at least one of them was able to come and go in his own house!

John found it difficult to understand how that could be. Many of his servants had worked for him for years, and some for his parents before him. He would have sworn that every one of them was loyal. Why had this person turned against him? What had he done that deserved this?

John had puzzled over it, but could find no answer. Perhaps his enemy had bribed one of the maids to place Andrea's things amongst his, hoping to unnerve him? It had certainly given him a nasty shock the first time, but afterwards he had begun to suspect what was going on. When he returned home he would ask his housekeeper if any new maids had been taken on in the past few months.

And why was his enemy trying to ruin him? Was it because Andrea had taken her own life? He had wondered if Sir Andrew had written his own letter in order to threaten him, and yet he could not truly think it. His father-in-law had known that her child was not John's—how could he blame John for the fit of despair that had driven her to take her own life?

Who else would want revenge for her death? John could think of no one. She did not have any brothers or sisters, and her mother had died when she was but a child.

So perhaps it was nothing to do with Andrea. Perhaps she was merely the tool being used against him. John frowned as he slowed his horses to a steadier pace. He had no idea where to start looking for clues. He could tell Tobbold what had happened so far, but he could give him no help in solving the mystery.

It was possible that this nonsense might be something to do with Sir Courtney Welch—or even Sir Montague Forsythe. John had been involved in both those affairs. He had helped when Charles had been desperate to discover his sister's whereabouts after Forsythe had had her abducted, and John had also played a big part in scuppering Sir Courtney's attempt to force Arabella into marrying him. It was also possible that he had trodden on someone's toes for quite another reason, though he did not know of anyone who had a right to hate him. He had not insulted anyone, nor had he ruined another gentleman at the card tables.

It was a warm spring day, but John felt the chill of winter enter his heart. The future looked bleak indeed. It was hopeless. How could he ever discover who his enemy was, let alone prove his innocence to the world? He had no answers to the questions others would ask of him. All he did know for certain was that he could not ask any woman to marry him while this shadow hung over him. Only a selfish man would think of his own happiness when it might bring harm to the woman he admired more than any other.

Yet had he the right to ignore Sarah? He had once given her to understand that he was in love with her. In the rose arbour she had seemed to invite him to speak, and a part of him had longed to oblige her—but he did not wish to bring her down. If he were to be disgraced—or, worse, accused of murder—it could ruin her life.

John knew that he must conquer the guilt he felt concerning his wife. It was true that he had not been able to give her the love she needed. Kindness and concern were all very well in their way—but was it his neglect in making their marriage a true one that had driven Andrea to take her life? Or was there some reason of which he had no knowledge?

Only when he had settled his own mind would he be able to think of making plans for the future.

## Chapter Three

'I am sorry you are not coming with us,' Sarah said as she kissed Arabella's cheek that morning. 'I shall miss you, but I understand why you would rather remain here.' She glanced at her mother, who was ordering the servants about unnecessarily and hovering in a flustered manner as their baggage was stowed on the coach. 'I dare say you will be glad to have your home to yourself again, Belle.'

'No, not at all,' Arabella assured her with a smile. 'Mama does fuss a little, I admit, but she means well, Sarah. I know she is anxious for you to marry, but it is because she wants you to be happy—truly happy. And I think you are not.'

'I am happy enough,' Sarah told her, avoiding her sympathetic gaze. 'But I shall not be happy if Mama pushes me into marriage with a man I do not love.'

'Charles will not allow that, I promise you,' Arabella said and kissed her cheek. 'If your mama is difficult, tell us, Sarah. Charles will stand by you, though it is his dearest wish to see you happily settled—but only with the gentleman of your choice.'

'Thank you, you have been so kind,' Sarah said. 'If it were not for you and Nana, I might have died when I was so ill. You took me in when I did not know my own name and made me want to live again.'

'We are as sisters,' Arabella said and smiled at her. 'I know your heart as well as you do, Sarah. I shall not embarrass you, but you must not give up hope, dearest. John is in some kind of trouble at the moment but I am sure that he still cares for you.'

'Oh, Belle…' Sarah's throat was tight with tears. She embraced her sister-in-law once more and then turned as her mother called to her impatiently. 'I am coming, Mama.'

Their farewells over, Sarah climbed into the carriage after her mother and waved to Arabella from the window. Charles was standing by her side, his arm about her waist. He lifted his hand in salute, then looked down at his wife, bending his head to kiss her briefly on her forehead. They were smiling at each other, lost in their own private world. Sarah sat back against the squabs, a little sigh issuing from her lips.

'Charles might have come up with us,' Mrs Hunter said. 'I am sure Arabella would not have minded.'

'He will come in a few days,' Sarah said. 'We do not need him, Mama. We managed well enough in Italy, if you recall.'

'In Italy we had the Conte to look after us,' Mrs Hunter said with a touch of asperity. 'Such a perfect gentleman, such exquisite manners—'

Sarah played with the strings of her velvet reticule. Her mother had not stopped talking about the Conte di Ceasares, and the chance Sarah had wasted, since his letter had arrived.

'He was very kind,' Sarah admitted. 'But I did not love him, Mama. Surely you wish me to be happy?'

'It is because I wish you to be happy that I am reminding you of what you have lost. You are such a stubborn girl,' Mrs Hunter said. 'Well, I am giving you your chance. If you do not take it, you will have only yourself to blame if you sink into a lonely old age, reduced to caring for your nephews and nieces. I shall not always be here for you.'

'Oh, Mama,' Sarah said with a smile. 'You will live for many years yet, I hope.'

'That is as may be,' her mother said. 'Think about your situation if you do not marry, Sarah. Do you always wish to be a guest in other people's homes? Surely you wish for a home and children?'

'Yes, of course,' Sarah said. 'But please allow me time to make up my mind, Mama. I do not wish to make a mistake about something as important as marriage.'

Mrs Hunter gave her a meaningful look. 'Time is shorter than you think, Sarah. You will be one and twenty in a few months; if you are not careful, you may find yourself left on the shelf.'

Sarah did not answer. She turned to glance out of the window. They had left the estate now and were travelling through open countryside. The moors at this point were wide and slightly undulating with only a few scrubby bushes and stunted trees on the horizon. She glanced back at her mother, who had closed her eyes and, being an indifferent traveller, was possibly already wishing that they were at the end of their journey.

In her heart Sarah knew that her mama was right. Her life would be as empty as the bleak moors if she did not marry. It was perhaps her duty to keep an open mind on the subject of marriage.

'It is so good to see you again,' Lady Tate said, giving Sarah a kiss on her cheek. 'Both Tilda and I have been looking forward to your visit.'

'Is Tilda here?' Sarah asked as the housekeeper helped her off with her travelling cloak. 'It seems ages since you left Italy to come home, Aunt Hester. Arabella sends her love, as does Charles. He is coming up for a few days soon, but Arabella does not wish to travel at the moment.'

'I had a letter from her,' Lady Tate said and smiled. Although Sarah was not actually her niece, she had always loved her and they were very close. 'I shall go down to the country in two months' time and stay for her confinement.'

'Sarah, my dearest…' Tilda came out into the hall then, and Sarah went to greet her as Lady Tate turned to Mrs Hunter. 'You are here at last. It seems an age since we were together in Italy.'

They embraced and then Tilda accompanied Sarah up to her room, chattering about various invitations that had already come in. Lady Tate had let it be known that her great friend Selina Hunter and her daughter Sarah were to visit her, and, as the Season was just beginning, the cards had begun to pile up.

'It is good to see you,' Sarah said. 'I am glad to see that the scars have healed considerably, Tilda.'

Tilda put a hand to her face and smiled wryly. 'I was never a great beauty, my dear. The smallpox has not ruined my chances of a great marriage, for I never had any. I am just so grateful to be alive—and I owe that to you, Sarah. Had you not cared for me so devotedly, I am sure I should have died.'

'I dare say one of the maids would have done all

I did,' Sarah replied modestly. 'But I did not wish to leave you to a stranger's care, Tilda.'

'It was fortunate for me,' Tilda said. 'A servant might have cared for me, but not as lovingly, my dear. I shall never forget your kindness and, if ever I may be of service to you…'

'Thank you,' Sarah said and shook her head. She did not wish Tilda to feel obliged to her. 'But I do not think there is anything I need—except a suitable husband. Mama is still cross with me because I refused the Conte in Italy—but though I liked him very well, I did not love him.'

'There was someone else,' Tilda said and frowned. 'Mr Elworthy married, did he not? I think he is a widower of some months now.'

'Yes, I have seen John,' Sarah said and her eyes clouded with disappointment. 'I believe he is still grieving for his wife.'

'I do not think it was a love match between them,' Tilda said and looked thoughtful. She had heard some disturbing rumours concerning Mr Elworthy quite recently, but did not know whether to believe them. She would certainly say nothing to Sarah for the moment. 'It may be that he thinks you still prefer not to marry, my dear.'

'Perhaps…' Sarah wrinkled her smooth brow. 'Yet I do not believe he can have thought that… Perhaps it is just too soon.' Perhaps she had misunderstood him and he had never cared for her as more than a friend.

'Too soon for propriety? Yes, he may think that, because he has always been a perfect gentleman and behaves just as he ought,' Tilda said. She could not think that the man who had done so much to help Arabella and Sarah could possibly have done anything to harm his wife, and decided to dismiss the rumour from her mind. 'Perhaps you will meet him again soon.'

'He did say he would come up for Lady Cavendish's ball,' Sarah said. 'I have promised to save two dances for him.'

'There you are, then,' Tilda said and smiled at her affectionately. 'When he sees you looking ravishing and dancing with other gentlemen, he will realise that he cares, and then I am sure he will ask you to marry him. Besides, you will meet a lot of gentlemen in the next few weeks and you may meet someone who sweeps you off your feet and makes you fall madly in love with him.'

'Yes, perhaps,' Sarah said, though she did not think it likely. 'Now, tell me, Tilda, what have you been reading? I have a book of poetry in my trunk that I believe you will like…'

'Have you read *Northanger Abbey?*' Tilda asked. 'I have been rereading it again, and I like it very well. Some people do not like it as well as her earlier books, of course. I think it is sad that Miss Austen has only been truly acknowledged since her death. Why do you imagine she was forced to publish under an assumed name while she lived?'

'I have no idea, for her secret was known to many besides her family and friends,' Sarah said. 'I have read all her books, but I think I might like to read *Northanger Abbey* again when you have finished it, Tilda.'

'Then of course you shall,' her friend promised, smiling at her. 'I am so glad that you have come to visit with us, Sarah. We shall have plenty of time to talk…'

'Oh, yes,' Sarah agreed. 'I am sure that we shall…'

They had been in town four days, most of which had been spent shopping or visiting the seamstress to have fittings for all the new clothes her mama seemed to think she needed before she was fit to be seen in town. This morning, Sarah had escaped before her mama was up. Accompanying Tilda to the library to change Lady Tate's books, she lingered to look into the window of a fashionable milliner's just as a gentleman came out carrying a bandbox.

'Miss Redmond,' he said, tipping his hat. 'And can it be Miss Hunter?'

Sarah glanced at his face and smiled. 'Captain

Hernshaw, how nice to see you,' she said. 'Are you on a visit home or have you left your post in Rome?'

'I have been called back,' Captain Hernshaw said. 'I believe I am to be offered a safe seat for the Whigs at a by-election. It is in my uncle's gift apparently, and the voting will be a mere formality. He would like me home to oversee the family affairs from time to time, and I may further my political career, which is of course my wish.'

'I see,' Sarah replied. 'I fear I have little knowledge of such things, sir, though I am sure it is an interesting career for a gentleman and I wish you well of it. I am truly glad to see you again. We are giving a small dance at the end of this month. I hope you will come?'

'Yes, of course,' he said. 'I shall look forward to it. I dare say we shall meet quite often, Miss Hunter—though I go down to the country for a few days next week. I shall return the week after and shall hope to see you then.'

'Yes, that will be pleasant,' Sarah said. 'Good day, sir. We must not delay you.'

'No, indeed. As you see, I have been shopping.' He indicated the bandbox he was carrying. 'A small gift for my sister. Rosemary is just seventeen and this will be her come-out into society.'

'And you have bought her a new bonnet,' Sarah said. 'You are a kind brother, Captain Hernshaw.'

'It is a surprise. I must hope that she will like it,' he said and tipped his hat to her before walking away.

'What a pleasant gentleman he is,' Tilda remarked as they moved on, crossing the road towards the lending library, where for a small subscription they were able to choose from an interesting selection of books. 'I can never forget how swiftly he dispatched that awful man who tried to kill you and then attacked Arabella. I am sure we have Captain Hernshaw to thank for her not being badly hurt or even killed.' She gave a shudder as a shiver of ice ran down her spine.

'Yes, he showed great skill and presence of mind,' Sarah agreed. 'I have always thought him very pleasant.' She had not told Tilda that she thought that Captain Hernshaw had been on the verge of proposing to her in Rome, for she was a modest girl and did not like to appear to brag of such things.

'Well, I dare say there are quite a few pleasant gentlemen in town,' Tilda said and smiled for she had noticed that someone was staring at them from a passing carriage. She touched Sarah's arm after it had gone past them. 'That was the Duke of Pentyre, my dear. I think he was looking at you just now. He seemed quite taken with what he saw.'

'No, was he?' Sarah laughed softly. 'I am sure you

are mistaken, Tilda dear. I have never met the duke and I am sure there are lots of pretty girls in London just now. I do not imagine that he finds me particularly special.'

'Oh, I do not know,' Tilda said. She thought that her companion was very much out of the ordinary. She had more of an air about her than most of the naïve young ladies brought to town by their hopeful mamas—and was perhaps just the type of woman to catch the eye of some of the more seasoned campaigners. Gentlemen who had been on the town for several years, but had escaped the matrimonial net, were perhaps now looking for a suitable wife with whom to set up their nursery. She did not know much of the duke—his was an Irish title—but she understood that he also had large estates in England, and that he was thought to be very wealthy. 'I believe that a lot of gentlemen will find you rather special, my dear.'

'That is because you are prejudiced in my favour, dearest Tilda,' Sarah said and squeezed her arm. 'Ah, here we are. I wonder if there are any new books today. I think I should like to read something of Lord Byron's if they have it…'

Sarah glanced at herself in the full-length cheval mirror in her bedroom, turning this way and that to admire her gown. It was a simple muslin, but draped with spangled gauze so that it sparkled in the candlelight. Her hair had been swept up on top of her head, though spirals of fair hair curled down her neck and clustered about her face. It had been dressed with white silk flowers and pearls and she had a simple strand of pearls linked with gold around her wrist. Her long gloves were white with a touch of pink embroidery at the edges.

'You look very well, my dear,' Mrs Hunter said, entering behind her. 'Yes, I like that ensemble. I was not sure when Madame Deloir suggested it. I thought it might look rather too sophisticated, but she was right. It does suit you, makes you look a little out of the ordinary.'

'Thank you, Mama,' Sarah said. 'Did you come to fetch me? I am ready now.' She picked up a spray of pink and white roses, which had been ordered for her by her brother, who had come up to town that very day. 'It was thoughtful of Charles to send these for me.'

'I dare say you will receive several floral tributes after this evening,' her mother said with a look of satisfaction. 'Hester was telling me that we have all been invited to a ball to be given by the Duke of Pentyre and hosted by Lady Jersey next week. She had not expected to be asked, but news of your arrival must have begun to circulate, dearest.'

It was their first important evening engagement. Until now they had dined with a few of Lady Tate's friends and attended one small card party and a musical affair. This was Sarah's first experience of an English ball in a private house, and she was both excited and nervous.

'Everyone has been kind, Mama,' Sarah said now. 'It was good of Lady Moore to invite us this evening, was it not?'

'Lady Moore and I knew one another years ago,' Mrs Hunter replied. 'However, the invitation from the Duke of Pentyre was unexpected at this early stage, Sarah. We must feel flattered for I would imagine that only the very best of society will be there.'

'Oh…' Sarah turned aside so that her mother should not see that her cheeks were warm. 'Well, I am sure it is most kind of the duke and Lady Jersey.'

'Yes, indeed it is,' Mrs Hunter said. 'Well, let us go down, my dear. We do not wish to keep the others waiting.'

Sarah walked obediently in her mother's wake. Lady Tate and Tilda were already in the hall being helped on with their evening cloaks by the housekeeper. Tilda smiled as she watched Sarah come down the stairs to join them.

'You look quite beautiful,' she said. 'That gown is a triumph, Sarah dear.'

'Thank you,' Sarah replied. 'It is rather lovely, isn't it?'

'I am sure any gown would look lovely on you, Sarah,' Lady Tate told her with a look of approval. 'Are we all ready? I know that Coachman is ready for us…'

She led the way outside to where her town carriage was waiting to convey them to the house of Lady Moore, which was a few streets away. Sarah knew that they could have walked there in the time it took to make the carriage and horses ready, but it was impossible—their dainty evening shoes would gather the filth of the pavements and it would not be wise for four ladies to be abroad in London at night without an escort. In their own carriage, with their grooms and coachman, they were perfectly safe. They were unlikely to be accosted by the bands of wild young men who sometimes roamed the streets looking for victims to persecute, and highwaymen usually haunted only the lonely country roads.

Sarah listened to the chatter of her companions. She had little to say, for she was feeling apprehensive. Would she be left standing at the side of the room for more than one dance? She had few acquaintance in London, though she had met some ladies, friends of her mother's and Lady Tate's, but only a sprinkling of gentlemen as yet—and most of them were either married or quite elderly.

The house was lit up outside and link boys waited with their lanterns to show the way for the ladies as they stepped down from the carriage. A red carpet had been laid down for them so that they did not soil their slippers. Inside the house, maids took their wraps from them and they were directed to the main stairs, leading up to the first floor. Sarah could hear music playing as they reached the top and followed other guests to what was a large drawing room, which had been turned into a ballroom for the evening. Double doors had been folded back to give access from a second parlour, where the guests were mingling and drinking champagne.

That evening was only a small affair, with no more than fifty guests invited, not one of the huge crushes that would take place later in the season. Lady Moore had, as she made clear in her invitation, asked her close friends to a *little* dance for her niece Julia. She smiled as Sarah was brought forward to be introduced.

'Ah, Miss Hunter—Sarah, my dear. I want you to meet Julia. She is a little younger than you, perhaps, but I hope you may become friends.' She looked approvingly at her niece. 'This is Miss Sarah Hunter, Julia. Why do you not go with her now, my love? Most of our guests are here and I shall greet the latecomers alone. There is no need for you to miss the dancing, for it has already begun.'

'Thank you, Aunt,' Julia said and nodded to Sarah. 'If you would like to come with me, Miss Hunter. I must confess that I am glad to have your company. Aunt Mary tells me that it is your first dance in London and it is mine too. We may give each other courage perhaps?'

'Yes, of course,' Sarah replied and smiled at her. She was a pretty girl with dark hair and not as tall as Sarah, but she seemed friendly and willing to be entertained. 'I should like that, Julia. I do not know many people in town yet.'

'Nor I,' Julia said. 'My aunt is very pleased with herself for she has captured one or two notable persons. The duke has not yet arrived, but he has said that he will come.'

'Oh…' Sarah was at a loss. 'I am sorry—I do not know who you mean.'

'My aunt's cousin—the Duke of Pentyre,' Julia said. 'He is a rather distant cousin really, several times removed, but she does not mention that in company. She sent him an invitation, but did not think he would attend—he often refuses more prestigious affairs than this, you know.'

'He sounds rather proud.'

'Yes, perhaps. I have only met him once and he just stared through me. I was, of course, only a child then, but I did not truly like him. Aunt Mary is always talking of him, but I do not think I should like to marry him.'

'Why is that?' Sarah asked, a little surprised at the confidence.

'Oh…no reason, just that he frightens me,' Julia said and gave a nervous giggle. 'But I am talking too much. It is because I am anxious, I suppose.'

'Not at all.'

Sarah shook her head and gave her new friend an encouraging smile. They had entered the ballroom now and, glancing round, she saw that ten couples were dancing, while a sprinkling of gentlemen stood talking.

They had been noticed! Sarah took a deep breath as three gentlemen came towards them, inclining their heads respectfully to Julia.

'Miss Moore, may I beg a dance with you?' one of them said and then looked at Sarah, his eyebrows raised. 'I do not believe I have had the honour?'

'Lord Henry Arnold,' Julia said. 'May I present Miss Sarah Hunter… Sir Matthew, Lord Bingham…'

The first introductions over, Sarah was asked to dance by all three gentlemen, beginning with Lord Bingham. She danced next with Lord Arnold and continued with Sir Matthew. Returning to her mama after the third dance, she was besieged by eager gentlemen. Her mama introduced those she was acquainted with and Lady Tate made her known to some others. It was not long before her card was filled and her fears of being a wallflower long forgotten.

She and Julia had stood together between dances, getting to know each other. It was therefore almost two hours later that Sarah returned from dancing with Lord Bingham for the second time to discover a tall and distinguished gentleman standing with her mama and Lady Tate.

'Ah, Sarah my dear,' Mrs Hunter said. 'The duke was delayed earlier and has but now arrived. He asked if he might dance with you and I was obliged to tell him that your card was filled. However, I said that I was sure you would allow him to take you into supper, my dear.'

Sarah dipped a curtsy. The gentleman was perhaps in his early forties, still attractive, if not wildly handsome, and, as he smiled at her, she thought that he had a pleasant manner.

'I shall be obliged, your Grace,' she replied. 'I have been asked to take supper by several gentlemen and found it difficult to choose without offence—but I believe you may claim to have precedence.'

'By virtue of my rank?' he asked, one mobile eyebrow lifting in wry amusement. 'I would prefer that I was your personal choice, Miss Hunter—but shall accept that I must earn your good opinion.'

'Oh, no, sir,' Sarah said and laughed softly. 'I am sure that it ought not to be a case of earning my good opinion, for we do not know one another and I can have formed no opinion as yet.'

'Beautiful and sensible,' the duke said approvingly. 'I believe you are to attend my own small affair, Miss Hunter. I must ask that you will save at least one dance for me.'

'Oh, I think I may spare two—one to make up for the disappointment of this evening, if you wish it, sir?'

'Thank you.' His eyes were warm with amusement. 'It will do very well, Miss Hunter. I shall claim you for supper.'

'Thank you,' she said. There was no time to say more, for her next partner had arrived and she could only smile vaguely at the duke before she was led away.

'You have a charming daughter,' the duke said, glancing at Mrs Hunter. 'I shall hope that we may meet often in the future.'

'There, Selina,' Lady Tate whispered as he walked away. 'I think Sarah has made a conquest. What a fine thing it would be for her if he were to make her an offer.'

'I had thought…the Conte di Ceasares, you know,' Mrs Hunter said, her eyes on the retreating back of the duke. 'But I suppose he is not such a catch as the Duke of Pentyre.'

'Surely it is for Sarah to marry a man she truly cares for and respects,' Tilda said in hushed tones. 'Are you certain that the duke would be a wise choice for her, Mrs Hunter?'

'Whatever can you mean?' Mrs Hunter said, a sharp note in her voice. 'He is everything a girl like Sarah could wish for, I am sure.'

'But what do you know of him—except that he is a duke and wealthy?'

'He is received and respected universally,' Lady Tate said. 'There is no doubt of it, Tilda. He would be an excellent match for Sarah.'

'Perhaps.' Tilda was unconvinced, but did not continue her protest. She might have more to say at an appropriate time. The duke must be at least twenty years older than Sarah, and she was sure in her own mind that the girl was in love with John Elworthy. She for one would not like to see Sarah forced into marriage just because the man was rich and well born.

Sarah had not given the possibility a thought. She was enjoying herself far more than she had thought she would, meeting lots of new friends and receiving many compliments on her gown, her appearance and her manners. In fact, it could be said that the only other girl in the room to receive as much attention was Julia, whose dance it was.

They had by now become firm friends and had promised to meet to go walking or shopping together as often as it could be managed, though with the Season beginning to get truly under way both had invitations for all manner of affairs. Picnics, dinners, musical evenings, card parties and dancing were just a few of the ingenious ideas the influential hostesses had come up with—to say nothing of the outdoor events, carriage drives and outings to the race meetings that the gentlemen enjoyed so much.

At the end of that dance, it was time for supper and as she left the floor she was approached by several eager gentlemen. However, they parted as a deep voice claimed her, allowing the duke through to offer her his arm.

'Miss Hunter. I believe we are promised for supper?'

'Yes, thank you, sir.'

Sarah laid her hand on his arm, allowing him to lead her through to the supper room, where she discovered that a table awaited them. It was already laden with several platters of the choicest delicacies and two servants hovered, waiting to serve them. Sarah knew that most of the ladies and gentlemen had gone to the buffet to serve themselves, but she was being treated as though she were someone special. It was because she was partnered by the duke, of course.

'Is everything to your liking?' he asked. 'Please say if there is something you would prefer. I am certain it can be brought.'

'I think I should be hard to please if I could not be pleased with this, sir,' Sarah said and looked at the servant hovering. 'I should like a little salmon and some green peas, if you please.'

'Will you have some wine? Or would you prefer champagne?'

Sarah smiled at the duke. 'I think champagne, if it is no trouble.'

'Of course,' he said and nodded to the other waiter, who went off at once to procure it for her. 'I understand you have been travelling in Italy until recently, Miss Hunter?'

'We returned home a few weeks ago,' Sarah said. 'We stayed there for more than two years.'

'You like living abroad?'

'I made many friends,' Sarah said. 'But I am quite happy to be home again.'

'I understand that you went away for your health?'

Sarah felt her cheeks become slightly warm. 'I was very ill at one time, sir. Mama thought it best to take me away.' She touched the wing of white at her right temple self-consciously. It was a constant reminder of a time that she had tried hard to forget.

'I trust you are better now?'

'Yes, thank you. I am quite well.'

'I thought so,' he said. 'I think you will be a success this season, Miss Hunter. I may even say that you will be the latest rage. You have something about you that is uncommon.'

'You are very kind to say so, sir.'

'I never say what I do not mean.'

Sarah looked into his eyes and felt a tingle at the base of her neck. He seemed a very pleasant, charming man, but there was something about him that made her uneasy.

'Then I shall thank you for the compliment, sir.'

The duke continued to make small talk throughout supper. However, as the guests began to make their way back to the ballroom, he took his leave of Sarah and Mrs Hunter, who had come to join them.

'I am pleased to have made your acquaintance, ma'am—and yours, Miss Hunter. I shall hope that we meet again soon.'

'We have just been given vouchers for Almack's next week,' Mrs Hunter said, looking rather like the cat that has stolen the cream. 'I believe you attend sometimes, sir?'

'Yes, I do,' he said and inclined his head. 'But I dare say we shall meet everywhere, Mrs Hunter.'

She watched as he walked away from them, her eyes glowing as she looked back at Sarah. 'That means we shall be invited *everywhere*. Mark my words, Sarah, the invitations will pour in now.'

Mrs Hunter was proved right; if they had received a nice flow of invitations before, they were inundated with them now. When there was more than one affair on a certain night, it was only possible to attend them all by leaving one event after an hour or so to move on to the next. It became a mad social whirl and Sarah's feet seemed to hardly touch the floor as she went from one large, prestigious affair to another. If it was not a private ball or soirée, it was a card party, masked rout or a visit to Vauxhall with a party of friends. Sarah found it exciting but also tiring, and sometimes wished for more leisure to spend with her true friends.

Mrs Hunter, however, had not stopped wearing a smile since they had been invited to a dinner and cards at Lady Mountbank's house, for she was one of the leading hostesses of the Season, and a lady known to ignore those who did not come out of the top drawer. While the Hunters were a good county family and well respected, they were not titled and had not expected to be invited into the homes of the most influential hostesses. Mrs Hunter had hoped that the invitations to the large balls might come their way, but now they were being asked to the more intimate affairs that she had not dreamed of. It was, of course, the Duke of Pentyre's influence, something she never failed to impress on her daughter.

'He is taken with you, Sarah,' she told her daughter on the morning of his own ball. 'I dare say he is not yet ready to speak, but if you are sensible he will do so by the end of the Season.'

'You cannot be sure of that,' Sarah said, avoiding her mother's gaze. She was already aware that the duke had shown her considerable favour and that because of it several rather haughty hostesses had gone out of their way to be more than kind to her. She was, as he had predicted, becoming all the rage, and could not enter a drawing room without being immediately surrounded by both ladies and gentlemen. 'We should not take his intentions for granted, Mama. After all, he might have married before this had he wished.'

'Gentlemen often prefer to wait to take a wife,' her mother told her. 'I think he has it in mind to set up his family, Sarah. No doubt he feels it is time to make sure of his heir.'

Sarah did not argue further. She had hoped that this would not happen, that she would be given time to discover if there was a gentleman she particularly liked among her new acquaintances. However, it seemed that Mrs Hunter had recovered from her disappointment that Sarah had not taken the Conte and was now set on her becoming a duchess.

She spent that morning driving to the park with Julia Moore and two gentlemen, and enjoyed herself a great deal. Neither of the gentlemen had shown a particular preference for her. Indeed, she believed she had been included in the party so that she might accompany Julia, and that suited her very well. She had no idea that several gentlemen who might have offered for her were watching to see what happened. It was already being rumoured in the clubs that Pentyre meant to have her, and it was generally felt that he was a bad man to cross.

He was known to have been wild in his youth, though much reformed of late. His fortune was intact, thanks to his skill and luck at the card tables, but he was a crack shot and few would risk offending him and being called out.

After saying goodbye to her friends outside Lady Tate's house, Sarah went into the parlour to discover that Elizabeth Cavendish was visiting. Elizabeth smiled at her.

'At last I have found you at home,' she said. 'I have called twice, Sarah, but you were out. I wanted to ask if you will come to a reading tomorrow afternoon?'

'Yes, thank you,' Sarah said before her mother could refuse. 'I had kept it free, because we have been out every day and shall not be home until the early hours of the morning.'

'Ah yes, you are to attend Pentyre's ball, are you not?' Elizabeth said and frowned. 'We were invited, but Daniel declined. We had a previous engagement.'

'Could you not have come on?' Mrs Hunter said. 'I think almost everyone will be there.'

'I am sure it will be a sad crush,' Elizabeth agreed. 'However, Daniel does not particularly care for Pentyre—some dispute in the past, I believe.'

'I have found him charming,' Mrs Hunter said. 'He seems very taken with Sarah, you know.'

'Indeed?' Elizabeth frowned, but made no comment. She would ask Daniel for more particulars before she spoke to Mrs Hunter. If she had understood her husband correctly, Pentyre was not the husband for Sarah, but she would not say anything before she had all the facts.

'Well, I must take my leave,' she said and kissed Sarah on the cheek. 'I shall see you tomorrow?'

'Yes, certainly,' Sarah said. 'I did not realise you

were in town. We have been receiving so many cards and I have not seen them all…but I knew you were due to arrive any day and I have looked forward to seeing you.'

'I hope that we shall meet often,' Elizabeth said. 'But at least you will be coming to our ball next week.'

'Yes, of course,' Sarah replied. She walked out to the hall with Elizabeth. 'I would not miss it for the world.' She hesitated, and then, 'Have you heard from Mr Elworthy?'

'Oh, yes,' Elizabeth said. 'Has he not called on you? He came up yesterday and is to stay until after my ball. He is our guest and you may see him tomorrow if he cares to join us for a few minutes. We shall be mostly ladies, of course, but he may come in for a while—if only at teatime.'

'John is in London?' Sarah's heart leaped with excitement. In all the chaos of the social whirl she had managed to put him out of her thoughts for a while—at least, she had pushed her unhappiness to the back of her mind. Now the idea that she might see him the next day filled her with anticipation. 'I do hope he will come, Elizabeth.'

'Yes, so do I,' her friend said and squeezed her hand. 'I shall do my best for you, dearest. And now I really must go…'

Returning to the parlour at the back of the house, Sarah was thoughtful. She was glad that she had kept the following afternoon free. It would be interesting to sit with Elizabeth and her friends and hear some readings—but it would be wonderful if John were to join them.

'I really cannot see what the Earl of Cavendish can find to dislike about Pentyre,' Mrs Hunter was saying to Lady Tate as she walked in and sat down in a chair that looked out at the garden.

'I did hear something—' Tilda said and stopped as the two older ladies turned to look at her. 'It was just that he had been a little wild when he was younger, though I am not sure what that means exactly.'

'A reformed rake makes the best husband,' Mrs Hunter said, giving Tilda a sour look. 'I am sure a lot of gentlemen could be described in that way, Tilda.'

Sarah did not listen to Tilda's reply or the conversation that went on behind her. All she could think of was the possibility of seeing John Elworthy the next day.

Would he think she had changed since she came up to town? She had been given so many compliments on her appearance that she thought her fashionable clothes must have given her a new touch. Perhaps John would find her attractive now. Or was he still too much in love with his wife to care?

'Sarah—are you attending?' Mrs Hunter spoke to her sharply. 'I was saying that you ought to go up and rest. You want to look your best for this evening, do you not?'

'Yes, Mama, of course.' Sarah rose and went out of the room obediently. Usually, she would have protested that she was not tired, but today she was glad of the excuse to be alone so that she could think about meeting John the following day.

## Chapter Four

It was the most glittering occasion that Sarah had so far attended. Three large reception rooms were overflowing with guests, the rich hue of their clothes and jewels like butterflies fluttering in a gaudy herbaceous border. Overhead, huge chandeliers were a blaze of light, the glitter of crystal baubles adding to the brilliance of the scene.

Sarah's party moved slowly through the reception rooms towards the gallery, where the sound of music could be heard. The French windows had been thrown open to let in some air, for the overcrowded rooms were already warm and the scent of strong perfume was heavy on the air. Such a crush would guarantee the success of the evening, though Sarah could not help thinking that the smaller dances she had attended were more enjoyable.

However, several gentlemen, who were eager to dance with her, came immediately to greet her, and, mindful that she had promised the Duke of Pentyre two dances, she filled them in herself for later in the evening. She was soon dancing with gentlemen she had met before at various affairs, laughing up at them, caught by the pleasure of charming company. Her card was filled for the whole evening before an hour had passed, and she was not even aware that someone came to the door of the gallery to watch for a few minutes. He left a short time later without greeting her or her companions. Had she been aware that John Elworthy had paid a brief visit to the ball without seeking her out, it might have dimmed her pleasure in the evening, but she did not catch sight of him and so she was able to dance and laugh with her friends in a carefree manner.

The Duke of Pentyre claimed Sarah for the two dances promised, and she found him charming. He danced well and treated her just as a gentleman ought, returning her to her mama after their dance. At supper Sarah's party found a table reserved for them and servants to wait on them, though the duke paid merely a fleeting visit to inquire if they had all they needed. As the host he was bestowing attention on as many of his guests as possible, though he did find time to ask Sarah if she would drive with him in the park the next afternoon.

'Forgive me, sir, but I am already engaged,' she told him with a smile. 'Perhaps another day?'

'Yes, of course,' he replied easily. 'When are you at home? I shall call on your mama.'

'On Tuesday afternoons, sir,' Sarah said. 'I know Mama would be honoured to receive you should you wish to call.'

'Then I shall,' he promised and moved on.

'I warned you not to engage yourself for tomorrow,' Mrs Hunter said when he had left them. 'You might have gone driving with him if you had not been so foolish.'

'But I am looking forward to Elizabeth's reading afternoon,' Sarah said. 'The duke will call on you, Mama—and I shall go driving with him another day.'

'Yes, I suppose it will not do to seem too available,' Mrs Hunter said, looking thoughtful. 'After all, you have met only a few times. We cannot be certain of his intentions yet.'

'We have some weeks before we go home,' Sarah said. 'Surely there is no hurry for anything, Mama?'

Mrs Hunter gave her a direct look, but said no more. People were beginning to drift back to the ballroom and Sarah's next partner had come to look for her. Mrs Hunter and Lady Tate sat on a little longer at the supper table.

'I think he seems interested in her,' she said reflectively. 'Will he come up to scratch, do you think, Hester?'

'Perhaps,' Lady Tate said and looked thoughtful. 'I believe John Elworthy was here briefly this evening. Did you see him? He was watching Sarah…'

'Watching Sarah?' Mrs Hunter's eyes slanted round to look at her. 'I know she liked him once, but he married someone else. Besides, I should wish more for Sarah. Mr Elworthy is a pleasant gentleman, I grant you that, but the duke would be so much better for her.'

'Perhaps,' Lady Tate said. 'But you should not push her, Selina. It only makes her uneasy. I am sure Sarah will receive more than one offer before long. Allow her to choose for herself, my dear.'

'I want her to be happy,' Mrs Hunter said and took out her lace kerchief, pleating it nervously between her fingers and dabbing at the corners of her eyes. 'Most of all I want her to be safe. I cannot forget that other business, Hester. If the gossips were to hear of it, it might mean the end of her chances.'

'Ah, I see,' Lady Tate said. 'I doubt that will happen, Selina. It was some time ago and must be forgotten. Besides, so few knew of it that I cannot think it likely. No, my dear, be patient—I do not believe that Sarah will disappoint you.'

* * *

John left the Duke of Pentyre's ball and walked through the dimly lit streets in the direction of the Earl of Cavendish's town house in a fashionable garden square. He had been undecided whether to attend the ball that evening, but at the last minute looked in on the off-chance of seeing Sarah. He had watched her from afar, seeing that she looked happy and was enjoying herself with her friends. It was not surprising that she had become so popular, for she was beautiful. Since arriving in town, he had been hearing her name everywhere he went, and knew that several gentlemen were betting openly on Pentyre to win her.

The idea of Sarah married to the duke brought a frown to John's face. Daniel could not stomach the man and said that he was a ruthless rake, a little too lucky at the card tables, and had once been seen often in the company of Sir Montague Forsythe.

'You do not think that he…?' John's blood had run cold when Daniel told him. 'Was he a member of that hellish gang who kidnapped Sarah and meant to sacrifice her in their foul rituals?'

'No, I do not think it—at least, I do not know,' Daniel said, a thoughtful expression on his face. 'His name was never spoken of in connection with that affair. However, I know for a fact that his tastes are perverted. There was a disturbing tale circulating about him some years ago. It has been forgotten now, of course, but I have warned Charles not to allow his sister to become too involved with him. I am sure that he would not give his permission to the match—unless, of course, Sarah was in love with him. He may well have reformed for all I can tell. What I actually know of his activities was some years ago. A man may change, I suppose.'

'Yes, perhaps,' John agreed, though like Daniel he felt doubtful. 'But still…I would not wish such a match for her.'

'No, nor I were she my sister,' Daniel had told him. 'But what of you, John? What news of your affair?'

'Nothing as yet,' John said. 'I have not as yet received another letter and Andrea's things have stopped appearing in my rooms since I spoke to the housekeeper. I believe it must have been one of the maids, and I think Mrs Raven may have dismissed her.'

'That is good,' Daniel said. 'Perhaps it will fade away now, John. Whoever was trying to cause trouble for you may simply give up. But you must not relax your guard—and watch your back just in case….'

Afterwards, John wondered whether it was instinct

or Daniel's advice that warned him later that night. He had been lost in thought, but all of a sudden he was aware of something happening behind him. He turned swiftly and saw that a man dressed in dark clothes had crept up behind him. His arm was raised, a heavy club about to be brought down on John's head.

John leapt at him, wrestling with him for the club as the fellow grunted and struck out with his feet in an effort to bring John down. However, the element of surprise had been lost and the rogue soon discovered that his mark was not as easy as he had imagined. When John landed a punch on his chin, the ruffian went staggering back, his cudgel falling from his hand. John kicked it away and the other man hesitated, then turned tail and went running off into the night, clearly thinking him not worth the effort of robbing.

John continued his walk. He had been in little real danger for he had a loaded pistol in his greatcoat pocket and might have used it if he had chosen—but had the attack been meant only as robbery? Was his attacker a villain of the streets taking his chance to rob an unwary gentleman—or had there been something more sinister behind the attempt?

He was thoughtful as he reached Cavendish Place and went inside. The letters had stopped, as had the attempt to make him think that Andrea was haunting him—but perhaps his enemy had decided to try a different tactic?

Who was he—and what had John done to arouse his hatred? It was a mystery he could not yet solve, though certain suspicions were beginning to take shape at the back of his mind.

Sarah had chosen a deep sea-green walking gown for her appointment with Elizabeth that afternoon. It had a high waist and a wide sash of a deeper green, and she wore a short jacket that fastened over her breasts with silk frogging and fitted neatly into her waist. Her bonnet was of a fine straw decorated with ribbons to match her gown and tied at the side in a large bow, her hair hanging down in a bunch of artfully arranged ringlets. All of which gave her a fashionable touch, setting off her pretty face to advantage.

Tilda had decided to accompany her. They walked the short distance to Elizabeth's house, for it was a lovely day and it was good to be in the sunshine. Admitted to the house, they both took off their bonnets and outer garments, going into the front parlour on the first floor to meet their hostess and those of her guests that had already arrived.

Sarah glanced around the room hopefully for John, but there was no sign of him. However, she had not expected that he would attend the meeting in its entirety and was not too disappointed. It was primarily a ladies' affair and she met several of her friends, but also some older ladies that she had not been introduced to before. More ladies were arriving all the time and there were twenty present when the first reading began with some lines from Byron's *Childe Harold's Pilgrimage.* A discussion then ensued as to whether his later work was of an equal standard, with some liking *The Corsair* and others very much against.

'I have always believed him the equal of Scott,' Lady Barrie said. She was a young matron, confident and lively. Her eyes sparkled with mischief, for she had meant to provoke a reaction. 'And for me he far eclipses Wordsworth—'

'Oh, no, how can you say so?' Sarah exclaimed. 'Mr Wordsworth has written some wonderful poetry. I love the Lucy poems and *Lyrical Ballads* is always by my bedside.'

'Have you read *The Excursion?*' Lady Barrie asked. 'It is not the quality of earlier work and I am not the only one to think it. Besides, Byron has such passion, such a zest for life…'

'Yes, I do not disagree with that,' Sarah said. 'But some of Mr Wordsworth's work is so romantic… Byron is a little dark and haunted, do you not agree?'

This was bound to cause a storm of words since

Byron's poetry was always controversial. And so the afternoon was soon spent in readings and heated discussion, after which the ladies took tea in high good humour with each other, all harsh words forgotten as they reverted to their social manners.

Sarah had looked for John but he did not join them for tea, and she could not help but be disappointed as she took her leave of Elizabeth a little later. It had been an enjoyable afternoon, but her hopes had come to nothing. However, as she and Tilda stepped into the warmth of a lazy summer afternoon, she saw that John was making his way across the square towards the house and waited until he came to them.

'Good afternoon, ladies,' he said, lifting his hat to them. 'Is your meeting over? I had hoped that I might be back in time to take tea with you, but my business kept me later than I had expected.'

'We had a lively meeting,' Sarah said, her face glowing from the pleasure of seeing him again. 'Will you walk with us a little way, sir? Or have you further business?'

'For the moment, none,' John said. 'Shall we walk to the garden? We may sit there in the sun for a little. It is warm and quite balmy.'

'Yes, thank you,' Sarah said, and took the arm he

offered. Tilda had stopped to speak with one of the other ladies. 'We shall not be far away, dearest.'

'You seem to get on very well with Miss Redmond these days,' John said, glancing down at her face. He thought that she was more beautiful now than he had ever seen her, and felt a surge of longing to hold her in his arms. 'I did not think that was always the case?'

'Oh, everything changed after Tilda was kidnapped,' Sarah said. 'She understood me better and…in Italy we became close friends.'

John nodded. They had reached the wooden bench in the garden and sat down. For a moment they were silent as they listened to a thrush trilling from the branch of a tree, feeling at ease together. Tilly had lingered on the far side of the square, and was kept talking to various ladies leaving the house.

'I am looking forward to Elizabeth's ball,' Sarah said, gazing up at him. 'You have not forgotten your promise to me, sir?'

'How could I?' John asked, his gaze intent on her face. He realised that he wanted very much to dance with her, to hold her close, hear her laughter and inhale the intoxicating perfume of her skin. Surely there was no sin in letting himself admit the feelings he had for her? 'I am looking forward to it, Sarah— and I hope you will keep two dances for me. I know that you have many admirers now, but your promise was made before you came to town.'

Sarah glowed in the warmth of his smile. Her heart had begun to race wildly and she was sure that he felt something for her.

'And it shall be kept,' Sarah told him. 'No matter who asks, I shall not give your dances away.'

'Good,' he said and reached for her hand, holding it with a firm gentle grip. His touch sent a tingle winging down her spine, making her want to melt into his arms. 'We are friends, are we not, Sarah? We have always liked one another, have we not?'

'Yes, of course.' Sarah hesitated, then, 'It might perhaps have been more once had I not been such a foolish child—' She caught her breath as she saw the look in his eyes.

'None of that business was your doing,' John said and smiled at her so tenderly that her heart caught. He did care for her! In that moment she felt the barriers swept away and it was as it had been between them at Arabella's home that last summer before she went to Italy. 'Have you put the nightmares of that time behind you?'

'Yes, I have. They are completely gone.'

'I am glad of it,' John said. He wondered if he dared to speak, but hesitated and in that moment Tilda came up to them. 'Ah, here is Miss Redmond.'

He stood up and inclined his head. 'I shall look forward to seeing you both at Elizabeth's ball.'

'Yes, of course,' Tilda said and looked awkward. 'If I am interrupting anything, I can walk on alone—'

'No, of course not,' John said. 'It will keep for another day. I shall call one day, Sarah. Please give my regards to your mama.'

'Thank you,' Sarah said and smiled at Tilda. 'You are right, we must be getting back or Mama will worry. And we have a dinner engagement for this evening. I shall look forward to seeing you soon, Mr Elworthy.'

'Your servant, ladies.' John tipped his hat to them and walked across the square.

Sarah linked arms with Tilda. 'Thank you for taking your time,' she said. 'I think we have come to a better understanding. Mr Elworthy did not actually say anything definite, but he seemed to be more his own self—far less anxious than he was when we were staying with Arabella a few weeks back.'

'Good.' Tilda nodded comfortably. 'I thought you appeared to get on well—and Mr Elworthy is a perfect gentleman, Sarah. It is only a year since his wife died in unfortunate circumstances. He could not be expected to do anything that might seem precipitate.'

'I have thought perhaps he was afraid to speak too soon,' Sarah said, looking happy. She had wondered if it was all too late, but now she had hope again. 'But I believe that he will ask me, Tilda. I was afraid he might not, but now I think he may.'

'And why not?' Tilda asked looking at her affectionately. 'You are beautiful, kind, intelligent and warm-hearted. Any man with half a brain would want you for his wife.'

Sarah's laughter tinkled like bells. 'I have not so many admirers—at least, not of a serious kind. I know it is not long since we came to London, but Julia Moore has been here about the same length of time and she has had two proposals already.'

'Julia is quite an heiress,' Tilda said, looking thoughtful.

'Is that why gentlemen ask one to marry them, then?' Sarah's eyes narrowed in thought. 'It seems so cold and calculating…'

'Not all the time.' Tilda pulled a face. 'It is a consideration for some, especially those that need to replenish their fortunes. However, you are not without fortune, my dear. I do not think that is the reason you have not received any offers just yet. It might have something to do with your Mama's obvious preference for the Duke of Pentyre.'

Sarah looked at her, a startled expression on her face. 'No, do you think so? I had thought one or two gentlemen might speak before this, because they seemed interested at first and then less so—but I imagined I must have disappointed in some way.'

'I doubt that is the case,' Tilda told her with a smile of affection. 'Did you wish for their offers?'

'No, of course not. There is only one gentleman I wish to offer for me, Tilda. I would refuse any other…at least I did consider the Conte di Ceasares, because I thought I must marry. I do not think I should care to marry the duke even if he is as wealthy as Mama says…'

'I think it would be wiser not,' Tilda said. 'I sometimes hear things, Sarah…things that you might not. People tend not to notice me sitting quietly in my corner. They make indiscreet remarks that they would not say if they realised they were overheard. I have heard things about the Duke of Pentyre that make me think he would not be a good husband for you, my dear.' Tilda had also heard gossip about John Elworthy, but, knowing him as she did, she was inclined to dismiss it as tittle-tattle.

'Oh…will you tell me?' Sarah raised her brows.

'Not unless it becomes necessary,' Tilda said a little primly. 'I do not wish to be accused of spreading gossip. Your mama would not be pleased with me and that might upset Hester—but should it be a case of your good, then I shall speak out and accept the consequences.'

Sarah squeezed her arm. 'I dare say it will not matter. Mama gets a little cross with me because I show no interest in the duke, but if John asks me to be his wife she must agree. I know Charles would support me and he is my guardian after all.'

'And so he should, my dear,' Tilda agreed. 'I am sure there could be no objection to an alliance with Mr Elworthy. He is one of the nicest men I have ever met.'

'Yes, isn't he?' Sarah said happily. 'I feel so much better now that I have seen him again, Tilda. I shall pray that he asks me to marry him on the night of Elizabeth's ball…'

John and Sarah did not meet again until the night of Elizabeth's ball, though she found his card on the silver salver in the hall after returning from her drive with the Duke of Pentyre. She had enjoyed herself, for the duke had been all that he should be, and his groom had accompanied them, which meant that the needs of propriety had been more than met during their short outing to the park.

They had talked mainly of horses, which were one of the duke's passions. It seemed that he bred his horses in Ireland but kept a string of them at Newmarket with a trainer. He had seemed pleased that Sarah liked to ride and told her that she was a good judge when she admired the cattle he was driving that day.

'You seem an admirable young lady, Miss Hunter,' he told her after they had been driving for some time in the park. 'The kind of lady that would make a suitable wife for almost any gentleman.'

'You are very kind, sir,' Sarah replied carefully. 'But should not marriage be based on affection and respect—if not love? I do not believe that true happiness can come through arranged contracts, do you?'

The duke's eyes were thoughtful as he looked at her. She looked older than her years, because of those wings of white at her temples, and her steady manner. However, she was still quite young. He had had it in mind to approach her mama quite soon, but now she had given him pause for thought. If she wished to be wooed, it might be best to proceed more slowly.

'It must depend upon one's idea of happiness, I suppose,' he said and smiled at her before changing the subject to one concerning a play that was being performed at the Haymarket Theatre.

Sarah was guiltily aware that he might have been on the verge of proposing to her; from her mama's expectant looks on her return, it was clear that she had also hoped for it. However, Sarah parried Mrs Hunter's questions by saying that the drive had been most enjoyable, and that the duke had said he might call on them one day.

'Very well, Sarah,' her mother said, but her eyes were thoughtful as they dwelled on her daughter. 'I hope you are not keeping anything from me—but I shall say no more for the moment.'

Sarah did not reply. She felt that she was treading on dangerous ground—if the duke should speak to her mama, pressure would be brought to bear, unless she had an alternative offer. She could only hope that John might speak at Elizabeth's ball.

She counted the days, but at last it arrived, and, as she dressed in a new gown of white silk with spangled drapery across the bodice, her heart was beating so fast that she felt breathless. In a short time she would see him, speak to him—dance with him. She seemed to have been anticipating this night for ever, and the short drive set her nerves racing.

John was almost the first person she saw. He was standing near Elizabeth and Daniel as they greeted their guests and appeared to be waiting for someone. As he saw her, his eyes lit from within and he came to greet her and her companions with a smile.

'Lady Tate, Mrs Hunter and Tilda…' he said and then turned his gaze on Sarah. 'May I be permitted to say that you look truly beautiful tonight, Miss Hunter.'

'Thank you, sir, you are very kind,' Sarah said and

her heart leaped with excitement as he bestowed a gentle smile on her. 'I have been keeping this gown for this evening, because it is my favourite.'

'And it becomes you well,' John said. 'I trust you have saved my dances for me?'

'Oh, yes,' she replied, a faint flush in her cheeks. 'The first waltz of the evening, and the supper dance.'

'They will do very well,' he said and turned to her mother. 'Do you stay long in town, Mrs Hunter?'

'Oh, another three or four weeks,' she said vaguely. 'I have not perfectly made up my mind.'

'You must dine with us next week, Mr Elworthy,' Lady Tate said. 'And you know we are always at home on Tuesdays.'

'Thank you, ma'am, I shall certainly dine with you— and I shall remember that you are at home on Tuesday.'

'Come along, Sarah,' Mrs Hunter said. 'We must move on and greet some of our other friends.'

Sarah reluctantly obeyed. Julia Moore and some others of her friends were already gathered in the ballroom, and Sarah was immediately asked if she would dance, which she agreed to with pleasure. Her card was soon filled, and before she knew it John was claiming her for the first waltz.

He gazed down at her as he placed his hand at her waist, sending a little tremor of delight winging through her. 'You are very popular, Miss Hunter. I believe you have become what they call all the craze.'

'Oh, no, have I?' Sarah laughed. 'The Duke of Pentyre said that I would. Perhaps it is his influence. I am sure that it is because of his kindness that we are invited everywhere.'

'Pentyre?' John's gaze became fixed on her face, his eyes intent and questioning. 'Are you much acquainted with him?'

'We seem to meet often,' she replied. 'He is a charming gentleman—but then, there are many very pleasant gentlemen in London at the moment.'

She looked up at him so ingenuously that John was reassured. He had not mistaken that look in her eyes when they sat for a few moments in the square opposite Elizabeth's house. He was sure that she felt as he did, and that he had only to speak to be accepted. At the back of his mind, the guilt he had nursed for months stirred, but he crushed it ruthlessly. He was innocent of Andrea's death. Surely there was nothing to prevent his seeking happiness with someone else?

He smiled down at her, 'Yes, I dare say you have received many compliments.'

'Oh, yes, lots,' Sarah said with complete frankness. 'However, I do not regard them, sir. I think that most of them are gallantry and nothing more.'

'Will you think it gallantry if I tell you that I think you as lovely in nature as you are in looks?'

'Oh, no,' she replied and laughed. 'For you are one of the most honest people I know. Elizabeth always says it and so does Arabella. You are known for it, Mr Elworthy.'

John's smile lit his eyes. 'I have good friends. I am very fortunate.'

'Lady Tate is planning an excursion to Vauxhall next week. Shall you be one of the party, Mr Elworthy?'

'I think perhaps I may,' John told her. 'I had not planned to stay on above a few days, but I think I may extend my visit for a little longer.'

Sarah smiled. She sensed that he intended to prolong his visit for her sake and she felt relaxed and happy. John might not ask her to be his wife this evening, but she was sure that he would speak soon.

They finished their dance and John returned her to her friends. She was claimed almost immediately by her next partner and went from one to another happily until the supper dance. John came to her again and they danced, talking easily of various friends and the further delights the season was about to offer them.

After their dance John offered her his arm, taking her into the long room where a delicious buffet supper had been laid out. They chose a few trifles together and wandered over to sit close to the long French windows that opened out onto the garden at the back of the house. Sarah toyed with a wine syllabub, but John ate nothing, merely sipping at a glass of champagne. When he saw that Sarah was not hungry, he stood up.

'Shall we take a turn on the terrace?' he asked. 'I should like to speak with you alone if I may.'

'Yes, of course,' she agreed, her heart beating wildly. She stood up, gazing at him with eyes that told of what was in her heart. However, just as they were about to leave the supper room, a footman came towards them. He handed John a letter on a silver salver.

John took it with a little frown, breaking the wax seal to scan its contents. A gasp escaped him and a little nerve flicked in his cheek.

'Is something wrong, Mr Elworthy?' Sarah asked. 'Is it bad news?'

'Yes, I am afraid it is,' John said. 'It means that we must postpone our talk, Sarah. I am sorry, but I have to return home at once.'

'Oh, no,' Sarah said, disappointment sharp in her voice. She had looked forward to this evening so much and now it was to end too soon. 'Must you really go this very evening?'

'My son is ill,' John told her, his eyes dark with

emotion. 'It seems they fear for his life. I must go immediately. Forgive me, Sarah. I am not sure when I shall see you again. I can only hope that it is not too long…'

Sarah watched him walk away from her. The disappointment was so great that she did not know how she stopped herself from bursting into tears. She turned away and went out on to the balcony, needing to be alone for a few minutes.

It was there that Elizabeth found her a little later. She knew at once that Sarah was in some distress.

'Are you ill, dearest?'

'No, not ill,' Sarah replied in a muffled voice. 'John left early. He received bad news from home.'

'Daniel told me. John took his leave of him. It was a pity that the news should come this evening—but John has been very protective of the boy since Andrea's death. He feels responsible for the child.'

'Yes, of course. I understand, but…' Sarah sighed. She could not tell anyone that she had been expecting a proposal of marriage—it would look very brazen of her. 'I had been so looking forward to this evening.' She lifted her head, knowing that she must return to the ballroom. 'Well, I dare say I shall see him again one day.'

Despite her brave attempt to hide her disappointment, Elizabeth knew what she was feeling underneath and it made her thoughtful. She did not say anything more to Sarah for the moment, but she believed that she might be able to come up with a plan that would enable Sarah to see John much sooner than she might think.

Sarah rejoined her friends in time for the next dance to begin. For the rest of the evening her smiles and conversation were a little subdued, though she did her best to hide the heaviness of her heart. However, she was relieved when the ball was over and they were able to go home.

Mrs Hunter looked at her a little oddly as she said goodnight and went up to her room, but she did not ask any probing questions. The Duke of Pentyre had not so far come up to scratch and she wondered if she had misunderstood his intentions. Elizabeth had told her that Mr Elworthy had had bad news from home, and she thought she could guess at the reason for her daughter's quiet mood.

'I am not sure what to do for the best,' she remarked to Lady Tate the next afternoon when they were taking tea alone together. 'I had expected the duke might speak before this, but he has not... perhaps I read too much into his intentions...'

'You must be patient for a little,' Lady Tate said.

'These things cannot be rushed, my dear Selina. I know that you wish to see Sarah settled, but the Season is still quite young.'

'Yes, of course,' Mrs Hunter said. She glanced up as a footman came in bearing a letter on a silver salver, taking it with surprise. 'For me? Thank you, Henry.' Turning it over, she saw that it bore the seal of the Countess of Cavendish. 'Elizabeth Cavendish has written to me, Hester. I wonder why…' She broke the seal and read the first few lines, giving a little cry of surprise. 'Oh…how thoughtful…yes, it might be the very thing…'

'Good news, Selina?' Lady Tate asked.

'Yes, it is…at least, it might be,' Mrs Hunter replied. 'Elizabeth has very kindly asked if Sarah may accompany them when they return to the country this weekend. She says that she will send her back in their carriage in ten days' time…'

'Ah, yes, Elizabeth is so perceptive, isn't she?' Lady Tate nodded her head and smiled. 'It may be the very thing, Selina. Sarah was looking a little tired this morning. A few days in the good country air of Yorkshire might be just the thing for her, my dear.'

'And if she is not here for a while it may help to make up someone else's mind,' Mrs Hunter said. 'If the duke is thinking things over, he may realise that

Sarah has other admirers…' She looked well pleased with herself. 'Yes, I shall write at once and tell Elizabeth that Sarah will be pleased to stay with her for a few days.'

'Do you not think you should ask Sarah first?' Lady Tate said. 'She will be in very soon now, Selina. I am sure that she will wish to go, but perhaps you ought to be sure…'

'Yes, I shall ask her, of course, but my letter might as well be written, for I am certain of her answer.' She lifted her brows at her companion. 'I am not quite a fool, Hester. I may have ambitions for my daughter, but I know that she once liked Mr Elworthy very much—perhaps still does. I shall give her this opportunity to attach his affections, and I shall allow her to go without me in this instance. However, should she come home without an understanding, then I must do my best for her. I still have hope of the duke.'

'I do not think Sarah truly likes Pentyre.'

'Well, then she must make a push to secure Mr Elworthy—I am determined that she shall not be allowed to dwindle into a sad old age.'

'Selina! You must not say such things, my dear. Sarah is very young yet. I think you worry too much.'

'Perhaps…' A little shiver went through Mrs

Hunter. 'I do not forget what happened to her, Hester. She is my little girl. I want to see her married to a gentleman who will look after her and give her the kind of life she ought to have.'

'Yes, of course you do,' Lady Tate said. 'I am sure Mr Elworthy feels a deep affection for Sarah, and, given the chance, I believe that he will ask for her.'

'For her sake I hope that is so,' Mrs Hunter said. 'But if he does not, she must make up her mind to take either Pentyre or the Conte di Ceasares.'

'Oh, Selina,' Lady Tate said with a hint of reproach. 'Do not be too hasty or too harsh. Remember what Sarah has suffered, my dear.'

'I do remember it,' Mrs Hunter said. 'It haunts me night and day, Hester. I can never be at peace until I know that she is settled with a good husband to care for her. That is why I am determined that she must marry soon…'

'Will you accompany me to the library?' Sarah asked the following afternoon. 'It is a pleasant day for a walk and it would be nice to have your company, Tilda.'

'Yes, of course,' Tilda agreed, getting up at once from the desk she had been sitting at. 'These letters may wait.'

Sarah waited while Tilda fetched a bonnet and

pelisse and then they left the house together. The library was only a few streets away from Lady Tate's house, but it was only to be expected that they would meet some of their acquaintance.

'Ah, Miss Hunter,' Lady Barrie said. 'I see that you are on your way to the library. I have just been myself.' She hesitated, and then, 'I was wondering whether I ought to call, Miss Hunter. Someone linked your name with a certain gentleman and I thought I ought to make you aware of something I had heard…'

'Linked my name with a gentleman?' Sarah looked at her sharply. 'I am not sure I understand you, ma'am.'

'Oh, nothing in the least reprehensible,' Lady Barrie assured her. 'At least, as far as you are concerned…it was just some gossip about Mr Elworthy, but perhaps I should not…' She shook her head. 'No, forget I said anything. Oh, is that the time? I must fly…'

Sarah looked at Tilda as the other woman walked hurriedly past. 'What did she mean? Some gossip about Mr Elworthy?'

'Oh, dear,' Tilda said. 'I had heard it, of course, but I did not wish to tell you—I am sure it means nothing.'

'Please, Tilda, you must tell me,' Sarah begged. 'You know that I love John. If there is some wicked tale about him, I must know!'

'Well, it concerns his wife's death,' Tilda said reluctantly. 'It is all nonsense, of course, for she took her own life—but some people are saying that it was his fault…that he either drove her to it by being cruel to her or actually—' She stopped and shook her head. 'No, it is too ridiculous for words. You and I both know he would never do such a thing.'

'No, indeed he would not!' Sarah said angrily. 'How could anyone believe that John might harm his wife? It is ridiculous! I am glad that you do not believe it, Tilda. I only wish that Lady Barrie had dared to tell me for I should have told her that she was much mistaken.'

'Well, it maybe for the best that she did not,' Tilda said, 'for it would not do for you to be rude to her, dearest. After all, she does not have the benefit of knowing Mr Elworthy as we do.'

'No, that is true,' Sarah said, looking thoughtful. 'But I shall not believe this wicked tale, Tilda.'

'No, my love, and nor shall I,' Tilda said, linking arms with her again. 'Let us change our books and forget it.'

Sarah sat at her dressing table. A little frown creased her brow as she thought about the chance meeting with Lady Barrie the previous afternoon. She had dismissed the tale concerning John as nonsense to Tilly, but during that night she had had a terrible dream. She had seen a girl running away from a house in distress, running to the edge of a riverbank and then a man had come out of nowhere and…he had pushed the girl into the river.

She had woken in distress, knowing that she must have been dreaming of John's wife, her nightmare influenced by the story Tilda had told her about the gossip concerning Andrea's death. It was so horrible that she had jumped out of bed and lit a candle. Once the light filled the dark corners of the room she had felt much better. Of course it was all nonsense! Andrea had taken her own life. Arabella had explained the true story to her.

She did not believe a word of the gossip! Sarah refused to let such spiteful nonsense influence her. John was brave and decent, and she loved him. She would not think about it again.

Behind her the maids were busily sorting out the clothes she would be most likely to need in the country. Some of her things would remain here as she would be returning after a week or so spent with her friends. Sarah had been surprised and delighted that Elizabeth had asked her to accompany them back to Yorkshire, and even more surprised that her mother had allowed her to go alone.

'It is very good of you to permit me, Mama,' Sarah

said when shown the letter and told of her mother's agreement. 'But Elizabeth also invited you if you wished to come…'

'Yes, she was everything that is kind,' Mrs Hunter said. 'But I should prefer to remain here with Hester. You know that I am an indifferent traveller and it would not suit me to travel all that way simply for a few days. You may go and enjoy yourself, my dear. All I ask is that you behave in a way that I should think proper, Sarah.'

'Yes, Mama, of course. You must know that I shall not do anything of which you could disapprove.' She crossed her fingers behind her back, praying that her mama would not change her mind at the last moment and forbid her to go. If Mrs Hunter had heard that lying tale about John being responsible for his wife's death, it was unlikely that she would have given her permission for the visit, but fortunately she had not as yet.

'Well, no, I do not expect it,' Mrs Hunter said with a smile. Her heart caught as she looked at her lovely daughter, for the nightmare of her loss was always present. 'Remember that I care only for your happiness, my love. Everything I do or say is for your good. I want you to be well settled for the future.'

'Thank you, Mama,' Sarah said and kissed her cheek. 'I hope that I shall soon be able to make you proud of me.'

'I have never been less than proud,' Mrs Hunter said. 'I just want to see you happy and safe.'

'Oh, I shall be quite safe with Elizabeth and the Earl of Cavendish,' Sarah said, smiling at her mother.

She felt pleased as she thought of the opportunity that would now be afforded to her. John lived only a few miles distant from Elizabeth and Daniel's home. She was sure to meet him in the next few days. When he saw her he would speak. Surely he would speak this time?

Sarah knew that she was relying on it, for otherwise her mother would grow impatient and she would have to make another choice. The Duke of Pentyre was the only one to have shown interest in her these past few weeks, though he had not actually proposed to her. But she did not want to marry him. Her heart belonged elsewhere.

And no matter what dreadful rumours she heard concerning John, she would not believe them!

# Chapter Five

The journey to Cavendish Hall was accomplished very comfortably. One night had been spent at a respectable inn on the way to make things easier for the ladies, but the Earl's carriage was lightly sprung and his horses were some of the finest and fastest to be found anywhere. Sarah and Elizabeth enjoyed each other's company, and the earl rode just ahead of them most of the time. None the less, it was a relief to them all when they arrived at dusk that evening.

'Come along in, Sarah,' Elizabeth said. 'I enjoyed my visit to town as ever, but I must admit that I am always pleased to be at home. This is the first time you have stayed with us, of course, so I shall take you upstairs myself and show you where the various rooms are. We are very comfortable here. As you see, Cavendish Hall is not so very large. It is Dora's favourite home, but she is staying with friends at the moment so you will not meet her, which is a shame for I am certain she would have loved to see you.'

'Lady Isadora?' Sarah wrinkled her brow. 'I think we must have met some years ago, but it was a very long time—before…' She shook her head, because all that was over and forgotten. She did not allow herself to dwell on the past. 'It is a lovely house, Elizabeth: not too large and overpowering. I think those very big mansions must be difficult to heat in the winter.'

'Some of Daniel's other houses are much too big,' Elizabeth said with a smile. 'He has plans for rebuilding, but he will not tell me much yet for it is to be a surprise.'

'Oh, I love nice surprises,' Sarah said. A plump, smiling woman had come to greet them and was introduced as the housekeeper. She helped them off with their outer garments and asked if she should bring some refreshment to the parlour.

'Yes, please,' Elizabeth said. 'I am going to take Miss Hunter upstairs, but we shall come down in fifteen minutes.'

'There is a cold supper laid in the small dining room, ma'am,' Mrs Bates said. 'But I think Cook has some nice warm soup if you should care for it later?'

'We shall have some wine first and then perhaps the soup with our supper,' Elizabeth said. 'Come,

Sarah, let me show you to your room. It is very comfortable and the one I occupied when I came here as Lady Isadora's companion.'

'And then you fell in love with the earl,' Sarah said with a little smile. 'How very romantic!'

'It did not always seem romantic,' Elizabeth said with a wry smile as she recalled the turbulent weeks that had led up to Daniel's proposal. 'I did not believe that he would wish to marry his mother's companion—and, of course, there was all that sorry business with Sir Montague Forsythe. He had ruined and murdered my father, you know—and he kidnapped me when he wanted to punish Daniel for poking his nose into his affairs. That was after Daniel, Charles and some other friends had first kidnapped Mr Palmer. Until then they had not been able to prove that Forsythe was responsible for your abduction. However, he boasted of it to me when he thought I was at his mercy, and, as you know, Charles accidentally killed him in the struggle to prevent his escape.'

'Yes, I know. Charles told Arabella everything and she told me. I think you were very brave, Elizabeth.'

'As you have been in facing up to what happened and getting on with your life, Sarah. I believe that in times of trouble one does what one has to do,' Elizabeth told her. 'I knew that Daniel needed proof of that man's villainy, and I believed that he or his friends would come to rescue me—and they did, all of them. Daniel got there first, but Charles and John arrived soon after.'

'John was very brave when Sir Courtney tried to kidnap Arabella,' Sarah said, looking thoughtful. 'I am sure I never thanked him as I ought…'

'You were in great distress at the time,' Elizabeth said. 'John would have understood even if you said nothing.' She gave Sarah a look of affection. 'Love will find a way, my dear. It usually does, you know. Do not give up at the first fence.'

'No, I shall not,' Sarah said. 'I understand that John must feel distressed that his son is ill, especially as his wife died in such tragic circumstances.'

'Yes, her death was tragic,' Elizabeth said and hesitated, then, 'I do not think it was a love match, Sarah. I believe John married her for reasons other than love, though I cannot tell you more than that…it is not my affair. Besides, I speak only of my own observations. I know nothing for certain.'

'I see…' Sarah said, but in fact she did not. She had assumed at their first meeting that John was still in love with his wife. If that was not the case, then why had he seemed to hold back from her? Remembering the gossip Tilda had reluctantly imparted after Lady Barrie's odd insinuations, Sarah wondered. Surely it was not possible that John was somehow implicated in his wife's death? 'Yet he seems still to be grieving?' She looked at Elizabeth inquiringly.

'I dare say John will tell you the details if he wishes you to know,' Elizabeth said. 'It is his usual habit to visit us at least once or twice a week. He came home four days ahead of us and we must hope that his son is well on the way to recovery. I shall ask Daniel to ride over in a day or so and see how he goes on.'

'Yes, that would be kind,' Sarah said, and as they went into a charming bedchamber decorated in varying shades of green and blue, 'Oh, this is lovely. Thank you so much, Elizabeth.'

'I hope you will be comfortable, Sarah. I think you can find your way back?' Sarah nodded. 'I shall see you in a few minutes.'

Sarah looked around the room, which was at the front of the house and faced the south. It had a warm, welcoming atmosphere and she knew that she would be happy staying here with her kind hosts. All she wanted now was to be able to see John again. Now that he had seen his son, he would surely ride over to visit his friends. Here, in the country, they would have plenty of time to be alone—time enough for him to ask her to be his wife.

\* \* \*

'Did you see John?' Elizabeth asked her husband as he came into the house that afternoon. They had been at home for six days and nothing had been heard of their friend. 'How is the boy?'

'I do not know,' Daniel said with a frown. 'I was told that John was too busy to see me, and that he would visit when he could.'

'How very odd,' Elizabeth said and frowned. 'That is most unlike John. Have we done something to offend him, do you think?'

'I cannot think it,' Daniel said. 'It maybe that the child is very ill…and yet it was strange for I did not even enter the house. His housekeeper came out to meet me. She said that it was best I did not go in because I might bring the sickness to you and the twins.'

'Did she say what the sickness was?'

'Yes…apparently the child has the smallpox,' Daniel replied with a frown. 'I would have gone in, Elizabeth, for I do not fear it, but I thought of you and the children.'

'Oh, this is terrible,' Elizabeth said. 'Poor John. It is no wonder that he has not called on us. He must be in a state if his son is ill with something like that—' She broke off and looked at Sarah as she came into the room. 'It is bad news, Sarah. Daniel did not see John. His son has the smallpox and he sent word that Daniel should stay away for fear of bringing it to us.'

'The smallpox…' Sarah frowned and looked thoughtful. She did not speak for a moment or two, then, 'It would not affect me—but you were wise not to go in for Elizabeth and the children's sakes, sir. It is a most terrible disease.'

'Why do you say it does not affect you? Were you vaccinated as a child?' Elizabeth asked. Sarah explained that, although she had not been inoculated, she seemed never to take it from others. Elizabeth nodded. 'How very odd—but I have heard of such cases before, though very rarely.'

'Well, there is nothing more we can do for the moment,' Daniel said with a frown, 'but I shall ride over again in two days and see what is happening.'

'The child should have reached the crisis by now,' Sarah said. 'It is usually a matter of days. Once the pustules come through, the scabs form and then fall off—and then he will no longer be infectious. John may be able to speak to you next time, sir.'

Sarah was thoughtful as she accompanied Elizabeth on a leisurely walk in the garden. If John's son had survived, he would soon be on the way to recovery—but what of John? If he had nursed the boy himself, he might have taken it from him. She voiced her fears to Elizabeth, who looked at her oddly.

'What are you saying, Sarah?'

'If John nursed the boy personally he must have felt that his servants were not to be trusted. If he should take it himself…' She hesitated, but the look in her eyes spoke volumes.

'Yes, I see what you mean. If he could not trust them to nurse the boy, how much worse may he fare himself?' Elizabeth said, her eyes opening wide as she saw the girl's expression. 'You are not suggesting that…it is not to be thought of, Sarah! Your mama would never forgive me.'

'I nursed Tilda and I did not take it. If John were ill, Elizabeth, I should not hesitate to offer myself in his service.'

'You love him very much,' Elizabeth said, 'but I could not allow you to do it, Sarah. Your reputation would be ruined if word got out, and your mama would never forgive me.'

Sarah did not argue. She had already settled it in her own mind. If nothing was heard of John in two days' time, she would ride over to his estate and discover the situation for herself. And, if need be, she would do what was necessary to ensure that he was properly cared for…

* * *

It was actually three days before Sarah took the decision to visit John's estate. Nothing had been heard from John; though Daniel had spoken of riding over to see how he was, he had not yet done so. Sarah had spent the intervening time fluctuating between hope and despair. That morning she rose early and went down to the stables, requesting that the mare she had been allocated to ride be saddled and that the young groom who helped her should accompany her.

'Do you know the direction of Elworthy Hall?' she asked and the boy nodded his head.

'Yes, miss. I often ride over with a message from the earl.'

'Then you will please show me the way,' Sarah said and thanked him as he helped her into the saddle.

He looked at her curiously, but did as he was asked, taking her by what he claimed was the shortest route, which entailed riding across a stretch of rather bleak moorland. When they arrived at the house, which was much larger than the one she had just left, she thought it rather forbidding in appearance. It must have been built more than two centuries earlier and, being fashioned of grey stone with tiny mullioned windows and a crenellated tower at one end of the main structure, seemed slightly oppressive at first glance.

Sarah looked at the young lad accompanying her. 'Wait here, Jemmy. I may be a short time or perhaps a little longer, but I shall come out to you as soon as I can. Wait for me however long it takes. Do you understand me?'

'Yes, miss.' The groom was clearly puzzled, but prepared to obey. He was a little in awe of the beautiful young lady visiting with his master and very willing to serve her.

Sarah got down from her mare, giving the reins to him and walking up to the house. Inwardly she was trembling, but she lifted her head and, gathering her courage, gave the door a rap with the heavy iron knocker. After waiting for some minutes for an answer, she knocked again. The door was answered moments later by a scowling woman dressed in black. She was tall and thin, with a sour countenance, and her eyes narrowed as she saw Sarah.

'Impatience will get you nowhere,' she muttered. 'I can't do everything. What with answering the door and looking after him upstairs—and half the maids run off or down with the sickness themselves.'

'I heard that Mr Elworthy's son was ill,' Sarah said, rushing into speech in her anxiety. 'Is there anything I can do?'

'I doubt it,' the woman said, giving her a hard look. 'For he is better and it's the master that has gone down with it now. I warned him to leave the nursing to Mrs Beeson, but he must do it himself and now he is worse than the lad ever was, if you ask me.'

'John has taken the smallpox?' Sarah said, her stomach clenching with fear. 'Please, I must see him.'

'And who would you be, then, miss?'

'I am Mr Elworthy's betrothed,' Sarah lied without hesitation. 'Is he being properly looked after, ma'am? I do not mean to offend you, but if you are the housekeeper, as I think you must be, you cannot do everything.'

'There's nothing surer,' the woman said, her gaze narrowing in suspicion. 'It's the first I've heard of Mr Elworthy being engaged to be married.'

'It happened in London before he left in a hurry to return to his son,' Sarah said, hoping that her cheeks were not fiery red as she lied. 'Please, I must see him.'

'I'm not one to stop you,' the housekeeper said. 'To tell you the truth, miss, I'm run off my feet. Two of the maids went down with it and one died. Some of the others went home because they were frightened to take it. Mrs Beeson is the village midwife and she is doing her best—but she isn't always—' She stopped and pulled a wry face. 'But you'll be taking a risk if you go near him, miss, and that's the truth of it.'

'I do not think so. I am immune to it, you see.'

'Well, if you say so, you might as well come in. I haven't time to stand here arguing.'

Sarah stepped inside as the woman moved back to admit her. The hall was large with marble floor tiles, which gave a cold feeling to the house. At one point the ceiling rose to a circular dome with stained glass windows that shed coloured light over the tiles. It had the atmosphere of a church nave and Sarah shivered for a moment, almost expecting to hear the chanting of monks.

'It takes some like that,' the housekeeper said and nodded her head. 'It was a monastery that stood here once, miss, and the stone was taken from the church to build the house—that glass, too. The late mistress swore it was haunted, though I've never seen a ghost myself.' She looked at Sarah, seeming suddenly to change, her manner becoming less hostile. 'Well, if you're engaged to the master, I suppose there's no harm in your visiting him in his bedchamber—though I'm not sure he'll know you.'

'I must see him at once,' Sarah said. 'Please, will you take me up to him, ma'am?' She smiled at the woman. 'Forgive me, I do not know your name.'

'Mrs Raven. I've been with the master since he was a lad in short coats, miss, and I wouldn't desert him—no matter what anyone says. But I can't do it all, miss.'

'No, of course you can't,' Sarah said, following her as she led the way up the main staircase and along the gallery to what must be the west wing of the house, which had been built in the shape of an E— a popular style in the days of the Tudors. This house, however, must have been built right at the end of the sixteenth century, Sarah thought, and she could see that some attempts to modernise it had been made on the first floor. 'It is obvious that you need help, Mrs Raven. This is a big house and it must be difficult to keep it as well as you do.'

'Well, it wouldn't have been so bad if the girls hadn't run off the way they did,' Mrs Raven said, a little mollified by Sarah's sympathy. 'Not that you can blame them, what with one thing and another—but I shan't desert the master and that's my mind made up.'

'I am very glad to hear it,' Sarah said. The housekeeper had stopped outside one of the doors, a frown on her face. 'Is this John's room?'

'Yes, miss, these are his rooms.' Mrs Raven sighed. 'This is as far as I go, miss. I have my responsibilities, and I bring up his tray—but I can't nurse him. Heaven knows what would happen to this place if I was took sick!'

'Yes, I understand,' Sarah said and lifted her head proudly. 'Where shall I find you when I come down, Mrs Raven?'

'Just ring the bell in the hall, miss.'

'Thank you.' Sarah nodded to her and placed her hand on the old-fashioned latch, pressing down the flat handle to open the door. The first room she entered was clearly a gentleman's sitting room—it was furnished with a sofa and armchairs covered in a heavy crimson brocade. There were large gilt-framed mirrors on the walls and some pictures of a hunting scene with dogs, horses and the hunt followers. A large bookcase covered one wall of the room and there were several wine tables, an imposing mahogany partners' desk and an elbow chair. The atmosphere was a little dark and depressing, as was much of the house that Sarah had so far seen.

She glanced round, but walked straight through to the door at the far side. Opening it, she discovered that she was in a dressing room. At the moment it was strewn with items of clothing and looked as if someone had been searching for something. She frowned—John's servants had clearly neglected their duty to their master as he lay ill. She heard a coughing sound and went quickly through the small room into the next one.

She was now in the bedchamber. It was difficult to see, for heavy curtains had been drawn across the windows, shutting out the light. A fire was burning in the grate, which made the room feel over-warm and stuffy. Sarah went across to the bed. She could see that the man lying in it had thrown back his covers and was thrashing wildly in his fever. She bent over him, laying a hand to his brow. He was bathed in a fine sweat, and clearly out of his mind as he mumbled something and cried out, his body jerking up from the bed as if he were in pain.

'John dearest,' Sarah said, and pulled the sheet over him. Any doubts she might have been harbouring fled as she saw him. 'My poor darling, how ill you are. But you shall not be neglected now. I am with you and I shall not leave you again until you are better.'

Sarah could see that the pustules had not yet appeared on his body, which meant that he was in the early stages of the disease, as she had expected. It was this first stage of the illness, when red patches appeared in the mouth, that was the most dangerous, and the most infectious. If he lived through the next few days, he would probably recover, though he would almost certainly be scarred. All she could think of at the moment was that somehow she must make sure that he was made comfortable and everything possible was done to ensure his survival.

Sarah went over to the fireplace and, with the poker, raked some of the wood away from the centre of the fire so that it did not burn so fiercely. Then she walked to the window, and pulled back the heavy curtains, leaving only a thin silk drape to keep the room shaded. She looked at John once more and saw that he seemed to be resting a little easier. She would go back downstairs and tell Mrs Raven what she needed—and she would give her groom a message for Elizabeth. Then she would return to the sickroom and stay with John until the crisis was over.

Elizabeth was in her favourite sitting room when her housekeeper came in later that morning. She looked up and smiled, laying her needlework aside.

'Yes, Mrs Bates? You wanted something?'

'There's a young lad from the stables here, my lady. He says as he has a message from Miss Hunter…'

'A message from Sarah?' Elizabeth was immediately alert. She had been a little surprised at Sarah's decision to go riding so early, but now she felt apprehensive. 'Bring him in, Mrs Bates.'

'He has the smell of the stables about him, ma'am.'

'Never mind that, I shall see him.'

Elizabeth was on her feet when Jemmy walked in. He looked at her nervously. The housekeeper had been on at him about cleaning his boots and he was not at ease in the elegant drawing room.

'You have a message from Miss Hunter?'

'Yes, milady,' Jemmy said and pulled at his

forelock. 'She asked me to take her over to Elworthy Hall this mornin' early—and she made me wait. Then she came out and told me she was stayin', because Mr Elworthy was struck down with the smallpox. She said I should tell you that she would not return until all danger of infection was gone, and that she would think it kindly if you would send some of her things over. And there's some things she wants from your stillroom if you could spare them, milady—for the fever, she said.'

'Sarah is staying at Elworthy Hall…' Elizabeth frowned. 'The foolish girl! But it is my fault. I should have guessed what she would do if there was no news of him.' Elizabeth took a turn about the room, her mind working swiftly. There was little she could do—even if Daniel went to fetch Sarah back, it was unlikely that she would return with him. The girl had a mind of her own! After a few moments, she turned decisively to the young groom. They must make the best of the situation. 'I think I must do as she asks. Are you willing to be our go-between, Jemmy? You know that there is smallpox in the house. You should not go in, and stay well clear of anyone who comes out to give you a message. You do not want to take it to your family or your friends.'

'I've had the vaccination, ma'am,' Jemmy said. 'Lady Isadora offered it to all those on the estate who would take it some years back and Ma had all of us done. She said smallpox were a dreadful thing and that her mother and brother both died of it when she were a girl. I don't mind going 'cause I shan't take it—leastwise, them what has had the vaccination don't take it as bad.'

'I know there was a vogue for vaccination some years ago,' Elizabeth said. 'I did not have it myself, nor, I think, did the earl—though I believe Lady Isadora was one of the first to have it herself. It is perhaps a sensible thing to do and I believe I may have the children done when they are a little older, if my husband agrees.' She was thinking aloud, but suddenly recalled herself and smiled at the youth. 'Go to the kitchen and have something to eat, Jemmy—and then I shall send a bag with Miss Hunter's things for you to take when you have eaten.'

Daniel entered the room just after the boy left. He looked at his wife curiously. 'What was young Jemmy doing here?'

'He brought me a message from Sarah,' Elizabeth said. 'Early this morning she rode over to Elworthy Hall and she is staying to nurse John, who apparently has the smallpox.'

'The foolish girl!' Daniel exclaimed. 'Does she not know what she is doing? It is a vile sickness and kills too many—and the scarring is sometimes terrible.'

'When you first brought the news of the child's illness, Sarah told me that she is naturally immune to it,' Elizabeth said. 'Indeed, I have heard of people who manage to remain free of it though others around them fall sick. Jemmy says that Mama had him vaccinated when he was a small boy, and he is willing to be our go-between. He is to take some of Sarah's things and medicines she needs to her.'

'I suppose it would be useless to order her to return home?' Daniel nodded wryly as he saw his wife's face. 'No, I did not imagine she would listen. Sarah is not an innocent child any longer, whatever her mama may think. She learned the hard way, and I dare say she knows her own mind.'

'She loves John very much, Daniel.'

'That much is obvious,' he said. 'But do they have an understanding? She is throwing her reputation to the winds, Elizabeth. If this gets out…' He looked grim. 'It puts John in an impossible situation.'

'Why should it become common knowledge?' Elizabeth asked. 'I have no intention of telling anyone but you, dearest.'

'What of her mother?'

'I shall write and say that Sarah has had a little chill and ask permission for her to stay longer with us.'

Daniel frowned at her. 'You are treading on dangerous ground, my love. Mrs Hunter worries over her daughter. She may very well decide to post down here immediately.'

'I do not like to mislead her,' Elizabeth said. 'But if I told her the truth, she would come at once and demand that Sarah return with her.'

'That is very true,' Daniel said. 'Delay your letter for the moment, Elizabeth. We may be in a better position to write to her mama in a few days. All I hope is that the foolish girl does not take it from him!'

'I think she would not care, providing that she can make him well,' Elizabeth said and smiled at him lovingly. 'Do not tell me that you would not do the same in her shoes, Daniel, for I should not believe you.'

He laughed and shook his head. 'That is somewhat different, my love. This has made me think and I believe we should have the children in-oculated when they are older, Elizabeth. I have looked into it and it is done by means of a diluted solution of the cowpox. In some cases the patient will take a mild form of the disease, but it protects against the more virulent disease.'

'I think perhaps we should ask the doctor to vacci-nate us all,' Elizabeth said. 'I had not thought about it for years, because there had not been an outbreak—but now I believe it would be wise to take precautions.'

'Let us hope that Sarah knows what she is doing,' Daniel said. 'I dare not think what her mama would say if she should fall foul of it—or Charles, either!'

'Charles would not blame us—he knows that Sarah has a mind of her own—but her mama would not be so easily satisfied.'

Elizabeth was thoughtful. She had no intention of betraying Sarah to her mama, but she knew that, in keeping her whereabouts a secret, she was neglecting her duty. Mrs Hunter would be justifiably angry if she ever learned the truth. She must just hope that she would not…

Sarah bent over her patient, lifting him gently as she held a cup to his mouth and tried to get him to drink the mixture that Elizabeth had sent over. It was one commonly used for fevers of all kinds and would ease him if she could just get him to swallow enough. However, he would not open his mouth for her and the healing mixture was running down his chin.

'You'll never get it down him like that, my lovely,' a voice said from the doorway. 'I'll give 'ee a hand. You wants to squeeze his nose—like this, see.'

Sarah looked at the slatternly woman who had entered the bedchamber. She had not sent Mrs Beeson away, though she always had a faint odour of strong wine on her breath, and was not as clean in her habits as Sarah liked. However, she was the only person in the house who was prepared to enter the sickroom, and she was still taking care of John's son, who, Sarah had seen for herself, was well on the way to recovery. The pustules had come and gone on the child's body, leaving pitted marks that would remain as scars—though they might fade a little as he grew older. But at least he lived.

Mrs Beeson pinched John's nose with her thumb and forefinger. As he opened his mouth in order to breathe, she motioned to Sarah to tip her medicine on to his tongue, at the same time letting go of his nose. John spluttered and choked a little as the liquid trickled down his throat, but most of it went down.

'Thank you,' Sarah said, though she thought the old woman's methods a little unkind. 'He would not swallow and I am sure it will do him good.'

'He's done better since you came,' Sally Beeson said and gave a cackle of laughter. 'Stands to reason, don't it? A fine gentleman like that knows when he's got a pretty nurse fussing over 'im—likes that better than old Sally round 'im, I can tell 'ee.'

'He does not even know I am here,' Sarah said, her throat caught with tears. 'He is so hot and so ill, Mrs Beeson. Much worse than Tilda was when I nursed her in Italy.'

'Took it bad, the poor lad,' Sally said and cackled again. 'Had to nurse the boy in his arms, despite I tells 'im 'ee will take it from the child. Little Nathaniel weren't too bad when all's said and done, and that's the truth—but Mr Elworthy were like a man possessed. Nuthin' I says would 'ee listen to and this is the result of it.'

'I expect he loves his son,' Sarah said. 'Is that not natural enough?'

'Ah, 'twud be if it were all right and tight,' Sally said. 'But I ain't one to gossip and I knows when to keep my mouth shut. Not like some others I could mention. There's talk enough and I won't add to it, though maybe I knows more than some what thinks they knows it all. Here when she birthed the lad I was and there's nothing hid when the pain is bad. 'Sides, the lad were as big and healthy as they come…'

'What do you mean?' Sarah looked at her curiously. 'What do you know, Mrs Beeson?'

Sally shook her head at her. Sarah would have questioned her further, but at that moment John sat bolt upright in the bed. His eyes were wide open and staring, but she knew that he was not seeing her.

'Andrea!' he cried in an agonised voice. 'Forgive me! I beg you to forgive me. I did not mean to hurt you. I never meant you to die…' He gasped and fell back on the pillows, his eyes closed, lost to the fever once more.

Sarah bent over him, smoothing a lock of fair hair back from his forehead. She bathed his face with a cool cloth, and then turned to look at Mrs Beeson.

'I think he feels a little easier, Mrs Beeson. He is not as hot as he was before.'

'The pustules are coming through,' Sally said and picked up his arm, showing Sarah the red marks that were beginning to appear on John's flesh. 'Once they are out he should be through the worst of it, my lovely. A few days until the scabs fall off, and then he'll not be infectious to any. You'll save your man yet despite all.'

'Shall I?' Sarah looked at her and tears hovered. She had lived in dread these past days, for it had seemed to her that John might die despite her care. 'Do you think he will live, Mrs Beeson?'

'Shouldn't wonder at it. The first few days are the worst. I reckon as you've nearly weathered the storm, though it ain't certain yet. Give it another two or three days and we'll see what happens— maybe he'll slip away and maybe he'll recover.'

'I pray that he does recover,' Sarah said, wiping her sleeve across her face. She had hardly slept for the past four nights and was feeling very tired. She knew that she must lie down for a while.

'You go and rest, my lovely,' Sally Beeson said, seeing the signs of exhaustion on her pretty face. 'Don't want you going down sick, do we? I knows you says you don't take the smallpox, but you'm tired to death and that's no good. He won't want to see you lookin' washed out when he's over it, will he?'

'You will call me if anything should happen?'

'I'll call you if I needs you,' the old woman said. 'Sleep afore you kills yourself, my lovely.'

Sarah smiled at her and went through into the adjoining room. She thought it must have belonged to John's wife, for it had been refurbished in pretty shades of pink and cream and was much airier and lighter than his own bedchamber. That was furnished in dark browns, crimsons and gold and, though everything was of good quality, the furnishings had an air of outdated opulence that belonged to an earlier time.

Sarah had not ventured far from the west wing, because she had spent all her time with John, watching over him, bathing him and caring for him in every way she could. Mrs Beeson had helped her, but the other servants did not come near. Mrs Raven brought food, water and fresh bedding up to the rooms, but she would not enter. Sally Beeson dealt with the soiled linen, and Sarah knew that without her both John and his son might have been left to die in their own filth. Smallpox was such a feared disease that many people simply refused to nurse those who had taken it.

Sarah lay down on the bed and closed her eyes. She was very, very tired and it was not long before she slept.

When she awoke the afternoon had flown and it was nearly evening. She jumped up, washing and tidying herself swiftly before going back through to John's bedchamber.

Mrs Beeson had gone. Sarah was distressed that she had left John alone, for since her arrival they had contrived not to leave him for a moment. She knew that the woman must have slipped out to see to John's son, though Mrs Raven was taking care of him for some of the time now that he was no longer infectious.

Going over to the bed, Sarah put a hand to his forehead and discovered that he felt quite cool. It seemed that the fever had left him at last, though she could see that there were clusters of the unpleasant pustules over his face. For the moment there was little she could do except apply a cooling lotion to the lesions. Later, when the scabs had formed and gone, she could give him a special cream that she had bought from a doctor in Italy. It had helped

Tilda, though it was likely that some of the scars would never heal. He would never be quite as handsome as he had once been, but that did not change her feelings for him.

What did the scars matter when it seemed likely that he would live? Sarah knew that for her part they meant nothing. She was only thankful that he had not died. She smiled as he stirred and murmured a name in his sleep.

'Sarah….' he murmured softly. 'Stay with me, my love…do not leave me. I love you so…'

Sarah felt her throat tighten with emotion. It was her name he had spoken, not Andrea's. He was not aware that she was with him. Now that the fever had broken he was dreaming—and it was her that he thought of as he dreamed. She stroked his hair back from his face and smiled.

'I am here with you, my dearest. I love you. I love you so much, my darling John. Please get better, my love…please get better…' She turned as the door opened and Mrs Beeson entered. 'Why did you not call me before you left him?'

'It weren't necessary,' the old woman said. 'Sleepin' like a babe, he were, when I left 'im to see to the child. He'll pull through now, you marks my words. We'll have 'im up and about afore the month's out or Sally don't know her business.'

'It is clear that you do know it, Mrs Beeson,' Sarah told her gratefully. 'I should have found it hard to nurse him alone—and I do not know what might have happened had neither of us come to him.'

'Mrs Raven sent for me as soon as the boy were took bad,' Sally said with a grin that showed a row of blackened teeth. 'Doctor wouldn't come near more than the once, so she said, told her to nurse the babe, but she were afeared of it same as most of 'em are. You'm a brave one, my lovely. Ain't many as would risk their own lives for the sake of another the way you have.'

'I love him,' Sarah said. She blushed as she said it—she knew that she was laying herself open to ridicule and hurt by confessing her love. Yet her action in coming here uninvited had already said more than words. 'What else could I do, Mrs Beeson?'

'You call me Sally, my lovely. He's a lucky man, luckier than he knows—and he's a good man an all. You don't want to take notice of anythin' you might hear to the contrary. I seen him with 'er and the boy and I knows a thing or two.' Sally touched the side of her nose. 'Mrs Raven was asking if you was ready for your dinner?'

'Yes, please. I shall have it here on a tray—some soup and bread will do very well, thank you.'

'No, you won't, then,' Sally told her. 'He'll be all

right for a bit on his own now, my dear. There's a proper dinner waitin' for you in the dining room, and 'tis time as you started to eat decent food.'

Sarah glanced at the bed. It was true that John was resting comfortably. He was deeply asleep and she could do no good by staying here for the moment. 'Very well, Sally. I shall do as you say. I do feel hungry this evening, and it would be foolish of me to let my own health slide just as John is recovering, would it not?'

'You go down then and I'll pop in every now and then. You'm been here nearly a week now and seen nothing of the house. 'Tis time you had a look about you if you'm to be mistress 'ere.'

Sarah blushed and turned away from the old woman's bright, inquisitive eyes. She had told the housekeeper that she was John's betrothed to gain access to him while he was ill—but what would he think of her behaviour when he recovered and learned what she had done?

Sarah pushed her embarrassment to the back of her mind. When John recovered he would either ask her to marry him or he would not. If he did not, then she would leave this house never to return, so it did not matter what his servants thought of her.

She was not quite sure where her meal was laid out downstairs for she had seen only a little of the house as she was conducted upstairs to John's apartments. She wandered towards the back of the house, glancing into the empty rooms as she passed them, and then she heard voices and something made her hesitate.

'You should not have come back here,' a voice that Sarah recognised as Mrs Raven's said. 'If you cause more trouble I shall likely be dismissed for it. Especially as there's to be a new mistress in the house. He won't stand for more of your tricks.'

'I've nowhere else to go—and you've said yourself that you need more help in the house, Aunt Bessie. Let me stay for a while. I promise I shan't do anything more to upset things.'

'Well, it's the truth I need help, for half the maids fled when the boy went down with the smallpox, and one of them died of it—though Millie is on her feet again. Very well, you can stay, but if you make trouble I shall tell him it was you and why.'

'I'm sorry I did it. I promise I shan't again.'

'Get off to the kitchen, then. I've plenty of work needs doing.'

Sarah opened the door of the room in which she had heard the voices and found that Mrs Raven was alone. It seemed to be a small sitting room, with a door leading through to another room at the back, and she thought that she must have stumbled upon the housekeeper's private apartments.

'Forgive me. I was told that a meal had been laid for me and I was looking for the dining parlour.'

'Well, you won't find it back here, miss,' the housekeeper said. 'I'll take you and show you if you like. The family rooms are mostly on the first floor of the main section. The upper floor of the tower is unsafe and no one goes there these days, and some of the rooms in the east wing have been shut up for years.'

'Thank you,' Sarah said. 'I am sorry for intruding. Were you talking to someone just now?'

'Just one of the maids, miss. I've taken a new girl on to make up for those we've lost.' Mrs Raven led the way back up the stairs, turning to the right at the top. 'The dining parlour and the drawing room are here, miss. There is a small sitting room downstairs in the west wing that you might prefer to use in summer. It opens out on to the best part of the garden—and the breakfast parlour is there too. I laid your meal in the dining room because it was closer for you. I hope as Mr Elworthy is a little better, miss?'

'Yes, I believe so,' Sarah said. 'He may still be in the infectious stage so it might be best if you do not enter the bedchamber, but we think that he is through the worst.'

'I am relieved to hear it, miss,' the woman said. 'I

am sure it was very brave of you to come and nurse him—even if you are immune to the disease. The gossips will make the worst of it, Miss Hunter—and he already has something of a reputation.'

Sarah turned to look at her. 'What do you mean? Mr Elworthy is one of the most honest and decent gentlemen I know.'

'I must say I've always thought so myself, miss.' Mrs Raven sniffed. 'I dare say its all lies, but you know what folk are—they say there's no smoke without fire.'

'What are you hinting at?' Sarah's gaze narrowed. Was the housekeeper speaking of those vile rumours concerning John's wife? 'Please speak plainly if you will. If you have something to say, then say it.'

'It isn't for me to say one way or the other. If you haven't heard the rumours, Miss Hunter, it's best you don't. I'm not one to spread gossip.'

'I must insist that you tell me what you mean!' Sarah took hold of her arm. She had no intention of telling the woman that she had heard gossip. 'You cannot make insinuations and then just leave it like that. If you have heard something important, please tell me now.'

'Well, perhaps it might be best to hear it from me,' Mrs Raven said. 'You must understand that it is not me making these accusations, Miss Hunter—

but I've heard it whispered that he killed Mrs Elworthy. I know it is a wicked lie, of course it is—but it is what they are saying anyway.'

'Oh, how could anyone say such a wicked thing!' This was even worse than the rumour Tilda had told her of in London. It made Sarah angry that people should say such things when he was unable to defend himself. 'I have never heard such nonsense. John would never, never do anything of the kind. I know he wouldn't.'

The housekeeper's expression was wooden. 'Well, I didn't say as he had, miss—but it's what some folks around here are saying. They say he drove her to her death, and some whisper that he either killed her or made the poor soul so wretched that she didn't know what she was doing. The opinion is divided, miss—and with him getting married so soon it is going to add fuel to the fire, if you ask me.'

'I see…' Sarah nodded, thoughtfully. It was true that if John remarried too soon it might lead to more speculation and gossip. They had arrived at the dining room and she thanked the housekeeper for providing such a nice meal for her, which was set out on the long mahogany sideboard under silver covers. 'Thank you, Mrs Raven. I am glad you told me what is being said, but I must tell you that it is a wicked lie and should not be believed.'

'Yes, miss. I dare say you are right,' Mrs Raven said. 'I'll leave you to enjoy your meal, then.'

'Yes, thank you.'

Sarah went to the sideboard and began to look underneath the covers, discovering scrambled eggs, cold ham and green beans, also a dish of crispy fried potatoes, all of which smelled delicious. She helped herself to a little of the egg, potatoes and ham and took the plate to her solitary place at the table. She began to eat, determined that she would not let the spiteful gossip upset her. John couldn't have done anything that would have made his wife take her own life…could he? Despite her feelings for John, she knew a flicker of doubt, but squashed it almost immediately. The man she loved was incapable of doing anything ungenerous or evil!

Her thoughts turned to Mrs Raven. The housekeeper had lied about the person she had been speaking to in her room earlier. Obviously, her niece had been dismissed once for wrongdoing, but she had taken her back into employment. Sarah wondered what the girl had done and whether she could be trusted not to do it again.

Mrs Beeson had hinted at something being untoward in the house, and now Mrs Raven's gossip, added to what she had heard in London, seemed to indicate that John's marriage had not been all that it should be. Mrs Beeson had warned her to take no notice of any gossip she heard, but Mrs Raven seemed to be suggesting that there might be something in the whispers.

Despite herself, Sarah could not help wondering just what had made Andrea so unhappy that she had taken her own life. A little shiver ran down her spine for she felt something dark and hidden, some terrible secret that had driven a woman to desperation.

Was it something in this house? Or was there something outside her marriage, some secret in Andrea's past, that had made her wish to die?

# Chapter Six

John's fever returned during the night, though it was not as virulent as it had been, and he seemed more amenable to taking his medicine. For another two days he wavered between delirium and moments when he seemed to know what was going on around him, though he was too weak and ill to talk to anyone, other than the occasional whisper of thanks for some service performed for him. It was on the morning of the next day, when Sarah went in after having left him to rest for a few hours, that she saw he was at last free of the fever. He lay propped up against the pillows, his eyes open, but clearly still too weak to try to sit up.

'Are you better, John?' Sarah asked as she went over to him. She smiled as she laid a hand on his brow and found it cooler than of late. 'I believe you have come through this, my dear friend. Some of the scabs have formed and in another day or so you will no longer be infectious.'

'Sarah…' John's voice was a rasp, his throat dry and sore. 'I thought it must have been a dream…the fever talking. I believed I had imagined that you were here when I was so ill.'

'I came when I heard you had been nursing Nathaniel yourself,' Sarah said. She smiled at him lovingly. 'I was afraid that you might take it from him, and you did. I knew that you must have been afraid for him, which meant that you were unsure of your servants, so I was determined to care of you myself. I have been here for several days.'

'I am very grateful for all that you have done,' John whispered in a weak voice. 'But it was a terrible risk, Sarah. I pray to God that you have not taken it from me.'

'I nursed Tilda through the smallpox when we were in Italy, and also two little children who lived near by. It seems that I am naturally immune to it, John. I do not know why, but I believe I am not the only one.'

He closed his eyes, clearly too weak to remonstrate further with her. 'I should like a little water, if you please.'

'Yes, of course,' Sarah said and went over to the table near the window that looked out at the back of the house. She poured some of the water that stood waiting in a jug and brought it back to him. Sitting on the bed beside him, she put her arm beneath his shoulders, lifting him so that he could drink a few sips. She smiled as he lay back against the pillows with a sigh. 'Good. That is the first time you have taken anything from me willingly. You did not like Elizabeth's fever mixture, John, but I believe it has done you a great deal of good.'

'Elizabeth is not here?'

'No, she could not come for fear of taking the smallpox to her children, but she sent the things she knew I should need. Was that not kind of her?'

'Yes, indeed,' John said. His eyelids flickered, but he made an effort to open his eyes again and look at her. 'You were reckless to come here, Sarah, but I do thank you for it, my dear. I shall never be able to repay you for your kindness.'

'I do not need repayment, nor do I care what others may say or think of me,' Sarah said. 'Had I not come, Mrs Beeson would have done her best, but she could not care for both you and little Nathaniel. And none of the other servants would come near you. Indeed, some of them fled to their homes in dread of it when your son first took the smallpox.'

'Is Nat better?' John asked with a little sigh. 'He seemed to be recovering, but I became too ill to care for him...'

'He is much better and beginning to be quite lively. I think that Mrs Raven has found a girl to be his nurse for she does not have the time to care for him herself,' Sarah said. 'The child has some scars on his face, John, but not as many as he might have had—and they may fade in time.'

John put a hand to his own face, his fingers exploring, discovering the scabs that had formed, but not yet fallen from the pustules. 'I dare say I look less than handsome these days.'

'Oh, you will have some scars, as Tilda has,' Sarah said in a practical tone. 'But there are ointments that may help you—and it does not matter. We must thank God that you are alive, John.'

'I think my recovery owes thanks to you and Mrs Beeson,' John told her with a wry look. 'But perhaps it was God who brought you to me, Sarah.'

'I hope you do not think me too presumptuous,' Sarah said a little hesitantly. 'I know there was nothing spoken between us and perhaps I have been a little hasty…'

'Nothing said, but everything understood,' John said, reaching for her hand before she could finish, and holding it tightly. 'You knew that I meant to ask you to be my wife—and I do so now, my dearest. Please do me the honour of becoming my wife, Sarah. I have a deep regard for you and I shall be the happiest man alive if you will be mine.'

'Oh, John, you know I shall marry you if you want

me,' Sarah said and smiled mistily. Those tiny doubts that had lingered at the back of her mind had fled as soon as he woke and smiled at her. Whatever lay behind the mystery of Andrea's death, she did not believe that the blame lay at John's door. 'I did think that you cared for me—that you meant to ask. I told your housekeeper that we were engaged so that she would let me in to the house so that I could care for you, but you did not have to ask. No one else but Elizabeth and Daniel know that I have been here with you. I would not have you feel obliged to say it.'

John shook his head. He was feeling too ill to say more at the moment, but he knew that her reputation was already damaged beyond repair, making it impossible for her to stay single, but it might be rescued by their marriage. People would always whisper, but their true friends would understand.

'I want to marry you, Sarah. You must know that I have always loved you, even before you went away to Italy. I felt a deep fondness for you when you were a child, but when we met again after your abduction, I fell in love with you and I have loved you ever since. You must believe me, Sarah.'

There was something close to desperation in his eyes at that moment. She sensed some deep underlying grief or guilt…as if he were haunted by his memories.

Then why had he married Andrea? Sarah was

tempted to ask, but she saw that his eyes were closing. He was too weak to go on talking and she knew she must keep her questions for another time. After all, it hardly mattered why John had married. The past must be put behind them, as she had put the distress and terror of her abduction behind her. They had the rest of their lives to talk and to care for one another. 'I shall leave you to sleep now, my dearest love. And when you wake again we shall give you some of the good nourishing broth your cook has had been preparing these past two days…'

She smiled as he sank back against the pillows, clearly exhausted. His proposal had granted her dearest wish, and yet she had a mounting sense of apprehension…a feeling that something was not quite as it ought to be. John's wife had killed herself and there must have been a reason. Who or what had driven her to such a terrible act?

After that day John gradually began to recover his strength. Sarah continued to nurse him, sharing the time spent at his side with Mrs Beeson, but leaving most of the more intimate tasks to the older woman. She thought that John might have felt embarrassed if she had continued to wash and tend him as she had while he was in the fever. Now, she contented herself by tidying his room, sitting with him, reading to him and bringing his tray to the bedside; at first he needed help to eat the nourishing soup and bread that was brought up for him, but then, one morning, he took the spoon from her and managed to feed himself. He asked if he might have something more interesting than broth, and she brought him some cold beef and pickles, and from that moment on he began to make huge strides. It was a week after the fever finally broke that he was able to get out of bed and walk about. The scabs had all gone, leaving pitted scars on his face, arms and body, but he was no longer infectious and now Mrs Raven had begun to venture inside his apartments.

Now that John was so much better, Sarah spent some of her day with Nathaniel. He was a lively child and his nurse seemed to find it difficult to cope with him. She was inclined to shout at him when he was naughty, and one morning when Sarah entered the room she saw the girl slap him.

'Please do not do that, Ruth,' she told the girl, receiving a resentful stare. Ruth had not realised she was there and her face was sulky. 'Nathaniel is not to be smacked. If he does something naughty, you will please tell me or his father, and we shall decide on his punishment—if any.'

'He threw one of his lead soldiers at me. It hit my

cheek,' Ruth said, a note of defiance in her voice. 'He must be taught manners, miss.'

'Not by you,' Sarah said sharply. 'You are employed to take care of him, not to be the judge, jury and executioner. You may continue in your duties for the moment, but I shall speak to Mrs Raven about replacing you in the nursery.'

'Are you dismissing me?' Ruth's gaze narrowed in dislike.

'No. I am sure that Mrs Raven can find a place for you somewhere else, but we need a young girl who likes children—someone to play with him.'

She left the nursery, going to Mrs Raven's sitting room. She knocked and waited, and after a few moments, the housekeeper opened the door.

'Was there something you wanted, Miss Hunter? I was taking the chance of a breather for a few minutes. I've been on the go all morning.'

'We need a proper nurse for Nathaniel,' Sarah told her. 'Ruth isn't suitable. I want a new girl—and I should like to see her myself before she is taken on.'

Mrs Raven gave her a hard stare, but there was something about Sarah at that moment that made her keep her thoughts to herself. 'I could send to the village, Miss Hunter. I think the Vicar's youngest daughter might take the post of nurse-governess. I heard tell as she was looking for a place, but didn't want to go too far from home, because her mother is an invalid and she wants to get home sometimes to see her.'

'You will ask the young lady to call,' Sarah said. 'Have all the maids that went home returned yet?'

'Some of them,' Mrs Raven said. 'We could do with a few more, though.'

'Well, then, I think you should put out feelers, Mrs Raven. We do not want to be short of servants. It is a very big house and it would be better to have more rather than less.'

'Have you asked Mr Elworthy about this, Miss Hunter?'

'Mr Elworthy is not yet well enough to be bothered with such things,' Sarah said, 'but I assure you that he will think as I do in the matter of his son's nurse.'

'Yes, miss, if you say so.' There was a hint of resentment in the housekeeper's expression. 'I'll send for Miss Harrington today—though I doubt she has any experience worth speaking of.'

'If she is kind and patient, we shall overlook the lack of experience for the moment,' Sarah said. 'When Mr Elworthy is well again, I dare say he will advertise in London for an experienced nanny.'

'I did say as he ought to months back,' Mrs Raven said, 'but he seemed content with the girl we had.'

'What happened to her?'

'Annie was the first to go down with the smallpox, miss. She took it real bad and died afore we rightly knew what was wrong with her. I dare say the boy had it from her.'

'That is sad,' Sarah said with a little shake of her head. She knew that it happened all too often. They had been lucky that both Nathaniel and John had recovered from the terrible disease. 'Please ask Miss Harrington to come as soon as possible and I will see her myself.'

'Yes, Miss Hunter.' Mrs Raven looked at her sourly. 'Do you want me to refer to you on all matters to do with the maids in future, miss?'

'No, of course not. I should not dream of interfering with your authority,' Sarah said. 'But the child's nurse is a different matter. Ruth is not suitable.'

Mrs Raven's eyes gleamed, but she said no more. Sarah left her to go upstairs to John's apartments. He had come through into his sitting room and was sitting with a light cover over his legs and a book of poetry open on his lap. He smiled as she entered, holding out his hand to her.

'I am poor company for you at the moment, Sarah my love. I think you could return to Elizabeth's house now. I shall ride over in a few days and then we shall announce our engagement in *The Times*.' He looked at her left hand, which was still bare of an engagement ring. 'I want to buy you a ring for yourself, Sarah. Most of the family jewels are in the bank in London, though they are heavy, old-fashioned things and will need refashioning for you. Do you mind waiting until I am able to venture as far as London? I believe there is a ring somewhere in the house, but it was Andrea's and I would prefer not to give you that…'

'I am quite content to wait,' Sarah assured him. 'I wanted to speak to you about a nurse for Nathaniel. Ruth is too sharp with him. I do not think her suitable. I have asked Mrs Raven to send for the Vicar's daughter, who is looking for a post near to her home. I think she has not much experience, but later you can engage an experienced nanny if you choose.'

'I am glad you have done something about it,' John said. 'The last girl was kind, but not particularly skilled. I believe Miss Harrington has a little experience in the nursery. She will do very well for the moment.' He frowned as he looked about him. 'I meant to do so many things when I married Andrea, but somehow they did not get done. This house is dark and dull and needs to be brought up to date.'

'I wonder that you do not have a manservant, John.'

'Bartley retired a few months back,' John said and sighed. 'He had been my father's man before he was mine. After he became too old to do his duties… well, I am afraid I let things slip. Andrea had died and things were difficult. You are right, Sarah. I shall advertise for a manservant and a nanny. I dare say we shall need more than one girl once we set up our nursery. If you have any other ideas, please feel free to tell me. I once intended to refurbish the house entirely. Perhaps I would do better to pull it down bit by bit and rebuild.'

'It is a little gloomy as it is,' Sarah agreed with a smile. 'But I think that a change of colours and furnishings might make a big difference. Perhaps we should see what could be done with it first?'

'Yes, you are right. I shall set it in hand as soon as I am able.' John smiled at her. 'When would you wish to be married, dearest?'

'Oh…perhaps in a month or so,' Sarah said, blushing. 'You need time to get well and I must buy my bride clothes.'

'I must write to Charles,' John said. 'I hope he will not be angered by the situation, Sarah.' He gave her a serious look. 'I really think you should return to Elizabeth's house now. The period of infection is at an end—if you had been going to take it from me it would have shown by now.'

'I told you that I was immune,' Sarah said. 'I shall go tomorrow—perhaps in the afternoon. I want to speak to Miss Harrington and make sure that everything is settled here before I leave.' She smiled at him. 'I shall miss seeing you every day, dearest—but I think you are right. While you were so ill it did not matter that I stayed here, but now…mama would not approve.' Her mother would not have approved of her coming here in the first place, but there was no need for her to know anything about it.

'It might be better if you went today, Sarah. I am well enough to manage alone now.'

'I wish to see Miss Harrington,' Sarah said. 'I shall stay one more night, John—what harm can it do?'


'Where is Sarah?' Mrs Hunter said. She glared at Elizabeth. 'I have had no word from her in weeks. She ought to have been in London more than a week ago. I demand to see my daughter.'

'Sarah isn't here,' Elizabeth said. 'Forgive me, Mrs Hunter. I did not wish to worry you…'

'She has not been abducted again?' Mrs Hunter's face was white with shock. 'Oh, I knew that something was wrong! I wrote to Charles and told him that he should come down here but in his reply, he said that his sister would be perfectly safe with his friends.'

'And she is safe,' Elizabeth said. 'I had a note from her only yesterday. She intends to return to us this afternoon.'

'Return?' Mrs Hunter stared at her in outrage. 'I thought she was staying with you. Where has she gone? I did not give my permission for her to go elsewhere!'

'Please sit down,' Elizabeth said and took a deep breath. 'I must explain to you. Sarah is quite safe. She went over to Mr Elworthy's home when he was very ill with the smallpox and she stayed to nurse him. Apparently some of the servants had run off and she felt that he was being neglected by those that remained.'

'Sarah went to the home of an unmarried gentleman?' Mrs Hunter stared at her in horror. 'I cannot believe that she would do such a thing—or that you would let her, Lady Cavendish. How could you allow her to ruin herself?'

'Sarah was most insistent that she would not take the smallpox…' Elizabeth faltered as she saw the expression on Mrs Hunter's face and knew herself at fault. 'She does have a mind of her own. I did not know that she intended going, for she slipped out early in the morning. If I had demanded that she return, I do not think she would have obeyed me.'

'You should have sent for me at once!'

'I thought it best to say as little as possible about the situation,' Elizabeth said. 'Sarah told me in her letter that John has asked her to marry him, and that she has agreed to be his wife.'

'That is the least he could do!' Mrs Hunter said, outraged. 'But I am not at all certain that I wish for this marriage. Sarah has behaved disgracefully. No one has consulted me—and I think Charles would have told me if Mr Elworthy had written to ask his permission.'

'I dare say he means to do so as soon as he is able,' Elizabeth said. 'He has been very ill, Mrs Hunter. I am sure that nothing improper has occurred. John is too much the gentleman to allow Sarah's reputation to suffer from his carelessness.'

'Indeed?' Mrs Hunter's face was set in stone. 'Well, that is not what I have been hearing recently. There is a tale circulating that distresses me very much. I have heard that there is some doubt about his wife's death—that perhaps it was not suicide, but a deliberate act on the part of an unknown person. And some go further…they hint that Mr Elworthy might have had a hand in her death.'

'That is not true,' Elizabeth said. 'Daniel and Charles both know of the rumours. We had hoped that they would not become common knowledge, but I can assure you that none of us believes one word of that monstrous lie.'

'Well, you may wish to take his part, but I am not sure that I can do so with an easy heart. Had it not been for these rumours I should not have minded if

Sarah married that gentleman—but this changes things. Mud clings and, no matter if he is innocent, it will shadow him all his life, and Sarah if she marries him. It will reflect badly on her. I am not prepared to let that happen. I shall take her back to London with me and hope that the news of her scandalous behaviour can be hushed up.' She smiled oddly. 'The Duke of Pentyre spoke to me a few days ago. He asked if I thought Sarah would accept an offer from him, and I told him that I would discover her feelings on the matter. I posted up to Yorkshire immediately. I think Sarah should return to London and do her best to make sure of him while she has the chance.'

'But Sarah loves John and he loves her,' Elizabeth said. 'Surely you will not deny them now that they have an understanding?'

'Sarah is my daughter. I think that you must allow me to know what is best for her, Lady Cavendish.'

'Perhaps if you were to go over and speak to John yourself—'

'No, I do not think so,' Mrs Hunter said. 'I believe you said that Sarah is to return here today?' Elizabeth nodded. 'I would be grateful if you will have her things packed. We shall go back to London immediately. I do not wish to impose on your hospitality longer than necessary.'

'Forgive me. I see that you believe I have neglected my duty towards Sarah. I should perhaps have told you sooner, Mrs Hunter—but I believed that a happy outcome would set all to rights, which it has. They have agreed to marry. Why will you not let them have their way?'

'If Mr Elworthy is able to prove his innocence, I may change my mind—but it is my hope that Sarah will be wed to Pentyre within the month.'

Elizabeth stared at her stubborn face. It was clear that she was very angry, and perhaps she had a right to be—Elizabeth *had* neglected her duty to Mrs Hunter. She ought to have made her aware of her daughter's whereabouts before this and she knew herself in the wrong. She had hoped that John would recover and ask Sarah to be his wife, which he had—but it seemed that that was not enough for Mrs Hunter.

There was nothing she could do for the moment, but she would speak to Daniel, ask him to call on Charles and hope that he could soothe his mother's ruffled feathers. She could certainly not prevent Mrs Hunter from taking her daughter back to town with her—but she could and would make John aware of the situation.

'But, Mama,' Sarah said, looking at her in desperation when they met later that day, 'John has asked me to marry him. We are engaged. You cannot force me to marry the duke. I shall refuse him—even if he still cares to ask me once it is known where I have been the past three weeks.'

'It will not be known,' Mrs Hunter told her sharply. 'Lady Cavendish will not speak of it and we must hope that it does not leak out—at least until you are safely married, Sarah. The duke means to ask you as soon as we are in town again and, if you are sensible, you will thank him for his offer. You threw away your chances in Italy, please do not make the same mistake again.'

'But I have told you that I wish to marry John Elworthy. I have given him my promise.'

'Mr Elworthy may have murdered his wife or at least driven her to her death,' Mrs Hunter said, giving her a severe look. 'The rumours are everywhere, Sarah. Had I known before you left town, I should not have permitted you to come here. I should be failing in my duty to you, Sarah, if I allowed you to marry such a man.'

'It is a lie,' Sarah cried. 'I know that there is some gossip, but it is not true. How could you believe such a terrible story, Mama? John would never do such a wicked thing. I *know* he would not.'

'It may be a lie or it may be true,' Mrs Hunter said. 'But there is no smoke without fire, Sarah. Why did his wife kill herself? Have you asked him? Have you asked yourself? There must have been a reason—perhaps some unkindness on his side. Men are not always what they appear in public. You do not truly know this man. I would not wish my daughter to end by throwing herself into the river.'

'I should not, Mama. Truly, I should not. I love John and he loves me. I can never marry anyone else. Besides, I have given him my promise.'

'No contract has been signed. If you wish to make me happy, you will marry the duke and put this nonsense from your mind. You know how I worry for your sake, Sarah. Have you no regard for my nerves?'

'I do not wish to marry the duke. I love John…' Sarah said, tears starting to her eyes. 'Mama, you are unfair. Please do not make me choose between you and John.'

'I have told you that a marriage between you and that man is out of the question. I should never sleep peacefully in my bed for worrying. If you care for me at all, Sarah, you will oblige me in this. Marry the duke and be sensible.'

'I cannot marry him,' Sarah said, her throat tight with emotion. 'Please do not ask it of me, Mama. I do not regard this cruel rumour that John was responsible for Andrea's death, and neither does Charles. He will support me in this, I know he will.'

'We shall see,' Mrs Hunter said. 'Say your farewell to Lady Cavendish, Sarah. We are returning to London at once. It is my belief that once you have time for reflection, you will realise that I have acted for your own good.'

'Mama…' Sarah's throat was tight with emotion. Why would her mother not listen? Why would she not understand that Sarah's love for John had stood the test of time? She would rather remain unwed than marry another man—but how could she marry John when her mother was so set against it?

She approached Elizabeth, offering her hand, her eyes wide and dark with distress. Elizabeth embraced her, whispering against her ear.

'John shall hear of this and Daniel is already on his way to speak to Charles. Have courage, dearest. Charles will talk to her and all will be well.'

Sarah nodded, her lips murmuring a silent thank you.

'Come along, Sarah,' her mother's voice said sharply from behind her. 'I want to set out immediately. The sooner we are in London the better. I shall invite the duke to call and, if you know your duty to me, your engagement will be announced immediately.'

Sarah did not answer, but she could do nothing other than follow her mama outside. She took her place in the carriage, sitting back against the squabs and closing her eyes. A tear squeezed from beneath her lashes, trickling down her cheek and into her mouth. What would she do if Charles did not come? Perhaps he would agree with her mama that she would be better married to the Duke of Pentyre.

'Damn it, why did you let her do it?' Charles demanded of his friend when told the news. 'She is so impulsive and obstinate—but it was the right thing to do. Of course it was. If John was being neglected by his servants, he might have died…yes, I understand why she thought it necessary. It is exactly what I would expect of my sister, even if it was reckless. Mama is a fool. It will be much better to announce their engagement. If any of this comes out, Pentyre would be entitled to withdraw even if it had been announced—and that would mean an even bigger scandal. Besides, I do not wish my sister to marry that man. Indeed, I shall not allow it. I wish, though, that you had told me of this before, Daniel. I might have spoken to Mama, prepared her for what was happening.'

'Yes, perhaps I should have done,' the earl agreed. 'Elizabeth told Sarah she must not go, of course, but after she did we both realised that there was little we could do. We hoped that it might come out all right, and of course it did. John asked her to marry him, as you would expect in the circumstances, and if Mrs Hunter had agreed to it we might have contained the gossip to our own locality. You are right, however. I ought to have written to you. Please accept my apologies, Charles.'

'It is not necessary to apologise, I know your loyalty was to Sarah in this case. Mama is behaving very foolishly,' Charles said. 'I shall post up to town at once and talk to her. You know my opinion of Pentyre for it is much as your own. The man may be a reformed character—but John is worth ten of him!'

'I agree entirely,' Daniel said. 'If I had thought Sarah in any danger I should have sent for you at once, but I knew she must be safe with John. He can always be relied on to do the right thing.'

'Yes, well, let us hope that I am in time to prevent Mama from doing anything foolish.'

'Sarah, I have received a letter from the duke,' Mrs Hunter said on the morning after their arrival in London. 'He will call on us this afternoon. You will receive him—and, if you do not wish to upset me, you will accept his offer. I have always done my best for you, Sarah. Surely you will oblige me? It would make me so happy to see you married to a man worthy of you.'

'Please do not say such things to me,' Sarah begged. 'You know that I love you, Mama—but I cannot marry the duke. I love John…'

'You are an ungrateful girl,' Mrs Hunter said, holding a kerchief to her eyes. 'After all the worry over your abduction…and now you wish to marry a man of whom I can never approve. If you cared for me, you would take the duke and make me happy.'

'Mama, you are unkind,' Sarah said. 'You know that I care for you, but I cannot…will not marry the duke…'

Sarah turned and walked from the room, her heart heavy. Her mother was forcing her to choose between her duty to her and her love for John. But she could not give him up, she could not…and yet, unless Charles could persuade her mother, there was no hope of her marriage taking place.

'Ah, Pentyre,' Charles said as he saw the duke leaving White's club just after noon that same day. 'I was hoping that I might find you here. May I have a moment or two of your time?'

'Hunter…' The duke's brows lifted as he saw the expression on the other's face. He was aware that Charles Hunter did not approve of him, which was why he had approached Sarah's mama rather than her brother. 'I have an appointment with Mrs Hunter—your mama—this afternoon.'

'Yes, I thought you might have,' Charles said and smiled coldly. 'Let us walk together for a moment, sir. I rather think it might prove to be a waste of your time to call on Mrs Hunter, Pentyre. You see, I have given my permission for Sarah to marry John Elworthy. I believe my mother may have misled you, but you should rather have approached me than her—Sarah is my ward and she shall not marry unless it is with my permission.'

'You are very blunt, sir,' the duke said, looking offended. 'I do not believe that I have made an offer for Miss Hunter as yet.'

'If I have misread your intention, I apologise,' Charles replied. 'It was to save you embarrassment that I sought you out, for my sister would have refused you had you offered. She is in love with John.'

'Indeed?' Pentyre was very angry. He had let it be known that he expected to marry the girl and would lose face over the wretched business. 'Then Mrs Hunter has misled me and I shall not waste my time in calling upon her.' He glared at Charles. 'I know that you do not like me, Hunter—but I should advise you not to make an enemy of me. I do not forget a slight.'

'No, no, I have no wish to be enemies,' Charles said. 'My mother was at fault. She knew that there was a long-standing agreement between them—but she was flattered by your attentions to her daughter and hoped to see her elevated to the peerage. Had Sarah's heart not been engaged, it might have done very well, sir.' Charles was at his most charming as he soothed ruffled feathers—he had learned the hard way that it was best not to make enemies. Misplaced arrogance could lead to bitter regret.

'I see…' Pentyre frowned. He was not completely convinced, but saw that it would appear foolish on his part if he were to fall out with the Hunters over this business. Besides, there were other ways of paying them back for the slight he had received. A word here and there, a raised eyebrow and they would find that they were no longer invited every-where. 'Well, thank you for telling me, Hunter. I should not have liked to be refused by Miss Hunter.'

Charles offered his hand. He disliked Pentyre, believed that the man was of bad character and cer-tainly not fit as a husband for Sarah, but he wanted to brush through the affair as easily as he could.

'I am glad I was in time,' he said. 'I am sure you will not regret this, Pentyre.'

'It is to be hoped that Miss Hunter does not regret her choice,' the duke said, a spiteful note in his voice. 'I am not one for gossip, Hunter—but there are certain tales that make one fear for her happiness as Elworthy's wife.'

'Lies,' Charles said, holding on to his temper with

difficulty. 'I assure you that there is not a grain of truth in any of them.'

'Let us hope so for your sister's sake,' the duke said. He tipped his hat to Charles and walked away.

Charles stared after him. He hoped that he had managed to cool Pentyre's anger, but placed no trust in the man's goodwill. He had saved Sarah from an embarrassing interview, but now he must calm his mama's outrage—and he must see what could be done to scotch the rumours concerning John.

It could not matter to his friends what people said, but it might be uncomfortable for Sarah if she were not to be generally received. Daniel already had agents searching for clues as to the identity of the person who had spread the malicious lies. There must be some reason for it—but Charles could not see what John's enemy hoped to achieve. He pushed the problem to the back of his mind. One thing at a time! He must speak to his mama and Sarah.

Sarah had been summoned to the parlour to find that her brother was already there. Her face lit up as she saw him and she ran to embrace him, a shimmer of tears in her eyes.

'Charles,' she said shakily. 'I am so glad you have come.'

'Your brother has chosen to override me in this

business,' Mrs Hunter said, looking at Sarah. 'You both know how I feel about this matter. I cannot agree to the marriage, because John Elworthy has been accused of murder—'

'No, Mama, he has not,' Charles told her. 'There are wicked rumours that his wife might not have died by her own hand—but as yet no one has dared to accuse John.'

'They might as well have done given that everyone will think it,' Mrs Hunter said with a tearful look. 'I am most disappointed that you have taken against me, Charles. I think I might have looked for your support. I want only what is best for my daughter.'

'Pentyre is perhaps one of the worst you could have chosen,' Charles said, hard put to it to keep his temper. 'I know for a fact that he is a libertine, a hard gambler—and there are rumours of worse. I saw him in the company of Sir Montague Forsythe some years ago, and Sir Courtney Welch.'

'Oh, Charles!' Mrs Hunter looked horrified. 'This changes everything. Why did you not tell me this before? If I had known, I should certainly not have encouraged him to pay court to Sarah. You know I would not...' She looked tearfully at Sarah. 'I wanted you to be safe from those evil men. I have been haunted by the fear that they might try to take you again.'

'Most of them are dead, Mama,' Sarah said and turned to her, unmoved by her mother's tears. 'I shall be perfectly safe as John's wife.'

'Pentyre has apparently reformed,' Charles said with a shrug. 'I do not believe in blackening a man's character without cause—but I would never have agreed to a marriage, Mama. You should have consulted me before giving him to understand that his suit would be acceptable. He was angry and one can hardly blame him.'

'Yes, perhaps I should,' Mrs Hunter said and dried her eyes. She looked at Sarah. 'Perhaps I have been at fault, Sarah. I was very distressed when I learned that you had been living in Mr Elworthy's house unchaperoned. However, I still cannot like the idea of your marriage to Mr Elworthy…'

Sarah looked at her mother. Mrs Hunter had sat down on the sofa and was suddenly looking deflated, her shoulders hunched defensively.

'I am sorry to have upset you, Mama,' Sarah replied. 'But I could not oblige you by marrying the duke.'

'And nor should I have permitted it,' Charles said. 'You acted foolishly, Mama, and should rightly have applied to me.'

'That is unfair…' Mrs Hunter sniffed into a lace kerchief. 'I was thinking of what was best for

Sarah—' She broke off as a maid knocked and then entered. 'Yes, Marlene—what is it?'

'Mr Elworthy, ma'am,' the girl said just as John walked past her and into the room. 'He would not wait, ma'am…'

'Charles! Thank God you are here,' John said. 'I came as quickly as I could, but I was forced to break my journey last night. I fear I am not yet as well as I should wish…' He took a linen kerchief from his pocket and mopped at his forehead, which was prickled with beads of perspiration. 'Forgive me, I must sit down…'

'John dearest,' Sarah cried and went to him as he sank into an elbow chair, his face as white as chalk. She knelt on the floor beside him, looking up into his face anxiously. 'You should not have left your bed to come here like this. You are not well enough to make such a long journey.'

He took her hand, holding it to his cheek, his eyes intent on her face. 'Elizabeth told me how distressed you were, Sarah my love. I had to come at once.'

'Dearest John.' Sarah smiled at him. 'It is all right, for Charles has spoken to Mama—and I hope she will forgive me for distressing her…'

John glanced at Mrs Hunter, who had sat back in her chair and was fanning herself as if in a fluster. 'Please forgive Sarah for her impulsive action in coming to me, ma'am. I should not have allowed it had I known, but I was too ill—and when I recovered my senses it was too late, for the damage was done. However, it was always my intention to ask for Sarah's hand in marriage at the earliest opportunity—and she has done me the honour of accepting. I shall hope for your approval, ma'am—and yours, Charles?'

'You know that you have always had my approval for a match between you,' Charles said and smiled at him. 'I have already told Pentyre that you and Sarah are engaged, so it is too late to withdraw. I shall insert the news of your betrothal in *The Times* tomorrow and we shall give a small dance for you in a few days—or whenever you are well enough to attend it, John.'

Mrs Hunter said nothing, but Sarah knew that she was offended and hurt because her wishes had been ignored, and it took the edge from Sarah's pleasure. She wanted her mother to smile and be pleased, but it was clear from Mrs Hunter's expression that she was not happy with the situation.

'I shall be well enough in a day or so,' John said. 'I leave it to you to make the arrangements, Charles. I think the wedding should be called for a month's time. Do you wish for it here or at your country home, Sarah?'

'I think I should like to go home,' Sarah said. 'But

not for a few days. You must rest, John, and I think we should give a small dance, as Charles said—though I think that too could be held at home. We do not need to invite the whole of society, only the friends we truly like.'

'Very sensible,' Charles agreed with a look of approval. 'I shall stay one more night and then go home to make the arrangements. I do not care to be away from Belle too long at this time, and you are safe now, Sarah. You and mama may follow in a few days—and perhaps John will accompany you?'

'Yes, of course,' he said, smiling at Sarah. 'I am at your disposal, my dearest.'

'Oh, John,' Sarah said, and her face was soft with tenderness as she gazed up at him. 'Are you sure you are well enough to be up?'

'I am a little tired,' he told her. The truth would have been that he was close to exhaustion, but he knew that she was anxious. 'Do not worry, Sarah. I shall be much better in a day or two, I promise you.'

Mrs Hunter sniffed into her kerchief, but did not say anything. She had been shocked by her son's revelations concerning the Duke of Pentyre, but that did not mean she was entirely reconciled to the marriage. She listened to the plans for her daughter's wedding going on around her, but took no part in them. It was to be hoped the rumours of John's involvement in his wife's death would die down, but she was afraid that the news of his impending marriage might pour fat on the flames.

'Your news is disturbing,' John said when he and Charles were alone later that day. 'Do think the report is accurate?'

'Tobbold is an excellent man. If he says he thinks he may be on to something, I believe you can rely on him. Apparently, a stranger has been seen a few times in your village, and one old woman said that it was not the first time. She seems to think that he was there some months back, though she cannot be certain where or when she saw him.'

'But why does he wish to blacken my name?' John asked, looking puzzled. 'Tobbold said that he had the manner and bearing of a soldier—but I cannot think of anyone I might have offended to such a degree.'

'Forgive me,' Charles said hesitantly. 'This touches on your private affairs and I hesitate to ask—but is Nathaniel your son? I know that you care for him, love him as a father, but was he actually fathered by someone else?'

'Yes…' A flicker of pain crossed John's face. The guilt was still strong in him, guilt for having failed the woman he had married. 'I have not told you before, Charles, because I felt it disloyal to Andrea—

and I would not have it go further. She was with child when she came to me and begged for my help. She told me that she had been forced and was afraid to confess to her father.' John frowned, his eyes dark with memories 'She was just a child in my eyes. I felt sympathy for her and I told her I would marry her. It was an impulsive and perhaps a foolish thing to have done, for I did not love her as I ought. I tried to be kind to her, but she was unhappy. Our marriage was…well, it did not properly begin, and I think she felt desperate towards the end. I have blamed myself for her death. Had I been a better husband, she might not have been driven to take her own life.'

'Andrea told you that she was forced?' John nodded his head and Charles looked thoughtful. 'Supposing she lied to gain your sympathy? Just imagine this scenario for a moment: She had a lover and she lay with him because she loved him—' Charles held up his hand as John would have protested. 'No, let me finish. Just suppose that her lover was sent away, either by her father—or perhaps, if he were a soldier, by his commanding officer. Andrea is left alone and discovers that she is to have a child. She cannot contact her lover and so she turns to a friend—and he, being the perfect gentleman that you are, John, asks her to marry him. She accepts because she can see no way out of her difficulty, but then she begins to wish that she had been braver—that she had waited for her lover to return.'

John turned away, going over to the window to look out at the formal gardens at the front of the house. 'I cannot deny that the picture you have painted could be true,' he said, his back turned towards Charles. 'There were times when I thought she was trying to tell me something and I ignored her. You see, I too wished that I had waited. I knew that Andrea was not the woman I ought to have married. I did not love her as I ought and she sensed it, even though I tried to be kind. And yet why would this man…her lover…why would he try to ruin me like this? Why not demand a showdown, accuse me to my face? If it were me, I should want to thrash the man who had taken the woman I loved from me.'

'That is the mystery,' Charles said and looked thoughtful. 'I cannot imagine why he would spread these rumours. He may hate you for taking Andrea from him and he may blame you for her untimely death; he might even try to kill you—but I agree that he would have done better to speak to you man to man.'

'I should like to put an end to this,' John said. 'Sarah has been brave enough to consent to the wedding despite the tales, but I should like to clear my name—for her sake, if not my own.'

'My sister has more sense than to be put off by malicious gossip,' Charles said. 'If it were just the tales, I should not be concerned, John. However, I do not wish to see her a widow before she has hardly become a wife.'

John's gaze narrowed as he looked at him. 'You seriously think that my life might be at risk? If I believed that—' He broke off for a moment, and then, 'I did hesitate to ask Sarah at first, Charles. As soon as I saw her again I knew that I still loved her, but I held back. I was blaming myself for Andrea's death, and I was concerned about these rumours. I hesitated before asking Sarah to be my wife for her sake, but I was forced to go home when my son became ill. When she came to me like that, when she saved my life and risked everything for my sake—what else could I do? Had I not done so, your mother might have had her way and forced Sarah to marry Pentyre. I did what I had to do, Charles.'

'Yes, I know, and it was exactly what I would have expected of you, John. Sarah was reckless and, if you had not behaved as you ought, she would have been ruined. Besides, she loves you.'

'I love her,' John said. 'But if this threat is real…perhaps I should not have spoken. If Sarah is at risk…' His hands balled into clenched fists at the idea. John gave the impression of being a quiet man, of taking things in his stride, but there was a well of passion and anger inside him as he considered that someone might wish to harm the woman he loved. 'If something were to happen to her, I should never forgive myself!'

'We shall guard against that,' Charles said. 'Tobbold's men can keep a watch over her—but you must be careful too, John. I would not have anything happen to you, my friend.'

'It is Sarah that I am concerned for,' John said, looking doubtful. 'If I thought she was in danger I would withdraw despite what it would cost me. I think that perhaps I did her a disservice in asking her to be my wife, Charles. I should have waited until I got to the bottom of this business. And yet I really had no choice. Sarah's reputation would have been lost had I not spoken when I did…'

Outside the door, having just paused to knock, Sarah heard John's last words and drew her breath in sharply. What was John saying? It sounded as if he was explaining that he had asked her to marry him simply to save her from gossip.

She turned and walked away swiftly, not waiting to hear her brother's answer. It was as her mother had warned her! John had simply done the decent thing in asking her to marry him. The pain of that knowledge struck hard and deep, bringing a rush of tears to her eyes.

'But you love her, John,' Charles went on, unaware that a small part of their conversation had been overheard. 'This thing may never be truly finished. You cannot ruin both her life and your own simply because you have an enemy. No, my friend, you did the right thing. All I am saying is that you must be on your guard at all times. I do not think Sarah is at risk particularly. It is you this man hates and you he means to pursue until he has ruined you…'

Sarah was close to tears as she ran upstairs. If John had asked her to marry him simply because she had placed him in an impossible position, it would be too awful. No decent gentleman would do other than propose after what she had done for him. It was possible that John might have died if she had not nursed him so devotedly, although Mrs Beeson had done her best in difficult circumstances. Sarah had been impulsive and reckless, and her mama had had been right to be cross with her. She felt ashamed and guilty over her behaviour, especially if she had forced John into an awkward situation.

Yet surely he cared for her? He had said it and she believed him. Perhaps she had simply misunderstood what she had overheard. Blinking back her tears, she thrust the doubts to the back of her mind. She loved John and he loved her. She would not let doubts creep in to spoil her happiness.

## Chapter Seven

'I am so pleased for you, dear Sarah,' Tilda said, smiling at her. 'I have always liked Mr Elworthy. He seems such a quiet gentleman, but is so brave and kind—and I know he is very fond of you.'

The four of them were sitting in Lady Tate's pleasant parlour, which was at the back of the house and overlooked a long, narrow garden. Mrs Hunter and Lady Tate were discussing the wedding invitations, which had been delivered from the printing house that morning.

'It is not quite what I should have liked,' Mrs Hunter said in a plaintive voice. 'But you know I have been overruled by Charles. Sarah wants a small family wedding and perhaps in the circumstances that may be for the best.' She shot a look of reproach at her daughter. 'Quite how it has become known that Sarah spent some time alone at Mr Elworthy's house I do not understand, for I was promised faithfully that it would not.'

'I am sure that neither Elizabeth or the earl said anything, Mama,' Sarah assured her. 'Besides, none of our true friends will make anything of it. John was far too ill for anything improper to have happened. Some spiteful people may count the months until I have a child, but they will be disappointed.'

'Sarah!' Mrs Hunter was horrified. 'Young girls should not even know about these things. I am sure I did not until the day of my wedding.'

'Sarah is not a child,' Lady Tate told her soothingly. 'I believe that it is better for a gel to understand these things rather than marry in ignorance, as I did. Had I known what to expect, I might never have married Tate, for he was a coarse brute and I suffered in the marriage bed.'

'Hester!' Mrs Hunter looked affronted at this plain speaking. 'Well, I suppose I could not expect Sarah to be entirely ignorant—but it is vulgar to speak of these things. I do not know what the world is coming to these days.'

'We should be leaving, Mama,' Sarah reminded her. 'John is taking us to the theatre this evening.'

'I had not forgotten,' Mrs Hunter said with a little frown. She stood up and pulled on her gloves. 'You will come down for the wedding, Hester? And you,

Tilda? I shall need the support of my friends for my nerves are in a shocking state and I am not certain how many guests we shall have.'

'I am sure that everyone will want to be there,' Tilda said, though she knew that there was some quite unpleasant gossip circulating. 'All those who truly know and love Sarah are certain to want to see her married.'

'Well, I hope I shall not be disappointed.'

Sarah said goodbye to their friends and left the house with her mama. Their own house was only a few streets away and they had chosen to walk, as it was a pleasant day. They passed two gentlemen, who lifted their hats and murmured a polite greeting, but two ladies that Sarah knew only slightly crossed to the other side of the road before they could come up with them. From the expression on Mrs Hunter's face, it was clear that she thought they had been cut, though to her credit she said nothing of it.

As they entered the house, Sarah saw a letter addressed to her lying on a silver salver on the hall table. She picked it up and took it upstairs to read later.

'I shall rest for an hour,' Mrs Hunter told her, her expression making it clear that she was still a little out of sorts with her daughter. 'If I were you, I should do the same, Sarah.'

'Yes, Mama,' Sarah replied, though she had little intention of it. She had that day received some parcels from her dressmaker and other shops she had patronised, and she wanted to examine her purchases. She would try on the new gowns that had been delivered, though any slight alterations could be done when they got home.

She laid the sealed letter on her dressing table and began to look through the packages. Besides a yellow silk evening gown and a striped pelisse, there were items of pretty lingerie, silk stockings, some dancing slippers and two new bonnets. She spent some time happily examining her purchases.

It was almost an hour later that she opened her letter.

Reading the few brief lines penned there, Sarah gasped. Oh, how could anyone be so spiteful? She crumpled the paper in her hands and tossed it on to the bed in disgust. Then, her hands trembling with anger, she smoothed the paper out and read the message again.

*John Elworthy murdered his wife. If you marry him, he will be the cause of your death. Draw back now while you still can. A well wisher.*

'Oh, no, how wicked!' she spoke the words aloud. A sick feeling was churning in her stomach. She had never expected to receive such a letter. Who would send such a thing to her? It was spiteful and cruel and it made her want to weep for frustration. If the writer had had the courage to speak to her in person, she would have known how to answer, but this horrid letter could not be rebuffed. Its poison would simply lie there, insidious and damaging because it could not be denied in any meaningful way.

She stared at it for some minutes, feeling an icy chill at the nape of her neck, because despite herself she could not help feeling uneasy. Was the letter a warning or a threat? Was the writer saying that she should be wary of John or of something else? For a moment Sarah wondered if John had done something that might have caused his wife to take her own life. If Andrea had guessed that he did not love her, she might have been so miserable that she could no longer bear to live. And yet, knowing John as she did, Sarah could not believe that he would have been so cruel as to let his wife feel unloved. He would have been kind and generous, as he always was... and that meant that there was another reason for her unhappiness.

Sarah put the letter away. Had she not been feeling the strain between herself and her mama, she might have taken the letter to her at once. However, she knew that Mrs Hunter would use it to prove that she

had been right all along. She would try to persuade
Sarah to change her mind about the wedding.

So what ought she to do? She could certainly not
show the letter to John, for he would be distressed
by it and perhaps feel guilty that Sarah should have
been subjected to such spite. Perhaps she ought to
throw it away—and yet it might serve as proof one
day. Someone was clearly determined to cause
trouble for John. Only an enemy would write such
a terrible letter to John's intended wife.

Who could hate him so much and why? Sarah
pondered the question, but could come up with no so-
lutions. John had always seemed to her to be the
perfect gentleman, kind, thoughtful and generous.
She would not have thought that he had enemies—
although he had taken part in all that unpleasant
business with Sir Courtney Welch, when that wicked
man had plotted to kidnap Arabella for the sake of her
fortune. But it was Captain Hernshaw who had
actually shot Sir Courtney. If someone wanted
revenge for his death, they could equally have centred
their attentions on the captain or even Charles, who
had masterminded the plan to outwit him.

It was no use. She had no idea who could be
spreading these wicked lies, but she knew that
someone wished to harm John. For the moment she
had no idea why, but there was some mystery here.

She had first sensed it at the house, when John lay ill, but she had been too concerned for him to give it much thought. But now, because she refused to believe that John had killed Andrea, she realised that there must be some other solution to the mystery— a mystery that would haunt John until it was solved.

John had not yet told her anything about his first marriage, but she believed that he would when he was ready. She decided that she would wait before asking questions. She loved John and she trusted him. Whoever had sent her that wicked letter hated him, but he had failed in his purpose, for she would not draw back from her wedding. Indeed, she could not wait to leave for the country, thus bringing the day closer when she would be John's wife.

John presented Sarah with a small posy of pink roses to match her gown that evening, and he also had another surprise for her.

'I hope that you will like this, Sarah,' he said, slipping a beautiful ruby-and-diamond ring on to the third finger of her left hand. 'I have made arrangements for the family jewels to be brought out of the bank. We shall choose those you wish to have altered to your taste, and the others may return to the vault. What would you most wish to have as your wedding gift—diamonds or pearls?'

'I have very simple tastes in jewellery,' Sarah said and leaned forward to kiss his cheek shyly. She loved him so much, but they were still getting used to the idea of their engagement. 'Pearls would be lovely, if you approve?'

John drew her gently towards him, kissing her softly on the lips. His kiss was tender and sweet, making her pulse race with excitement as she responded to him with all her heart.

'Do you not know that I would approve of anything you chose, dearest Sarah?'

'Oh, John…' Sarah's eyes misted with tears of joy. She had longed for this moment, almost giving up all hope at one time, but now she thrilled to his nearness and the promise of happiness to come. 'You are too good to me.'

'I love you very much, dearest. You must know that?' His words carried the ring of sincerity, the look in his eyes seeming to caress her.

Before she could answer, Mrs Hunter came into the room. She saw how close they were standing and frowned in disapproval.

'John has just given me my ring,' Sarah said, holding out her hand for her mother to see. 'Is it not lovely?'

'It looks very well,' Mrs Hunter said in a grudging tone. 'Are we ready? We do not wish to be late.'

'The carriage awaits, ma'am,' John said, smiling

easily at his future mother-in-law. He was aware that she was not completely reconciled to their marriage, but determined not to allow her attitude towards him to spoil things for Sarah. 'Shall we go?'

Mrs Hunter swept out ahead of them. Her expression was one of resigned martyrdom. Clearly she had not forgiven any of them for going against her wishes. Her attitude threw a shadow over Sarah's happiness, for although she was marrying the man she loved she could not be completely happy while her mother continued to show her dislike of both John and the marriage.

Sarah took John's arm, smiling up at him. She was delighted with her beautiful ring and the prospect of marriage to the man she loved. And, however much it might hurt, she would not let her mama's disapproval—or the unknown writer of that wicked letter—spoil her pleasure.

It was a very pleasant evening despite Mrs Hunter's reserved manner. They met several of their friends at the theatre and Sarah could not detect any change in their manner towards either her or John. She said as much to her mother before she went to bed that night.

'Julia Moore told me that she would come for the dance and our wedding,' she said. 'Do you not think that shows people know these tales are scandalous lies, Mama?'

'Perhaps,' her mother replied with a shrug. 'Your friends may ignore the gossip—but you may find that you will not receive vouchers for Almack's unless these tales can be disproved.'

'I should be sorry if that were the case,' Sarah acknowledged. 'But it changes nothing. I can be happy at home in the country with John. Indeed, I believe I shall not want to visit London often. I can buy almost everything I need in York and send to town for anything else. I enjoy meeting my friends, Mama, but I do not care so very much for large society gatherings.' She smiled and changed the subject. 'You know that John is taking me to Scotland for a few days, Mama? A friend has offered us his hunting lodge.'

'Would you not have preferred to visit France or Italy?' Mrs Hunter's brows rose.

'I have only just returned home after more than two years abroad, Mama,' Sarah reminded her. 'Italy is beautiful and perhaps John will take me there one day. He asked me where I should like to go and I told him that I wanted to be at home for a few months. His house needs a great deal of attention and it will give me much pleasure to choose the silks for our new curtains, and the new colours and furnishings, for he has given me *carte blanche* to do as I please. When we have created a home to be proud of, we shall hold a large house party for our friends and neighbours.'

'Well, I suppose you will have your own way,' Mrs Hunter said darkly. 'Do not blame me if things do not work out as you hope, Sarah.'

'What can you mean, Mama?'

Her mother's gaze narrowed. 'Supposing there is some truth in this rumour, Sarah? There must surely be a reason for it having spread as it has. What will you do if you discover that your husband was in some way responsible for his first wife's death? How will you feel then?' She gripped her daughter's arm, suddenly intent. 'Will you not reconsider, Sarah? I know you think I am deliberately spoiling things for you—but I am frightened. I cannot shake the feeling that if you marry him your life may be in danger.' Tears stood in her eyes. 'I do love you, Sarah, even if you do not think it…'

'Oh, Mama…' Sarah said and shook her head. She felt that icy chill at her nape again, for, combined with the threatening letter she had received, her mother's doubts were enough to make her uneasy. 'Please do not worry. John would never harm me.'

'But something made that poor woman kill herself. What if you discovered that he was in some way responsible?'

'I shall not discover anything of the kind, for it is not true,' Sarah replied, her head high. 'John could never do anything so wicked. I do not know how you can think it, Mama. It is most unfair of you. You know how kind he has always been to us—how much he helped Charles when I was lost. I know Charles thinks highly of him, as do Arabella, Elizabeth and the earl.'

'Yes, I know he was a good friend to your brother, but… Oh, I do not know what to think,' her mother said and sighed. She gave a little shake of her head. 'Perhaps I have been wrong over this affair, Sarah. I am haunted by this fear and…perhaps I am foolish as your brother says. All I want is for you to be happy.'

'I shall be happy as John's wife.' Sarah moved towards her, her hand stretched out in supplication. 'Please do not let us quarrel any more, Mama. I know that you wanted to see me safely wed, because of what happened when I was abducted—but I shall be safe as John's wife.'

'I pray that you will be,' Mrs Hunter said, but her face was shadowed by doubt. 'I am sorry if I was unkind to you, Sarah. I was so angry at what you had done. Did you not think of what would happen if John had not asked you to marry him? Your reputation would have been lost. As it is, you may find that you are not welcome everywhere even after your marriage.'

'I know that I took a risk,' Sarah said honestly. 'If John had not asked me, I should have had to retire from public life completely, perhaps gone abroad for good—but if he had died I should not have cared what became of me. He is the only man I could bear to marry, Mama. I am sorry if you wanted me to become a duchess, but I could never have married the duke.'

'Oh, Sarah…' Mrs Elworthy looked at her in distress. 'I wonder if it is wise to love so completely. I fear that you will be hurt one day. At least John did the decent thing, though he could not have done less in the circumstances. Any gentleman would have done as much in his place.'

'John loves me, Mama. It was his intention to ask me to marry him even before I went to his home.'

'Yet he did not do so,' Mrs Hunter reminded her. 'He had opportunity enough, I think, before he was called to his son—but there, it hardly matters. He did as he ought in difficult circumstances and you are to be married. I must be content with that and forget my doubts.'

'You have no need to doubt him, Mama,' Sarah said, raising her head proudly. 'John loves me. I know he does.'

And yet, as she lay down to sleep that night, her mother's words came back to haunt her. Why had

John not spoken when they were both staying with Charles and Arabella? She had believed he meant to ask her on the night of Elizabeth's ball, but he had rushed home. And he hadn't wanted to give her Andrea's ring.

Was it possible that he had simply done the decent thing as her mother was suggesting? It was true that she did not know him well. Could he still be in love with Andrea despite his denials? Sarah had proved her love for him by going to his side when he was ill, nursing him and arranging a new nurse for his son. Had he decided that he ought to marry for the boy's sake? Had he believed it his duty to save Sarah from the scandal she had brought upon herself by her rash behaviour?

It was a small pinprick of hurt. Sarah struggled to put it from her mind. John loved her. He had kissed her so tenderly and told her that he had always loved her.

If that were true, why had he married Andrea? Why had Andrea taken her own life? It seemed strange that a young wife with a small child should be so unhappy that she could no longer bear her existence. There must be some secret in her past, some mystery that had caused her to throw herself in the river that day…unless she had not died by her own will…

Sarah tossed restlessly on her pillows. It was a

while before she managed to sleep, but at last she subdued her doubts. John loved her. He had sworn it and she believed him. To believe anything else was impossible—it would mean that he had lied to her and then he would not be the man she loved.

'I am so happy for you, dearest Sarah,' Arabella said, embracing her. 'I have always thought John was the man for you, and I know you will be happy with him.'

'Yes, I shall,' Sarah agreed for she had managed to put her doubts aside. She would have been foolish to allow them to mar her happiness, because everyone was doing so much to give her pleasure. 'You and Charles have been so good to me, Belle. I am really looking forward to the dance and then of course my wedding.'

They were alone in Sarah's bedchamber, and the room was cluttered with boxes and parcels, most of them gifts from friends and relatives. Sarah had hardly begun to unpack them yet for she had been too busy having fittings for her wedding gown and other items of her trousseau.

'Are you pleased with your wedding gown?' Arabella asked. It was at that moment lying on the bed, a fragile creation of white silk, lace and ribbons. 'I think it is beautiful and it looks well on you, dearest.'

'Yes, it is lovely,' Sarah said. 'I was not satisfied

until your dressmaker adjusted the waist, but now it looks just as it should.' She noticed that Arabella was looking tired. 'Are you feeling unwell? You are a little pale, Belle.'

'Oh, no, I am not ill,' Arabella said, 'but I think I ought to lie down for a few minutes. My doctor told me that I should rest in the afternoons.'

'Then you must do so,' Sarah said. 'It is too nice out for me to stay in. I think I shall go for a little walk if you are going to rest.'

'Yes, you do that,' Arabella said. 'I think Daniel and John will be back later this afternoon. They said that they would not stay more than one night in York.'

'Yes, I know. John said he had some business there and I believe Charles also needed to see someone on business?'

'Oh, yes, it will have been business of some kind,' Arabella said. 'Go for you walk then, Sarah. I shall see you at tea.'

Sarah picked up a paisley shawl and draped it over her shoulders, following her friend out into the hall. Arabella turned away to her own apartments and Sarah went down the stairs.

She left the house by means of the French windows in the small back parlour and walked across the lawns. Beyond the formal garden was an expanse of open parkland with specimen trees arranged in artful carelessness to look as if nature had always intended they should stand just so. The park had been landscaped during her grandfather's time, and the trees had grown to great heights, their branches dipping down to sweep the earth majestically.

At the far edge of the vista the lake gleamed in the sunshine. Sarah had always loved to visit the lake, sometimes to feed the swans that glided there so gracefully, at other times just to stand and watch the water as it rippled in the breeze.

That afternoon the water looked especially inviting as it reflected the blue of the sky overhead. It was not as blue as the lakes in Italy or the Mediterranean Sea, of course, but in its own way it was just as beautiful. On the far shore there was a haze of blue-green from the dense wood planted there, also by her grandfather. Pausing to shade her eyes from the sun, Sarah looked towards something dark moving at the edge of the wood.

A little shiver ran down her spine. Someone—a man—was standing in the trees. He wore riding breeches and a dark coat, his head bare. As she stood motionless, reminded of the morning that she had been so brutally abducted from her family, the man emerged from the trees. He came nearer to the opposite bank of the lake and stood staring across it at her. His action was deliberate, somehow threatening, as if he were somehow accusing her—but of what?

Sarah felt coldness spread all over her. She did not know why, but she sensed menace in the man. He was not from the estate, of that she felt certain—and from the way he dressed, she thought he might be a gentleman…or perhaps a soldier. There was something bold in his stance, something challenging, as if he were warning her, though of what she had no idea.

For a moment Sarah considered calling out to him, asking him what he wanted, why he was on her brother's land, but then he turned away, disappearing into the woods as if he had never been. Sarah had goose pimples all over. Someone must have walked over her grave!

The old saying made her feel uncomfortable as it popped into her head, and a little frightened. Yet what was there to be frightened of? It was a beautiful day and she was quite safe. No one had thrown a blanket over her head. She had not been abducted.

Yet somehow the pleasure in her walk had dimmed. She turned and walked back towards the house. Who was he, the stranger who had stared at her from the other side of the lake? Why had he stared at her that way? Or perhaps she was imagining it?

But he had certainly not been one of the estate workers. The woods were private property and he must have scaled a high wall to enter them—for what purpose?

As she neared the house, she saw that a curricle had drawn up and two men were getting out. She gave a little cry of pleasure, forgetting the odd incident at the lake as she ran to greet them.

'Charles! John! You are back…'

She ran to John, who caught her in his arms, holding her as she clung to him, his smile warm and gentle as he gazed down at her.

'Is something wrong, Sarah?' he asked, for he sensed that she was disturbed about something.

'Oh, no,' she said and laughed up at him. 'I am just pleased to see you.'

'He has been away for one night only,' Charles said, giving her a mocking smile. 'It is as well that you are to be married soon, Sarah!' He was laughing as he walked into the house ahead of them, leaving them to look at each other in delight and snatch a stolen kiss.

'I am foolish,' Sarah said. 'But I was just so pleased to see you.'

'I hope that you will always greet me as eagerly,' John said, and for a moment there were shadows in his eyes. 'But tell me, did something happen…something that bothers you?' He searched her face anxiously.

Sarah hesitated, wondering if she should tell him about the man in the woods—but what was there to tell really? She had seen a stranger on her brother's land. That was not so very unusual after all. People did occasionally stray on to the estate by mistake.

'No, nothing,' she said and reached up to kiss his cheek. 'Nothing at all, John. I had been for a walk and it was just so nice to see that you and Charles were back, that's all.'

There were only a few days until her wedding. Sarah was keeping her fingers crossed that nothing would go wrong. When they were married and nothing could prevent her being John's wife, then she would tell him about the stranger.

It was a happy evening. Arabella had invited some of her friends and neighbours to dinner and the company had blended well, Sarah receiving many warm wishes and congratulations on her coming marriage.

After dinner, when the gentlemen had finished with their port and joined the ladies in the parlour, Sarah was asked to play at the pianoforte. John came to stand at her shoulder, turning the pages, and then, when she had finished, he suggested a duet and sat down beside her on the stool. They gave a spirited performance, which was greeted with enthusiastic applause and cries for more at the end. They obliged for they were enjoying themselves, and rose only when the tea tray was brought in.

After this the gentlemen disappeared to the billiard room, and the ladies went upstairs to their rooms. Mrs Hunter came to say goodnight to Sarah as she was undressing.

'You played very nicely, Sarah,' she said. 'I was pleased to see that everything went well this evening. I have my reservations about your marriage, you know that—but I must admit that Mr Elworthy has very good manners, and he seems generally liked.'

'He is, Mama,' Sarah said. 'Please try to like John for my sake—and forgive us for going against you in the matter of the ceremony. I know you would have liked a grand affair in town.'

'Well, you are my only daughter,' Mrs Hunter said with a little sniff. 'But I suppose it will do well enough.'

Sarah smiled as she went out. She could only hope that her mama would be reconciled to the marriage, for she did not like to be at odds with her. Being a generous girl, she had forgiven her mother for her unkindness and all she wanted now was for everyone to be happy.

\* \* \*

'Oh, what a lot of cards and gifts you have,' Tilda said as she entered Sarah's bedchamber the next morning. She and Lady Tate had arrived the previous evening for the dance that was to be held that night. 'I found these on the hall table, Sarah, and so I thought I would bring them up for you.'

She deposited half a dozen small packages on the bed. Sarah was sitting up against the pillows. She had been drinking hot chocolate, which her maid had brought up for her earlier, because she had decided to stay in bed a little longer so as to be fresh for the evening. She reached out for the letters and smiled as she saw that one small package was from John, but the others were messages from friends who were coming to the wedding. She opened several, including John's latest gift, a pretty ruby pendant on a fine chain, and then picked up the last, a shudder running through her as she saw the writing.

Tilda had been looking at some of the gifts that had been set up on a table at one side of the room. They had arrived in the last week or so and would be displayed downstairs on the day of the wedding.

'What a beautiful little clock,' she said, touching a tiny enamelled carriage clock with her finger. 'I think that is French…' She turned and saw the expression of apprehension on Sarah's face. 'Is something the matter, my dear? Something in one of the letters I brought up to you?'

Sarah offered her the unopened letter wordlessly. She took it, broke the plain wax seal, and read the few lines with a frown. 'This is wicked, Sarah,' she said and read aloud, '"*I have warned you before. Draw back now before it is too late. He does not love you. He will never love you. Marry him and you will never cease to regret it. A well wisher.*" How could anybody send you such a wicked letter?'

'Oh, no, not again. It is horrible…' Sarah said and shivered. Emotion caught at her throat but she held back her desire to weep. She would not give way to tears, but the letter had thrown a cloud over her feeling of pleasure. 'Why would anyone write such stuff to me?'

'This is not the first you have had, is it?' Tilda turned it over and saw that it was not franked. 'It must have been delivered by hand. I think we should investigate a little further, Sarah. You must show this to Mr Hunter—or perhaps John.'

'No, not yet,' Sarah said. The letter had triggered that creeping feeling of unease again, but she did not want anyone to see that she was distressed. She lifted her head, forcing herself to smile. 'It is just someone being spiteful, Tilda. I do not want to upset John, and Charles would make such a fuss…'

'Better that he should know,' Tilda said. 'Wait until after the dance if you wish, but do tell Mr Hunter at least. This is a threat, Sarah, and you should not just brush it aside, especially if you have had others.'

'One other, and that was worse,' Sarah told her. 'It said that John was—' She shook her head. 'No, I shall not let whoever it is upset me. It is all a part of the malicious campaign to discredit John.'

'Yes, my dear, I believe it is,' Tilda said, feeling distressed. She did not like to see that look in Sarah's eyes when she had been so happy moments earlier. 'I do not believe a word of these lies, but someone must have a grudge against John. I wonder…' She looked thoughtful and then shook her head. 'I dare say Mr Hunter and John will already have thought of the possibility…'

'What possibility is that, Tilda?'

'It occurred to me that someone who would do these things must be jealous of John, Sarah. Might it possibly be that his first wife had an admirer or perhaps a lover? Could he be bitter because of what happened? If in his own mind he blames John…'

Sarah stared at her. 'Do you know, Tilda, I think you may have hit upon something. You should speak to John or my brother, tell them your thoughts on the matter.'

'Oh, no, my dear,' Tilda said and blushed. 'I am

sure that they do not need any advice from me. No doubt they have thought of all eventualities.'

'Perhaps…' Sarah said, but wondered if she ought to speak to her brother concerning the letters and Tilda's idea.

'You said you had more news?' Charles looked at his friend, brows raised. 'Does it concern the matter we spoke of in London?'

'Yes…' John frowned, his expression serious. 'Tobbold says that he has traced the man here—to the grounds of your home, Charles. He says he is sure it is the same man that was seen in my village a few weeks ago…'

'That means we are getting closer to solving the mystery.'

'Yes, perhaps,' John said. 'And yet I cannot help being anxious, Charles. The letters were one thing and I had almost put them from my mind, for though they were hurtful they could do no real harm. I did not murder Andrea and nothing can be proved to the contrary—but why is this fellow watching me? Does he have some wicked intent?'

'You mean will he attempt to kill you?'

'Or Sarah,' John said. 'You know that I love her dearly, Charles—but I have wondered if we should postpone the wedding until this is settled.'

'I do not see how that would help,' Charles replied. 'This thing may never be truly finished. You cannot ruin both your lives simply because you have an enemy. No, my friend, you did the right thing. All I am saying is that you must be on your guard at all times. I do not think Sarah is at risk particularly. It is you this man hates and you he means to pursue until he has ruined you…'

'I would be content if I thought it was only my life in danger,' John said, his eyes glinting. 'But if anything should happen to Sarah…I would kill him with my bare hands!'

Charles smiled. 'And I would applaud you, my friend. But if we are clever and make our plans, we may trap him without such drastic measures. I do not imagine Sarah would care to watch her husband die at the end of a rope.'

John glared at him and then laughed. 'No, I dare say you are right,' he said. 'And now, if you will excuse me, Charles, I shall go and find Sarah or she will think I have deserted her…'

Sarah went out into the garden, needing to be alone. Her thoughts were confused—the second letter had unsettled her once more, bringing back the doubts she had fought so hard to suppress these past days.

Why did the writer of the letter say that John

would never love her? Was her mother right in saying that she was rushing into this marriage with unseemly haste? She would not have given the letter a second thought had she not overheard her brother and Charles talking together that day in London. Try as she might, she had not quite been able to put it from her mind. Had John been saying that he had had no choice but to ask Sarah to marry him?

She *had* placed him in an impossible position. No decent gentleman would do other than propose after what she had done for him. It was possible that John might have died if she had not nursed him so devotedly, although Mrs Beeson had done her best in difficult circumstances. Sarah had been impulsive and reckless, and perhaps her mama had had been right to be cross with her. She felt a little ashamed and guilty over her behaviour, especially if she had forced John into an awkward situation.

Sarah's mind twisted this way and that, her emotions in a turmoil. She had been so sure that John loved her. Her throat was tight with emotion. Surely he did! Yet she could not help wondering if she had made it impossible for him to do anything else but ask her to be his wife. Was it possible that he still loved Andrea—was that what the letter had meant? John could never love her because his heart was with his wife in her grave? It was all so confusing! She had been told that John might be a murderer, that he might have driven his wife to take her own life because he was unkind to her—and now this last letter seemed to suggest that he still loved her. What was she to think? And yet…the writer of this letter clearly had mischief in mind…

She was still sitting alone in the rose garden when John came to her half an hour later. He stood watching her for a moment, wondering at the pensive expression on her face.

'A penny for your thoughts,' he said and sat down next to her on the wooden bench beneath an arch of roses. They hung down in clumps of heavy white blossom, the perfume strong and sweet on the early summer air. 'Is something troubling you, my love?' He reached for her hand and held it lightly in his. 'You would tell me if something had upset you, dearest?'

'I am not upset,' Sarah said, lifting her head, a gleam of pride in her eyes. She would not confess that she was tortured by her doubts. 'I was just sitting here, thinking how strange life is, John. If I had not gone to Italy when I did, you might not have married Andrea.'

'You are not distressed by the thought of my first wife?' he asked and stroked the back of her hand with the tip of one finger. 'I cared for her in my way, Sarah—but I did not feel for Andrea what I feel for you. I love Nat because he is a child and vulnerable. He needs my love because he has no mother and he will know no other father. It is my duty to care for him, and indeed, I have come to love him dearly. I hope you can accept that, dearest?'

'Oh, yes,' Sarah said easily. 'He is such a lovely little boy. I love him too, John, and I shall always care for him as if he is our son—even when we have others.' She blushed and avoided his gaze, her heart beating wildly. 'I do want to have children, don't you?'

'Yes, Sarah. I want very much to have your children, my darling. To live quietly with you and all our children is my dream of happiness. I am not an ambitious man. I have no dreams of fame or great riches, but I shall strive to provide a good life for you and our children.'

He sounded so sincere. How could she doubt him? Sarah lifted her eyes to his, seeing that his were warm with affection and perhaps more. She must believe in his sincerity, his love. She knew that she would have nothing to live for without him, and she must accept what he told her. There was no room for doubt if they were to be happy together.

'I am so glad, John,' she said and moved towards him invitingly. 'I can hardly wait until we are wed, my dearest.'

John reached out for her, pulling her against him. He put up his hand to trail his fingers down the side of her face, his touch sending shivers of delight down her spine. And then he kissed her. It was not the gentle kiss he had given her so often before, but hungry and demanding, seeming to draw her very soul from her body so that they became as one. She clung to him, her mind spiralling in dizzy delight as she imagined herself lying in his arms once they were wed. It seemed to her then that a prospect of unimaginable pleasure was opening out to her.

How foolish she was to doubt him for a moment!

'I shall stay for our dance, naturally,' John told her. 'But tomorrow I must go home for a quick visit, Sarah. I have put some alterations in hand and I want to see that my instructions are being carried out— but I shall return the day before the wedding.'

'Must you go?' Sarah asked wistfully. 'I shall hate to part with you, John, even for a few days.'

'I think I must,' he said and laughed softly. 'If I stayed I might be tempted to anticipate my wedding night. When you respond as you did just now, Sarah, I want to sweep you up in my arms and carry you straight to my bed.'

Sarah's eyes lit up and she smiled up at him. He had never spoken to her like this before, and she glimpsed the passionate, loving man beneath the gentlemanly manner John habitually showed her. Her perfect gentleman was perhaps bolder than she had imagined—and she could not wait to discover more of this new facet of his character.

'I do not think I should mind if you did, John' she whispered, her eyes dark with the intensity of her feelings. 'You have never kissed me quite like that before.'

'I did not wish to frighten you, my love,' John said. 'I do not forget that you were cruelly kidnapped and subjected to the wicked threats of that evil man Sir Montague Forsythe. I know you had nightmares about that night in the woods and I was determined that I would be patient and not demand more than you could give.'

'Those nightmares have gone,' Sarah said, knowing that it was true at last. 'You need not be anxious that I shall fear to be your true wife, John, for I shall not. I know that you must go home, but hurry back to me, my love.'

'We have the rest of today and this evening,' John said. 'And now, Sarah, I have a little gift for you.' He took a slender leather box from his coat pocket and gave it to her. 'I thought you might like to wear this for the dance this evening…'

She opened it to find a necklace of creamy white pearls with a heart-shaped drop made from small diamonds. 'Oh, John, it is a love heart,' she said. 'It is so beautiful. I shall treasure it always.'

'You must never forget that I love you,' John said and there was a fervent note in his voice as he reached out to touch her face. 'Please promise me that you will never run away from me, Sarah—never do anything foolish.'

He must be thinking of Andrea! There was such pain in his voice, such appeal in his eyes. Clearly he was still tortured by the memory of his wife's death for whatever reason. She leaned forward to kiss him on the lips.

'Of course I shall not run away from you, John. Why should I?' She smiled up at him as his arms closed about her once more. 'It is a beautiful gift and I love it. I shall always treasure it…all my life.'

They stood up, and, with John's arm about her, began to stroll back towards the house, neither of them aware that they were being watched by jealous eyes—eyes that burned with a bitter anger and hatred.

'You think you can escape your guilt,' the soldier muttered through lips that were white with anger. 'You killed her, John Elworthy, and you shall pay with your own life—but not before you suffer the torments of hell. You too shall know what it is like to lose all that you love before you beg me to let you die…'

## Chapter Eight

It was an evening of sheer delight for Sarah. After her tête-à-tête with John in the garden she had managed to put all her doubts aside, and she was determined to make it a happy time for her lover and her guests. She had arranged with Charles for her mother to be given a beautiful bouquet of flowers as well as a posy that evening, and she knew that he had given their mother a small gift of porcelain. Mrs Hunter had softened sufficiently to wish her daughter a happy evening, and Sarah had responded by embracing her warmly.

She opened the dance with John, feeling as if she were waltzing on air as he whirled her around the floor, the skirts of her lovely gown billowing about her like pale pink thistledown.

'Are you happy, dearest one? You look beautiful,' John told her, whispering against her hair as he held her close in the waltz. 'I am so proud of you, my darling. So very proud.'

'I am proud of you, John,' she said looking up at him. Her eyes were bright with excitement and sparkled in the light of the many candles. 'I do love you so very much…and I am very happy.'

It was true that one or two of the guests they had invited had not come, but none of them were particular friends. Since Mrs Hunter had invited almost everyone she knew, it was perhaps just as well that a few had cried off, for the reception rooms were overflowing with happy, laughing guests all intent on wishing Sarah and John happiness and enjoying themselves.

The champagne was flowing, the food offered to the guests by Arabella's cook was mouth-watering, and the music was delightful. Sarah's doubts had been stilled and she felt that she was that night happier than she had ever been.

At the end of the evening, she wandered out into the garden with John and he took her into his arms, kissing her with such tenderness and yet such hunger that she melted into his body, feeling as if she were dissolving with happiness.

'Soon we shall be married,' John whispered against her ear, his arm about her waist as they lingered beneath the stars for a few moments. 'I must go home tomorrow, as I told you, but the days will soon pass—and then we need never be alone again, my darling.'

'I long for that,' Sarah said, feeling as if she would melt with love as she heard the tender note in his voice. 'When we were in Italy I thought of you so often and then I heard that you had married and all my dreams were at an end.'

'If only I had known,' John said, torn with regret. 'It was my fault. I should have followed you to Italy, but I was afraid of pressing you into something that frightened you, Sarah. I thought that I should wait and then it was too late.'

'I was never frightened of you, John,' Sarah told him with a smile. 'Only of my nightmares. There was a time when I believed I should never marry. I was haunted by bad dreams and I did not think I could bear to be touched by any man, but then I began to realise that I had been lucky. Nothing so very terrible had happened to me—at least, it might have been far worse. Once I realised that I was no longer afraid, I began to think of you—and to wish that you had followed us to Italy.'

'If only I had, my love.' His voice carried a ring of anguish, making her aware of his own suffering these past months. 'You will never know how much I have regretted that I did not…'

John reached out to stroke her hair, his touch

making her shiver with pleasure. She knew that if he had asked she would have gone to him, become one with him that very night, but he did not ask. Instead he smiled, took her hand and led her back into the house to say goodnight to those of her guests who still lingered.

Sarah went to bed with the music, the magic of the evening and the sweetness of John's kisses playing through her mind. She tumbled into bed, feeling happy and at peace with herself, and soon fell into a dreamless sleep.

The day after the dance was naturally very quiet. Everyone was feeling a little tired, not inclined to do much other than sit about and talk and sip tea or wine. Sarah went for a little walk in the gardens, but she felt lonely because she was missing John and soon returned to the house to join Elizabeth, Arabella and Tilda, who were sewing together in one of the small parlours.

'You look lost,' Elizabeth said as Sarah picked up a book and then put it down again with a sigh. 'It will not be long to the wedding now, Sarah. If I were you, I should make a start on the thank-you letters, for they take for ever and when you get home you will have other things to do.'

'Yes, I shall,' Sarah agreed. She went over to the

desk by the window and took out some paper from the drawer. She had thanked most of her friends personally, of course, but the letters still needed to be done—especially to some relatives who lived long distances away and were too elderly to attend the wedding, but had sent beautiful gifts.

She spent more than an hour at her letter writing, and after lunch she joined some of the other ladies in a hand of cards. Dinner was more lively for the gentlemen were in good spirits, and the day ended with everyone laughing and happy.

Sarah woke early the next morning. The lethargy of the previous day had gone and she asked her maid to help her dress in her riding habit. Once ready, she left the house and walked down to the stables, where one of the grooms was only too happy to saddle a mare for his young mistress. He saddled a bay hunter for himself, because her brother had instructed that she must always be accompanied when out riding. Sarah did not object when he followed her from the stableyard. She intended to give her mare a good gallop and the groom would either keep up with her or not, but she did not object to his company.

'Yes, do come if you wish, William,' she said with a smile. 'It is a lovely day for riding.'

'Yes, miss. Thank you, miss.'

They set off at a gentle trot, leaving the park behind to ride out on to the moor, which bounded Charles's estate on one side. It was here that Sarah dug her heels in, letting her mare have its head. The sensation was like flying over the undulating ground and she could feel the wind in her face, her hair streaming in the wind. As usual she had not bothered with a hat and the feeling of absolute freedom was wonderful.

Her groom followed behind at a short distance. His horse was well able to keep up, but he did not try to race his mistress, merely keeping her in sight as she galloped ahead of him. It was as they were returning to the estate at a slightly slower pace that he caught a glimpse of someone in a small stand of trees. Instinct made him push forward to reach Sarah, but before he could do so the man in the trees raised his arm and fired in her direction.

The shot went wide, but it was enough to startle Sarah's mare. It shied, half-stopped, then reared up and nearly unseated its rider before taking off in a panic.

'Hang on, Miss Sarah,' William cried and set off in pursuit of the fear-maddened mare. 'Don't let her throw you…'

Sarah could not hear what he was saying, but instinct kept her in the saddle as the mare raced towards the trees, entering the wood and swerving this way and that, between them. Sarah was forced to duck her head as branches slapped into her face. It was a terrifying ride, for, no matter what she did, the mare would not be halted. It was only as they reached a clearing that her horse faltered when a fallen tree blocked their path, coming to an abrupt halt. Sarah managed somehow to hold on, leaning over the neck of the quivering beast, breathing almost as hard as her poor mare as she tried to soothe her.

A moment later the groom was there. He had hold of the bridle, gentling the mare as she started to shy again, his anxious eyes on Sarah as she sat gathering her breath before slipping from the saddle and walking a few steps to sit on the fallen tree trunk. She lowered her head to her hands, recovering her composure as she felt herself tremble. In a moment or two the feeling of fear receded and she raised her head, looking at the young groom standing respectfully near by.

'That was a close one, William,' she said. 'That stupid poacher frightened Rosie to death, poor creature. It was no wonder that she took off like that.'

'The wonder of it was that you were not killed, Miss Sarah,' William said. 'I thought he was going to shoot you, but his aim went wide.'

Sarah stared at him, her eyes widening. 'Did you see him? I thought it was a poacher shooting at a rabbit… Was that shot meant for me?'

'That's the way it seemed to me, miss,' William said. 'I can't say for sure, because his shot went wide if he meant to kill you—but perhaps it was merely meant to startle your horse. You could have been thrown and badly hurt, miss.'

'Yes, you are right,' Sarah said, biting her lip. Had it been a warning to her? Could the man she had imagined a poacher be the same one who had sent her those threatening letters? 'I have had a lucky escape, William. I think that if you will help me to mount again, I should like to go home now.'

'Yes, miss, of course.' He smiled at her as he came forward to help her back into the saddle. She had plenty of courage, that much was certain. 'That's it, Miss Sarah. It's always best to get back up after something like that, I reckon. You don't want to dwell on what might have happened.'

'I shan't,' Sarah said, lifting her head determinedly. 'William, I want you to promise me that you won't tell anyone else what happened this morning.'

'I shan't tell anyone but Mr Hunter,' William replied, a stubborn set to his mouth. 'I have to tell him, miss—it's my duty. If there is someone poaching on his land, he needs to know.' Besides,

William was pretty sure that shot had been fired at Sarah and her brother would need to be aware of it.

'Yes, tell Charles it was a poacher misfiring, William,' Sarah said with a nod of approval. 'That is what I shall tell him, for I am sure that that is all it was.'

She rode on ahead of him, her head high, shoulders straight. The incident had shaken her and it would be a while before she felt confident about riding out alone again. If William thought that the shot had been intended for her, it meant that whoever was out there was ruthless and would stop at nothing.

'Please do not go riding alone for a while,' Charles said to her later that day. They were alone in his study for he had asked to speak to her privately. 'If William is right, you could be in some danger, Sarah.'

'I believe it was just a poacher misfiring,' Sarah told him. 'Why should anyone want to kill me, Charles? I do not think that anyone has any reason to hate me.'

'Perhaps not you personally,' Charles said and frowned. 'But John would be devastated if anything happened to you, Sarah. It may be that his enemy hopes to get to him through you. You must promise me to be careful.'

'Yes, of course, but what you said about his enemy

using me…surely he would not?' Sarah felt cold all over. 'I know John has an enemy, but this is so cruel, evil…' She had not dreamed of anything so sinister, believing that the letters she had received were merely the work of someone who wished to spoil her pleasure in the wedding.

'What do you know of this wretched business, Sarah? Has John told you about the letters he received?'

'No…' Sarah hesitated, then, 'I have had two letters myself, Charles. They were quite wicked, and accused John of murdering his first wife…'

His eyes narrowed. 'Why did you not tell me this before?'

'I tried to ignore the first one,' Sarah confessed, 'but I was going to tell you when the second one came here, for it was not franked, which meant it must have been delivered by hand, but then I decided to forget them—I thought it was merely someone's spite.'

Charles frowned. 'Will you fetch the letters and show them to me now, please?'

'Yes, if you do not mind waiting.'

Sarah left him and went quickly up to her room, returning with the letters immediately. She handed them to him, biting her lip as she saw his look of anger as he read them.

'These are disgusting,' Charles said and returned

them to her. 'You must keep them in case they are needed as evidence, Sarah. My advice would be to show them to John. I think he should be aware of these threats to you.' He hesitated, then, 'I wonder if we ought to postpone the wedding…'

'No!' Sarah cried at once. 'That is why I have not shown them to anyone but Tilda. She brought the second one up to me the morning after she arrived. I do not wish to postpone my wedding, Charles. To do that would be to let this evil person win.'

'Yes, you are right,' Charles said. 'But I shall speak to John and make sure that he understands that you need protection. Had your groom not been with you today, there is no telling what might have happened. I know that you were not thrown, but you might have been. You might have lain unconscious for hours before you were found. You might even have died.'

'Do you think whoever it is wants to punish John?' Sarah had been trying to think who would want to do such a thing, but could not.

Charles looked at her steadily, his expression serious, thoughtful. 'Yes, it is my opinion that all this is aimed at John. When Sir Courtney tried to kidnap Arabella, he wanted revenge on her and he wanted her money—but, remember, Elizabeth was kidnapped to draw Daniel into a trap. It is possible that you might be harmed simply to destroy John. I believe that someone hates John very much, though I cannot tell why.'

'What can John have done to make his enemy hate him so much?' Sarah asked. 'I do not think he would harm anyone…unless he had good cause.'

'Some people become jealous for no reason or for reasons they have invented in their own minds,' Charles said. 'I can only presume that it may have something to do with John's first wife, though that is a guess.'

'Tilda said something of the sort,' Sarah mused, remembering. 'She thought that perhaps Andrea had had a lover…that he might be angry because she had married John. It is quite possible that he would blame John for her death, even though she took her own life.'

'Yes, that is possible,' Charles said. He knew that there were other possibilities that had nothing to do with John's first wife, but he did not wish to upset his sister. She seemed to have forgotten the trauma of her kidnap and the months that she had spent living on Arabella's estate, her memory lost. It was possible that someone who had once been connected with Sir Montague Forsythe had an axe to grind, though in that case it made no sense that John was the chosen victim. It was true that he had helped

Charles and Daniel unmask the rogues who had stolen Sarah, but his part in the affair had been small. 'I think you may be right, Sarah, but we ought to keep an open mind.'

'Yes, of course,' Sarah replied thoughtfully. 'I promise that I shall be careful, Charles. I shan't go riding alone without a groom, and I shall not take any foolish risks—but I do not wish to postpone my wedding.'

'No, well, we shall not,' Charles replied with a grim smile. 'I am glad to know the whole situation, Sarah. I had already put some measures in place, but I shall do more. We must all be watchful until this devil is brought to account.' He quirked his brow. 'If I were you, I should say nothing of this to Mama. I think she would have strong hysterics.'

'I am perfectly sure that she would,' Sarah said and laughed a little ruefully. 'Do not worry, Charles. I have no intention of telling her about the letters or the shot that went wide.'

'Good.' Charles gave her an encouraging smile. 'I think we shall manage this thing, Sarah, but you will have to be a brave, sensible girl—I do not think that this man will give up easily.'

'No,' Sarah said and looked grave. 'I think he is driven by whatever it is that ails him, and he will not give up until he either gets his way or is caught.'

\* \* \*

She was a better rider than he had imagined. Despite his hatred of John Elworthy, he had to admire the woman who was to be his wife. Sitting at the inn table, the soldier drank deeply of his ale. If it were not for the nightmares that haunted him, he might have given up his quest for revenge and taken himself off to join another regiment in some far-flung land.

There was little here for him now, he thought staring into his empty pewter tankard. Andrea's death hung over him like a dark shadow, nagging at his conscience. Sometimes he heard her cry out to him, begging him to save her, and he was like a soul in hell, burning in the fires for his sins.

She had promised to wait for him! Why had she married so soon after he was forced to leave her and return to his regiment? Why had she not stayed faithful?

His mind returned to the last time he had seen her, to the accusation in her eyes, the dark shadows and hollows in her cheeks. He had been shocked to see her thus, her eyes tortured and haunted—a pale spectre of the woman she had been when they had lain together in a secret place, confessing their love and taking its pleasures.

It was her husband who had done that to her! He

had seen the unhappiness in her, the look of defeat in her eyes as she saw him the day he had at last returned and sought her out at her husband's estate. At first he had thought she would run from him, but she did not. She had just stood staring at him, her body seeming frail and hopeless, as if she felt defeated by life. He had begged her to leave Elworthy, to go with him. It was true that as a younger son he had nothing but what he could earn as a mercenary or win at the card tables, but he would have found a way to give her at least some of the pretty things she liked.

He had pleaded with her, but she refused despite her unhappiness. He had begged and knelt to her, and she had turned her face aside and then he had become angry. The cruel words he had flung at her echoed in his head. Were they a part of the reason she had been driven to walk into the river? Or had she? Was he right in suspecting that someone had pushed her…that she had been murdered?

At first he had not been sure that her husband had killed her. It was his first instinct to blame Elworthy, but he had not been certain…now his suspicion had hardened into a firm belief.

John Elworthy showed the face of a perfect gentleman to the world—but he, Sergeant George Rathbone, knew the truth. He had been told that

Andrea's husband had cruelly deserted her, breaking her heart by his coldness, his indifference, until she had finally been driven to take her own life in her desperation—if she *had* taken it, and not been pushed into that river.

He had wondered why Elworthy would wish his wife dead, but now he had the evidence of his own eyes and ears. It had come from Elworthy's own mouth. He had made a mistake in marrying Andrea, because he loved someone else—and now he was going to marry the woman he loved.

Andrea was hardly cold in her grave and Elworthy was going to marry another woman. It seemed that they were very much in love and their happiness when together was plain to see. He had watched them kissing, holding hands and talking of the future. But why should they be allowed happiness when *she* was dead?

He had not tried to kill Sarah Hunter the morning he had seen her out riding. He had fired impulsively, meaning to frighten her, but he would have shed no tears if she had fallen and injured herself. His mouth twisted with anger. It was Elworthy he wanted to punish, not the woman, and by God he would do it!

Sarah heard John's voice as she approached the study that morning. He had returned a day sooner than he had promised and her heart gladdened at the thought that she would see him again before she had expected. She hesitated, remembering the conversation she had overheard once before, and then knocked at the door, before putting her head round to ask if she might come in.

'Sarah, my love,' John said, looking at her in concern. 'Are you all right? Charles told me happened. It is a mercy that you were not thrown from your horse and badly hurt.'

'It was probably a poacher misfiring,' Sarah said, wanting to brush over it as lightly as possible. She smiled at him as his lips touched her cheek. 'Besides, if the shot was meant for me, it went wide. I am none the worse for my adventure, as you see, dearest.'

'I thank God for it,' John said, capturing her hands in his and holding them tightly. His anxious eyes searched her face. 'Charles says that you do not wish to postpone the wedding, despite everything?'

'No, certainly not,' Sarah said. 'This person is merely trying to frighten us, John. We should be foolish to allow him to do so. Surely you do not wish to give into this kind of bullying?'

'For myself I care nothing of his spiteful tales and tricks,' John said, his eyes dark with anguish as he looked at her lovely face. 'However, I do not wish to put your life at risk, Sarah.'

'We must be brave,' Sarah said, gazing up at him with determination. 'I do not think this person meant to kill me, John. He must hate you for some reason, but we cannot allow him to rule our lives. Besides, we have no proof that the shot was intended for me. It could simply have been a poacher misfiring.'

'Sarah is right,' Charles said. 'Besides, look how it would seem if you were to postpone it now, John. Everyone would whisper behind her back. No, you cannot do it—you must go ahead with the wedding. I have spoken to Tobbold and he is doubling the men protecting the estate until after the wedding. He will send some of them to Scotland with you—and then to your own estate. However, he says that he thinks he may know the identity of your enemy, John.'

'I pray you, tell me at once!'

Charles shook his head. 'He has not confided in me yet, though I understand that he believes the man a soldier. He says that one of his men has seen someone and thinks he knows him; he is almost sure he that they fought together in France.'

'I need him caught and questioned,' John said. 'It puzzles me why he has set out on this personal vendetta—for I can think of no reason for it, try as I may.'

'You know I have a theory on that,' Charles said, 'but we shall not discuss that at this moment. Take

Sarah for a walk in the garden, John. She has not dared to venture far since that last incident—and I am sure that you wish to be alone.'

John offered Sarah his hand and they left the room together, going through the small sitting room that led to the gardens. It was pleasantly warm, though a few clouds had appeared and it was not as hot as it had been the previous day.

'I hope the weather will stay fine for our wedding,' Sarah said, glancing up at John as they walked. 'It would be a shame if it were to rain—especially for the estate people, who are looking forward to a feast in the grounds.'

'I'm sure it will be sunny,' John said, but his eyes were dark with anger as he looked at her. For the moment he was unable to share her pleasure in the wedding. 'Forgive me, Sarah. I feel as if I have brought danger into your life. Had I known this would happen, I should not—' He broke off and shook his head, clearly at odds with himself.

'Please do not blame yourself, John,' Sarah said. She raised her eyes to his, gazing at him fearlessly. 'I would still have done everything that I have done even had I known that you had an enemy. I refuse to allow him to spoil the happiness we have found together, my dearest.'

'You are very brave,' John said, his fingers tightening about hers. 'Some young ladies would have wanted to run back to their mamas in tears had they been subjected to such a frightening experience.'

'But I am not a very young lady,' Sarah said. 'I shall be twenty-one in a few months—and, besides, I feel older. I suffered when I was abducted, John, because I did not know what had happened to me—or even who I was—but I am not suffering now. I am determined that whoever is trying to threaten us shall not succeed in driving us apart.'

'Oh, Sarah, my dearest girl,' John said, his voice husky with emotion as he bent his head to kiss her on the lips. 'I am so fortunate to have found you. I thought I had lost you when you left for Italy. I married Andrea because…because she was a vulnerable child who needed my help. In the end I failed her, but it was begun with good intentions. I meant to be kind to her…'

'You could never be anything but kind, John.'

'I think Andrea believed otherwise at the end,' he said and his eyes were shadowed by grief. 'I did not love her as I ought, Sarah. I should never have married her, for I knew that I loved you—but I was hesitant and…' He shrugged his shoulders. 'I have not told you before, because I did not wish to be disloyal to Andrea—but our marriage was not a true marriage. I never did take her to my bed. The room next to mine was prepared for her, but she chose another in its stead—she said she was ill and needed to sleep alone. I did nothing to prevent her, and though, after her child was born, she gave me to understand that she was ready to become my wife in every way, I did not try to cross the chasm that had grown between us. You see, I had by this time learned to regret my marriage and to resent it. I am ashamed to admit it, but I wished to be free, and though I did my best to hide that from her, I think she may have sensed it.'

'Then you did not love her? Her son was not yours?' Sarah gazed up into his face as she understood the truth at last. 'Oh, John! When we first met again I believed that you were still in love with her. I thought that you did not speak because you could not forget her…'

John shook his head, reaching out to touch her cheek. 'Oh, no, it was not for love that I held back, but guilt, Sarah. I have always felt that I failed Andrea, that it was my fault she killed herself.'

'No, John how could it be?' Sarah smiled at him lovingly. 'She came to you in trouble, is that not so?' He nodded. 'And you helped her by asking her to marry you. That was the act of a true gentleman, John. If afterwards you were unable to love her, it was not your fault, dearest.'

'I did try,' John said. 'I wanted to make her safe, Sarah—but she changed after the child was born, becoming ever more moody and shrinking from me, her moods sometimes so dark that I feared for her sanity. I left her alone—and then one day she came to me dressed in her best and she smiled. She kissed me and said that she would like to move into the room next to mine.' He hesitated, and then went on, 'I told her that I thought we should wait—that she was not well and I was thinking of fetching a special doctor to her…'

'A special doctor?' Sarah asked. 'Do you mean…?'

'I thought she was suffering from some mental affliction,' he admitted. 'Oh, I do not think that I believed her mad—but she was restless, going from one mood to the next, and I thought it had made her ill. She was very thin, and I believe in some turmoil of heart and mind. It may have been my harsh words to her that day that sent her to the river in a fit of despair.'

'Oh, John,' Sarah looked at him sadly. 'Your words would not have been enough to drive her to take her own life had she not been ill—or unhappy. Have you asked yourself why she came to you for help?'

'She told me that she had been forced…'

'That would have been terrible had it been true,' Sarah said, her brow furrowed. 'But supposing that she had a lover and he had gone away? In her shame and fear, she turned to you for help and you gave her what she needed.'

'Yes, that is possible,' John said. 'If he returned and learned that she had killed herself…' He paused, frowning. 'I think that I might want to kill a man who had made you desperately unhappy, Sarah.'

'But you did not make Andrea unhappy,' Sarah argued. 'If she was haunted by her love for another man—and perhaps guilt because she understood that you had asked her to marry her out of kindness—it must have played upon her mind.' Sarah frowned. 'Did she have a difficult birth?'

'Yes, I believe it was hard for her. She was always slender in the hips. The doctor told me it would be best to wait at least a year before having another child. It was one of the reasons I did not make an effort to consummate the marriage.'

'I see…' Sarah took his hand, holding it to her cheek. 'I have heard that some women become ill and unhappy after giving birth to a child, John. I do not think the doctors have a name for it, but it is not as uncommon as you might imagine.'

'Elizabeth said as much to me once when I mentioned that Andrea was moody. She had not suffered from it herself, but she said that she had met others who felt it very badly. She said that it would pass in time, but that a doctor she knew of might be able to help.'

'So you were trying to help her again, but she misunderstood you,' Sarah said and smiled at him lovingly. 'There, I knew that you had nothing to reproach yourself for, John. I think we shall not talk of this again, dearest. It should be put aside. Nathaniel is your son, for you have taken him to your heart. The rest of this must be forgotten.'

'If we are allowed to forget it,' John said grimly. 'Whoever this fellow is, he is bent on mischief. I intend to double the men I have patrolling the estate when we return from Scotland, Sarah. I believe this man is dangerous and we shall not be entirely safe until he has been caught.'

'But we shall not allow him to disturb us other than to take care,' Sarah said. 'Do you agree?'

'Yes, if that is your wish,' John said and drew her close. He stood looking down into her lovely face, feeling the desire burn inside him, making him ache with the need to posses her. 'I do not think I could draw back at this stage, my darling. You are right. We must be married. There is nothing else we can do, because it would kill me to leave you now.'

'That is all I wish to hear from you,' Sarah said and stood on her toes to kiss him on the mouth. 'I cannot wait for our wedding day, my love.'

'Nor in truth can I,' John said, his arm about her waist as they strolled towards the house. He looked down at her, his eyes dark with some intense emotion. Sarah could only guess at what was going on in his mind, though she knew that his fear, his anxiety, was for her sake.

Sarah got her wish, for the morning of the wedding was both hot and dry, the sun rising high into a cloudless sky, as she looked out of the window of her bedchamber. She had stayed in bed a little longer for her breakfast had been brought up to her. She had not felt in the least hungry, but she managed to eat a roll with honey and butter, and to drink some of the hot strong chocolate that she liked.

A stream of female visitors had come to her bedroom as she lay propped up against the pillows, looking through some small packages and cards that had arrived that morning. Several gifts from friends had been delivered that very morning, and Sarah was delighted with a silver bangle from Julia Moore, which was personal and in addition to the beautiful porcelain tea service that had come from Julia's aunt.

She still had a pile of unopened gifts and letters when Tilda came in with a bunch of wild flowers she had picked for her. 'They had the dew on them this morning,' Tilda said, placing the little vase on her dressing table. 'They are not for you to carry, Sarah. John has sent a wonderful posy of roses and lilies for you, my dear. They are being kept cool downstairs, but someone will bring them up to you later.'

'Everyone is so kind,' Sarah said, indicating the pile of gifts she had not yet opened. 'I have not had time to undo them all.'

'Would you like me to open one or two for you?' Tilda asked, and when Sarah nodded, she picked up an oblong box wrapped in silver tissue. 'I wonder what is in here?' She pulled the ribbons opened and lifted the lid, shutting it quickly. 'Oh, no! That is awful. I shall take this away and dispose of it, Sarah. I do not know how anyone could be so wicked as to send this on your wedding day.'

'What is it?' Sarah asked, her face turning pale. She realised that whatever was in the box was unpleasant, and was glad that Tilda had opened it for her.

'It is a bouquet of deadly nightshade, and every part of the plant is poisonous to the touch. Had you opened this and touched it, not realising what it was, you might have fallen ill,' Tilda said. 'Fortunately, I recognised it at once and did not touch it. I'll open all your parcels, Sarah, and make sure that nothing like this is in any of them—though I doubt there will be more.'

'Take it to Charles,' Sarah said. 'He will want to know about this, Tilda. If he has the package, he may be able to discover how it was delivered.'

'Yes, very wise,' Tilda agreed and went out. 'I shall return shortly, Sarah.'

Sarah closed her eyes as the door closed behind her friend. It was so cruel of the person who had sent this thing to wrap it as a gift and sinister, for it she had eaten something after touching the posy she might have been ill. However, she was determined not to let the unpleasant incident frighten her, and she had already opened some more of the parcels by the time that Tilda returned to help her. They finished the task together, and were pleased that nothing else of an unpleasant nature had come to light.

Tilda did not refer to it again. She sat and talked with Sarah for a while, but got up and went out when Arabella came to take her place. Sarah did not distress her sister-in-law by telling her of the deadly night-shade Tilda had removed. Arabella was feeling the strain of carrying her child, though she did not complain—but she would have been horrified had she known that a deadly posy had been delivered to Sarah.

Arabella had brought her some beautiful lace and a pretty cameo brooch, though the main present of a silver tea-and-coffee service was already down-stairs in pride of place, ready to be shown to the guests with all the other lovely things that had been sent to John and Sarah.

They talked for a while, and then Elizabeth came. She was followed by Lady Tate and, last of all, Mrs Hunter. She handed Sarah a small flat velvet box.

'What is this, Mama?' Sarah asked. 'You have already given us so much—the silver cutlery and that beautiful Venetian glass.'

'This is just for you, Sarah,' her mother said. 'It is my way of saying sorry for what I said to you before…'

'Oh, Mama, that is all forgotten,' Sarah said and gave a cry of pleasure as she opened the box. Inside was a heavy silver chain with a jewelled crucifix. It was a large jewel and very grand. 'This is lovely, Mama. Was it yours? I do not think that I have seen it before.'

'It was sold to me when we were in Italy,' Mrs Hunter said. 'I was told that it had belonged to a saint in the sixteenth century, and had magical powers to protect the wearer, but I do not imagine that is true, Sarah. However, it is a valuable thing and I should like you to have it, my dear.' There was an odd look in her eyes, and Sarah knew that she was still uneasy about the marriage. It sent a little shiver down her spine, for it was unlike her mama to carry a worry this long. She must be truly concerned to have thought of giving Sarah such a gift.

Sarah thanked her, and got up to kiss her mother on the cheek. For a moment she felt a flicker of fear, her stomach churning because she knew that there was good reason for her mother's anxiety. Someone hated John. As his wife, she might also be in danger.

Thrusting the shadows to the back of her mind, Sarah rang the bell for her maid and asked for hot water to be brought up. It was time to dress for her wedding.

The sun continued to shine throughout the ceremony, sending rays of colour through the stained glass to form a pattern on the ancient grey flagstones of the church. Sarah's heart missed a beat as John turned to look at her, his gaze so serious and intent that it sent a little shiver running through her. Why did he look so on their wedding day?

However, as she took her place at his side, he smiled and all her feelings of vague unease fled in the blaze of happiness that his smile lit in her. The ceremony passed without Sarah truly realising it and before she knew it they were leaving the old church to be met with a shower of rose petals. Several children from the village offered her gifts of flowers and straw dolls, which were symbols of fertility and good luck at a wedding.

She accepted them all with smiling grace, and then they were in the carriage, being carried back to the house. Sarah turned to John, her heart beating very fast as he drew her into his arms, kissing her tenderly but with an underlying hunger.

'Whatever happens, always remember that I love you and would give my life for you, Sarah,' he said in a voice that rang with passion. The hand that reached up to touch her cheek trembled a little and Sarah wondered why he seemed to be in such distress. He had sworn that he loved her—that he had always loved her—so why should he look as if he were troubled? It was their wedding day. 'I shall love and protect you always, my darling.'

'Is something wrong, John?' she asked, a feeling of foreboding hanging over her. 'Can you not tell me what is troubling you?'

'Nothing troubles me, except my love for you,' John said. He was smiling now, as if the dark clouds had been banished to a small corner of his mind, and yet Sarah was convinced that something had happened—something was playing on his mind. 'You will always trust me, Sarah? Promise me that, whatever happens, you will not lose faith in my love?'

'I promise,' Sarah said and went willingly to his arms. As he kissed her, she felt the familiar stirring of love and desire and the odd doubts were thrust to the back of her mind. She was sure that something had happened to disturb John, but he did not wish to tell her—perhaps because he thought it might spoil her wedding day. 'I love you, John, and nothing can change that…'

'Good,' he said and let her go as the carriage pulled to a halt in front of the house. 'And now we must go and greet our guests.'

John watched as his new bride moved amongst her guests, greeting them with smiles and kisses. At that moment she was talking to his brother Philip and Lady Elworthy, who had travelled some distance to attend the wedding, and were more than delighted to see him married to an intelligent and pretty young woman.

John was proud of Sarah. However, at that moment his expression was not that of a happy bridegroom. His brow was furrowed with concern, and his eyes were shadowed with thoughts that did not belong here. He turned and walked away, going outside to stand alone on the terrace for a few moments as he tried to gather his thoughts.

'John—is something the matter?' Charles asked, coming up to him. 'You seem preoccupied. Uneasy…'

'I received another letter this morning,' John said, taking it from his coat pocket and offering it to his brother-in-law. 'What have I done, Charles? I should never have married Sarah. If anything happens to her because of me, I shall never forgive myself…'

Charles read the letter and frowned. 'It says that you should enjoy your wedding night for it may be the last time you know peace on this earth…'

'It is a threat,' John said, 'but is his malice directed at Sarah or me? We shall be quite isolated at the hunting lodge, Charles, and yet I do not wish to disappoint Sarah. I know she is looking forward to our trip to Scotland.'

'Does anyone else know of your intention to go to Scotland?'

'I have told no one outside the family.'

Charles nodded. 'Then there is a way to keep you safe, at least for your honeymoon, John. Listen, this is what we shall do…' He began to outline his plan, John nodding in agreement as he realised it was the best that they could do at this late stage.

Sarah had noticed John go outside. She knew that his mood was hardly one of unalloyed pleasure, and it bothered her. If something had happened, why did he not tell her? She would far rather know than be left to wonder. Or was he regretting their marriage? No, no, she would not allow the doubts to creep in again! John loved her and she loved him.

Walking to the open French windows, she saw that her brother and Charles were talking earnestly.

'A penny for them?' Hearing Arabella's voice at

her shoulder, Sarah turned to look at her. 'Why so pensive, dearest?'

'Charles and John seem concerned about something,' Sarah said. 'I dare say it is just business…' She shrugged and walked away from the window. 'I think everyone has enjoyed themselves, don't you?'

'Yes, I am sure of it,' Arabella said and smiled at her. 'Just remember that John loves you, Sarah. All this other stuff doesn't matter. You must just be patient and keep believing that everything will turn out well in the end.'

'Yes, of course,' Sarah said and smiled at her. 'Dearest Belle, you always manage to make things better. I think that perhaps I should go upstairs and change into my travelling gown, don't you?'

'Yes, I believe it is time,' Arabella said. 'I came to fetch you because your mama was saying that you ought to get changed. John will want to start soon if you are to reach your destination before nightfall.'

'I shall go up and change,' Sarah said, 'and then I shall come down and say goodbye to everyone.' She kissed Arabella on the cheek, walking away from her with her head held high.

As she went upstairs, her mother followed and so did Tilda. With her friends chattering, exclaiming on how pretty she looked in her travelling gown and making her laugh, Sarah had little time to brood, but when she went back downstairs to say goodbye to all their friends she saw John standing with Charles. His expression was so serious that it made her uneasy.

John was keeping something from her. She wished that he would not—it made her uneasy. She would much prefer that he told her exactly what was bothering him.

## Chapter Nine

Sarah looked out of the window as the carriage they were travelling in began to slow to a halt. She was puzzled because they had been travelling for no more than half an hour, and yet they were approaching an inn and it was clearly John's intention to stop.

'Why are we stopping here?' she asked, turning her head to look at him.

'Because Charles has arranged for us to change carriages here,' John said. 'He thought it best—to make sure that we are not followed, Sarah. After what happened this morning…' He frowned as her eyebrows rose. 'Charles told me about the posy of belladonna. Apparently, a young lad from the village delivered the parcel. He had no idea what it was, of course. He said that he was given a shilling to bring it to the house, but his description of the man who paid him was quite vague—he said it was a gentleman, but could tell Charles no more than that.'

Sarah looked at him intently. 'Is that why you looked so stern in church, John? Were you distressed by what my brother told you?'

'Yes, that was a nasty thing to happen,' John said. 'It was fortunate that Miss Redmond opened it, for she is a sensible woman, and it saved you from the harm that might have resulted, did it not?'

He had decided that it would be best if Sarah did not learn of the letter he had received. She would naturally be distressed and anxious for his sake, and he wanted to avoid giving her more worry over this unfortunate affair. Besides, he was struggling to make sense of it all in his own mind. Charles was sure that Andrea had had a lover, perhaps a soldier, and that it was he who was making these threats, but John had another theory of his own, and at the moment he was not quite sure how the pieces fit together.

'Tilda has been a good friend to me,' Sarah said. 'She was so grateful to me for nursing her when she had the smallpox, and I think she tries to look after me in her own way. I know she was very brave standing up to Mama for me when she thought I should marry the duke.'

John nodded. He smiled at her, but his eyes held an odd, distant expression that made Sarah wonder what he was thinking.

'Are you comfortable, dearest?' John asked,

helping her into the second carriage, which had been waiting at the inn for them. 'Our baggage was sent ahead with this coach to disguise our carriage. If we were being followed, whoever it is will see the carriage standing outside the inn, and when, after some hours, it is driven back to Charles's estate, it will be too late for anyone to follow our trail.'

'I am quite comfortable,' Sarah said. 'But this is all a little unsettling, John. It makes me anxious to think that you have an enemy.'

'I think it is just spitefulness,' John replied untruthfully. 'I dare say it will all blow over in time. Besides, we have people looking after us, Sarah. I am sorry that we had to resort to such cloak-and-dagger tactics, but your brother wanted to be sure that we should be able to enjoy our honeymoon without any nasty surprises.'

'Charles is very protective of me,' Sarah said and smiled. She decided that she must put all this unpleasantness from her mind. She was John's wife and it would be foolish to let anything spoil her happiness. 'But I am sure you are right, John. It is just someone being spiteful and no doubt they will tire of their sport soon enough and leave us alone.'

Sarah rose from the bed and walked over to the window, gazing out at the moon, which had just sailed out from behind a bank of clouds and was shining directly into their window.

They had not bothered to draw their curtains the previous night. The hunting lodge was situated in woods and very secluded. This was their second night at the idyllic cottage, and Sarah was feeling happier than she could ever have dreamed. Their lovemaking had been all that she could have desired, and any shadows from the past had been forgotten as soon as John drew her into his arms that first night. His touch had been so gentle, his kisses so sweet, that she had felt no fear as he led her gently along the path of sensual delight.

She was surely the most fortunate woman alive, Sarah thought as she gazed out at the night sky, watching the branches of trees sway in the breeze. It was a little cooler here in Scotland than it had been at home, but she did not mind, for it was a magical place and she had already become enchanted by the wonderful scenery.

The mountains and lakes had such a presence that she felt as if she were living in a world of splendour and majesty that had little to do with real life. This was a time apart, a time of learning to know her husband and loving him more each day, of leaving behind the past and becoming someone new. She was no longer the innocent girl who had known nothing of the pleasures of love, but a woman discovering her own sensuality in the arms of a passionate man. John was the truly gentle man she had always thought him, but he was also a strong, generous lover who had surprised her with the intensity of his desire.

Behind her John stirred, feeling the bed cold and sitting up as he realised that she was standing by the window. 'Is something wrong, my darling?' he asked, getting out of bed to come and join her by the window. He put his arms about her, kissing the back of her neck as they stood together gazing out at the moonlight. 'Couldn't you sleep?'

'I woke and saw that the moon was shining in at the window,' Sarah said, leaning back against him, feeling the strength of his body at her back, the heat of his flesh warming her. 'We forgot to draw the curtains, John.'

'We were in too much of a hurry,' John said and rubbed his face against the side of hers. She could feel the slight rasp of his unshaven cheek and she turned towards him, offering her lips for his kiss. 'Forgive me, my darling. I cannot seem to have enough of you, Sarah. I am like a starving man offered a feast…'

Sarah laughed huskily, pressing her body against his as she felt the heat of his arousal and knew that he wanted her again, as she wanted him. At this moment her body was singing with need and a strong, hot desire that made her moan a little as he bent down and swept her up into his arms, carrying her back to their bed.

They lay looking at each other for a while, kissing slowly; tiny, tantalising little kisses that only stoked the fires within. John's hand stroked the satin arch of her back, down over her buttocks, holding her close to him. She felt the heat of his arousal against her thigh, her legs opening to his seeking hand as he caressed her, bringing her to a state of sensual delight that had her gasping as he took her. She writhed and arched beneath him, giving herself up to the sweeping tide of desire that engulfed her, urging her on to a place that she had never been. And when at last it was over, she clung to him, her legs curling over his back, holding him to her as her body convulsed with pleasure.

Afterwards, they lay holding each other and talking until they both fell asleep once more, safe and secure in their love and the warmth of their bed.

In the morning they made love again. Later they parted to bathe and dress, Sarah eating soft rolls and honey in bed while John consumed a quantity of cold ham, pickles and bread in the breakfast parlour.

After that they went walking together until it was time to eat a light nuncheon, and in the afternoon John drove them to see more of the beautiful scenery.

They stood by the side of a lake, watching the dark ripple of the water as a breeze sent little waves skidding across the surface. Away on the side of the mountain they saw a proud stag, its head high, magnificent antlers outlined against a darkening sky. Sarah shivered as she felt the temperature drop all of a sudden and a few droplets of rain dimpled the water.

'I think it is going to rain,' John said. 'Perhaps we should go back, Sarah. Even in summer it can turn quite cold in the Highlands.'

'Yes, I think you are right,' Sarah said and turned towards the carriage. As she did so she saw a flash of something bright from amongst the trees that shadowed one edge of the lake. 'John…' she cried and something made her push him to one side. 'Be careful!'

The shot echoed in the clear air, seeming to reverberate from the mountain, achingly loud and somehow distorted so that it seemed to fill Sarah's head. She whirled around, but the flash of silver had gone and there was nothing to be seen but the blue-green haze of the ancient trees and the mist that seemed to be swirling over the water towards them, making what had been beautiful suddenly menacing and eerie.

'Who can it have been? A poacher misfiring?' Sarah looked at him anxiously as she saw his expression of anger. 'You do not think it was intentional? Oh, John…not here…after all our precautions…'

'Damn it!' John swore and grabbed Sarah's arm, hurrying her into the curricle and climbing up beside her. The shot had not come close enough to harm either of them, but it was clearly a warning—a warning that his enemy was always watching them. He would have gone after the man, but dare not risk it. John had no fear for himself, but he would not hazard Sarah's life. He knew that he must get her to safety first and consider what this meant afterwards. 'I cannot think it an accident, nor do I imagine it was a poacher. I had thought we were safe here, but it seems that I was wrong. We must go home, Sarah.'

Sarah glanced at his profile, seeing the stern set of his jaw and the grim expression in his eyes. 'Thank God he did not hit you, John.' She shivered, feeling an icy tingle at the nape of her neck. 'Surely it was not the man who fired at me that day at Charles's estate? How could he have found us? Why is he pursuing us like this?'

'I have no idea,' John said angrily. 'But it seems he has and that means we must go home, Sarah. I mean home to Elworthy. I can better protect you there. Here we are too isolated for safety.'

'Go home?' Sarah was stunned by what had happened. Their beautiful day had turned into a nightmare and she was filled with apprehension. 'But we were to stay for the rest of the week…'

'I know and I am sorry to disappoint you,' John said. There was something odd about him, something tight and angry, as if he were somehow blaming her—or shutting her out. 'We shall find other ways to amuse ourselves, Sarah. Perhaps another time we can return, when this business is all over. For the moment it is not safe. I should never forgive myself if anything happened here…you would be alone and vulnerable. No, we must return home immediately.'

Sarah was silent. The shimmering delight of the past few days was somehow shattered, leaving her feeling ill at ease. She had a feeling of foreboding, her mind haunted by a nameless fear that she refused to acknowledge.

Why had John's enemy followed them here? Why did he hate John so much that he was determined to destroy them? The thought flickered into Sarah's mind that perhaps some of the rumours concerning Andrea might be true, but she quashed it immediately. No, she would not let her mind be poisoned against him! She loved John and trust went hand in hand with love. He would never, never do anything to harm any woman, let alone the woman he had promised to care for and protect.

They hardly spoke to each other on the return to the hunting lodge. John gave immediate instructions to the servants to pack their belongings and follow, stopping only long enough for Sarah to pack a few things she needed on the journey.

He handed her into the carriage, telling her that it would be best to draw the curtains and try to get some sleep, but he did not climb in with her.

'I shall ride just ahead, Sarah,' he told her. 'We have grooms to accompany us, dearest, but I want to be ready in case we are attacked. Do not be scared. You are well protected.'

Sarah was not frightened for herself. She believed the shot had been meant for John, though she knew that it would have been easy for the assassin to kill first John and then her. She wanted to beg him to ride inside with her, but she knew that her plea would have been ignored. John had suddenly become a stranger, his manner cold, angry and tense. She could hardly believe that this was the same man who had made love to her so tenderly the previous night.

Why was he angry with her? Surely she had done nothing wrong? She had pushed him to one side, hoping that the shot would go wide, as it had. Indeed, it had fallen short for they were too far away from the would-be assassin. Perhaps the shot had never been meant to kill, but merely to taunt and frighten. Was it John's enemy's intention merely to spoil their happiness and create tension between them? Somehow the sending of that poisonous posy and spiteful letters did not seem in keeping with the attempt to shoot John. Was it possible that he had two enemies? And why were all these things happening now?

Sarah sat silent and tense within the carriage, her nerves stretched taught as she felt every bump in the road and wished that she could be back in their hunting lodge, wrapped in John's arms safe and warm. She had the oddest feeling that everything had changed and she was frightened. Not only of the assassin that had waited in the shadows, taking his chance to fire at them—but of this new silent, angry John. She did not know him. He wasn't the man she had married or the quiet, gentle man she loved so very much.

Sarah stepped from the carriage, feeling weary and exhausted by the journey. They had stopped only to change horses at the posting houses. Once John brought her a glass of wine and some bread and meat, but she had drunk only a few sips of the wine. The food would have stuck in her throat for her throat and chest felt tight and she found it difficult to hold back her tears.

John was speaking to his men, giving orders, hardly seeming to notice Sarah until he suddenly turned and saw her, his expression so reserved and cold that it sent a quiver down her spine.

'Do not stand here, Sarah,' he said sharply. 'Go up to the house. Mrs Raven will have your room ready and I shall be in shortly. I have things to do for the moment.'

It was not the homecoming she had imagined, the servants lined up to meet their new mistress and John leading her into the house, smiling and proud of his new bride. She approached the front door, which opened as she reached it. Mrs Raven bobbed a curtsy to her, her expression openly curious as her eyes swept over her. Sarah was conscious that her gown must be crumpled and that she had not stopped to change her linen before setting out on the journey. She felt dirty and dishevelled and not at all like the mistress of this great house.

'If the master had sent word you were returning early, we might have been more prepared to receive you, miss…ma'am,' Mrs Raven said, a hint of insolence in her tone. 'Your room has been prepared, of course, but there is no food ready and the girl who is to serve you does not arrive until the day after tomorrow. I'll send Ruth to you. She was a lady's maid once, so I dare say she will know what to do for you.'

'Thank you, Mrs Raven,' Sarah said, giving her a

straight look. 'My own maid will probably arrive in the morning. The baggage cannot be far behind us, I think.'

'Yes, ma'am. Shall I show you the way—or do you remember where to find the master's bedchamber?'

'Thank you, I believe I can find my own way, Mrs Raven.'

Sarah walked up the stairs, her head high. The housekeeper would not have dared to speak to her in that tone had John taken her into the house as she had expected he would. By returning early and riding off immediately, he had created the idea in Mrs Raven's head that he was not particularly interested in his new wife.

Her cheeks stinging with embarrassment and her eyes gritty with tears of disappointment, Sarah made her way to John's apartments and then through the connecting door into the apartments that had been refurbished for Andrea, but never used by her. She was immediately aware of a sweet perfume; it smelled of flowers and was very light and fresh. Sarah rather liked it, looking around for the bowl of flowers she thought must have been put here. However there were no flowers in the room, and she could not find the source of the scent. It just seemed to cling to everything, almost as though it had been sprayed recently on to covers and curtains. When she opened the large armoire, she discovered that the perfume was much stronger here—and then, tucked into a corner, she discovered a fine linen shift. Taking it out, she could smell that the perfume was very strong, more than would have been the case had it got there by someone simply wearing it. It must have been soaked in the perfume—but why?

She was still staring at the shift when the door opened and Ruth walked in. She smiled oddly as she saw what Sarah was holding.

'Did you find that in the armoire, Mrs Elworthy? I must have overlooked it. Forgive me. I shall put it where it belongs with the rest of her things in the attics.'

'I don't understand—what did you mean by saying that you had overlooked it? Did this belong to Andrea?'

'Yes, miss…I mean, ma'am,' Ruth said and her slanted eyes gleamed with a secret amusement. 'These were her rooms. I was told to clear everything out, but I must have missed this somehow. Do you want me to unpack for you, ma'am?'

John had told her that his first wife had never used this room. Was he lying or was it Ruth? If John had lied about that…but she had only the girl's word and it would be foolish to trust her. 'Thank you, I can manage for now,' Sarah said, rejecting her help. 'I have only this small bag until my baggage arrives, which should be in the morning.'

'Was there an accident to the coach, ma'am?'

Ruth looked at her, her dark eyes narrowed, almost impertinent.

Sarah had taken little notice of her the first time they met, for she had been interested only in making sure that Nathaniel was not tormented by his unkind nurse. Now she saw that the woman was not in the first flush of youth, though to a casual observer she looked no more than twenty-five or six—but she was perhaps nearer thirty. She might have been beautiful dressed in the right clothes with her hair dressed loosely about her face, instead of pulled back into a confining knot at the back of her head. Her dark eyes were sly and mocking and she seemed too confident for a servant who had once been dismissed.

'No, there was no accident. We decided to return earlier than we had intended, and the baggage was not packed. It will arrive tomorrow, I expect.'

'Yes, I expect so, ma'am,' Ruth said. 'But what will you wear in the meantime? You can hardly sit down to dine with the master in that gown?'

Sarah glanced down at herself, realising that she looked as if she had slept in her gown, which indeed she had, in the coach.

'Perhaps you would press it for me, Ruth? I have clean lingerie, but that is my only dress until the baggage arrives.'

'Yes, ma'am. It might look better for a press.'

Her tone suggested that it was highly unlikely, but Sarah decided to ignore it. Her personal maid would arrive the next day. Ellie had agreed to come with her and Sarah was glad of it—she had a distinct sense of being unwelcome in this house.

Oh, why hadn't John come in with her? Sarah took off her gown and handed it to Ruth, retiring behind a pretty Chinese screen to take off her other things.

'Please bring me some warm water when you return,' she said, but there was no answer, and when she poked her head round the screen she saw that the room was empty. 'Oh, bother!'

She came out from behind the screen, walking over to the washstand in the corner of the room. The water jug was empty. Clearly it had not been filled because they did not expect her to be here yet. Frowning, Sarah walked into the little dressing room that joined her bedchamber to John's. Here she found hot water in a can and cold water in the earthenware jug.

She frowned as she realised that the oversight in her own room was deliberate. Mrs Raven had sent up water for her master, but ignored the needs of her new mistress. Another hint, if Sarah needed it, that she was not welcome here.

She picked up the can of hot water and took it into her own room, using half of it. Returning it to the dressing room, she went through the same action again, carefully measuring cold water into her bowl so that she had enough to wash, but did not leave John without any. She had brought a bar of the soap she liked in her travelling bag, and she was able to wash and dress in a clean shift by the time Ruth returned with her gown.

Ruth had an expectant look in her eyes, but if she was waiting to be asked to fetch hot water she was disappointed. Sarah accepted her help with the gown, which fastened to the waist with little buttons at the back, and then gave her a cool nod.

'Thank you, Ruth. I shall not need you again for the moment. You may go.'

'Yes, ma'am,' Ruth said, a defiant light in her eyes. 'Mrs Raven said would you care for some soup in half an hour—or shall you wait for the master to return?'

'I hope that Mr Elworthy will be back by then,' Sarah said. 'However, if he does not return, I shall take my supper up here in the dining room, thank you.'

'Yes, ma'am, of course,' Ruth said, bobbed a slight curtsy and walked away.

Sarah stood staring after her. She had never had to deal with hostile servants before, and she was not quite sure what to do. Arabella's people were all devoted to her, and Mrs Hunter would not have stood for any nonsense. Sarah was unwilling to make a fuss the moment she arrived. She would feel better when Ellie was here, but in the meantime she would just have to make the best of things.

John did not return in half an hour and Sarah's supper tray was brought up to her. She ate her chicken soup and bread in solitary state at the dining-room table, feeling close to tears. This was not how it was supposed to be! John should be with her. She was certain that neither Mrs Raven or Ruth would have dared to use that tone to her had John brought her into the house as she had expected.

It was most distressing and she wasn't sure whether she most wanted to weep or get angry and shout. She had a book of poetry in her bag and she sat reading by the light of a candle in her sitting room until it grew quite late.

Where was John? What business was it that kept him out until this hour? When a clock chimed eleven downstairs in the hall, Sarah went into his bedchamber, curling up in a chair by the empty fireplace. Even though it was summer evening, she felt cold in the huge room and got up to drag a cover from the bed and wrap it around her as she hugged her knees.

She was very tired and eventually her intention to wait up for John was overcome by the need to sleep.

Her eyes closed and she put her head back against the wing of the chair and dozed.

She was sound asleep when John came in a little later. He frowned as he saw there was no fire. She must have been cold or she would not have taken a cover from the bed. Why had she not ordered a fire lit? He had imagined that she would find it easy to take charge of her new home. After all, she had brought it to his attention that Nathaniel needed a proper nurse and that he needed a manservant.

Sighing, John bent and lifted her into his arms. She looked younger and more vulnerable as she slept, and he realised that he ought to have seen her settled in the house before going off to his meeting with Daniel and Tobbold. The fact that his enemy had managed to follow them to Scotland despite their precautions was unsettling. It meant that whoever it was would not give up his campaign of hatred! John had quickly realised that he was dealing with a dangerous situation. He had been anxious to make certain that all the protective measures he had ordered were in place, but perhaps he should have taken a few minutes to see Sarah settled. She seemed to be confident and in control, but perhaps he had expected too much of her—as he had perhaps of Andrea. She had been even younger and more diffident than Sarah.

Carrying Sarah into her own bedchamber, he was aware of the strong perfume that seemed to hang in the air. It was a perfume he disliked, because it was Andrea's. He had ordered it removed from her bed-chamber with all her things—but it had no right to be here, because Andrea had never used these rooms. Someone must have done this deliberately and he could guess why!

He frowned and turned back, taking Sarah to his own bed and laying her gently down, pulling the cover over her. Was it starting again? He had thought all that nonsense had stopped after he had made Mrs Raven aware that he wouldn't put up with it. He wasn't sure who was trying to torment him by leaving Andrea's things about, but it had to stop. He was simply not prepared to keep a servant who did not obey his orders, and he would speak to Mrs Raven again in the morning.

For a moment he stood looking down at Sarah as she lay sleeping. He should never have given into temptation, never have married her. As his wife she was the one who would suffer if the assassin's shot found its mark next time. She would be a widow all too soon—and he was afraid that worse might happen. He had that evening told Daniel what was on his mind.

'Someone is determined to destroy me. I have

brought danger to Sarah. I knew at the start that it could happen, but…' he shook his head '…what else could I have done? She had near ruined herself for my sake. If I had turned aside, she would have been cast off by society. Besides, I love her, Daniel. I do not think I could bear it if anything happened to her because of me.'

'You must keep a watchful eye on her,' the earl said. 'Tobbold will have someone watch your back, and Sarah's, of course—but it sounds to me that there is more than one involved in this affair, John. This soldier, whoever he may be, does not have access to your house—unless he knows one of the servants, that is. Yet what you tell me is not something that I believe a man would do…it is more a woman's trick. Forgive me, I must ask—you have not in your loneliness taken one of the maids to your bed?'

'Damn you, Daniel! What do you take me for?' John said, shocked at the suggestion. 'That is not my idea of home comfort! If I visited an obliging lady— and that has been seldom enough since I left the army—it would be one who was married and wished for a discreet arrangement for our mutual benefit.'

'Yes, as I expected,' Daniel said with a rueful look. 'I did not mean to offend you, but it was a possibility. Jealous women may do anything and it could have been one of the maids leaving Andrea's things about the house.'

'Yes, perhaps you are right that one of the maids is playing tricks on me, but I would not have seduced a servant. I was not in love with Andrea, but I was fond of her. I cared for her in my own way and wanted her to be happy. To have slept with one of the maids under her own roof would have been a wicked insult. Unforgivable! I would never have done it to her.'

'Then whoever it is must have some other reason for making mischief.'

'I shall discover who it is and dismiss her!'

'Be careful, John. It is sometimes better to have an enemy where you can see him or her. If this woman has been paid to torment you, you should have her watched—see where she goes, who she meets. Ignore her tricks and do not let Sarah be upset by them. She cannot harm you if you stay strong in mind and purpose. It is the man who fired at you that worries me. If that shot had hit home…'

'It was not meant to,' John said. 'I think he is playing games, as a cat might with a mouse it has captured in its paws. I am meant to suffer torment, as perhaps he does if he loved Andrea. And yet you are right, I have been thinking that there is more to this than immediately meets the eye—Andrea may indeed have had a lover who hates me because she is dead.'

'Yes, that is perhaps the reason why he has not killed you before,' the earl said, looking thoughtful. 'Which means that it might not be you, but Sarah, who is in the most danger…'

Looking at his sleeping wife, John knew a moment of despair. He must keep Sarah safe. Somehow he must protect her…and he thought he had discovered the way to do it. If his enemy guessed that she meant the world to him she might be killed, but if he kept his distance, appeared more interested in his estate than his lovely new wife, perhaps she would be allowed to live.

It was a cruel choice, for he knew that any distance on his part would distress Sarah, but it was perhaps the only one he had for the moment…

Sarah awoke to find that she was lying on John's bed with the cover over her. Sitting up, she saw that one of the covers was lying on the chair where she had curled up the previous night, and she thought that John must have slept there. She frowned and wondered why he had not lain beside her. Why had he not woken her?

Getting up, Sarah went into her own room. She saw that someone had been in and pulled back her curtains. A tray of hot chocolate and biscuits was on a table near the window, but when she touched the pot she discovered that it had gone cold. Ruth—if it had been her—had simply brought it up and left it, neglecting to see if her mistress was in the next room.

This could not be allowed to go on. She knew that her own maid would arrive later that day, but it was time that she asserted her authority here. If she allowed this behaviour to continue, she would never be mistress in her own home. She gave the bellrope a determined pull. It was answered a few minutes later by Mrs Raven herself.

'Yes, ma'am?' she asked, a sullen expression on her face. 'Was there something else you wanted?'

'The chocolate is cold,' Sarah said. 'It was left in here and I was in my husband's room. Who brought it up?'

'That was Ruth, ma'am,' Mrs Raven said. 'I am sorry if she did not do as she ought, but I dare say she was in a hurry to leave. It is her day off. She has one day a month and she wanted to get away.'

'I understand that Ruth wants her day off. She is certainly entitled to it,' Sarah said. 'But could you not have sent someone else with it—someone who would have the good manners to let me know that it had been brought up?'

'I'll speak to her about it when she gets back,' Mrs Raven said. 'And I'll have one of the other girls bring you some more chocolate. I'm sorry you've been badly served, ma'am, but we are short-handed at the moment.'

'Do not trouble with the chocolate. I shall have my breakfast in the small parlour downstairs,' Sarah said. 'My own maid should be here later today, Mrs Raven—but you will please speak to Ruth. I am not prepared to put up with insolence from anyone.'

'As you say, ma'am,' the housekeeper said. 'You are the mistress here now, are you not?'

'Yes, I am,' Sarah said, 'and there will be some changes, Mrs Raven. I shall make an inspection of the house after I have taken breakfast, and I shall let you know what my intentions are when I have thought things over.'

'Yes, ma'am.' Mrs Raven inclined her head and went out, leaving Sarah to wash and dress. The water in the can was still warm, though not as hot as she would have liked, but she could put up with it for once.

Sarah dressed in a serviceable blue gown, wearing a crisp linen collar to set it off, and white cuffs. She wanted to look efficient, as the mistress of a house this large would need to be if it were to run as it ought. She was smiling to herself as she went downstairs. She *was* the mistress here. She would not dwell on the feeling of being unwelcome that she had experienced on her arrival. She did not need to put up with Ruth's impertinence, for she could dismiss her if need be.

'I have to be careful,' Ruth said as she looked at the man she had slipped away to meet. 'If I go too far, she will dismiss me. My aunt took a risk in having me back after he told her it had to stop. She told me that if she got another complaint from him, she would have to send me away for good.'

'Play your tricks on her…his new wife,' the man said and gave her a hard look. 'I gave you money for the child and I want results. He murdered Andrea! He has to pay for what he did.'

'I agreed to help you for the sake of my child,' Ruth said. 'She was ill and I needed the money for medicines and food. I was desperate when you found me, near to starving, and I would have done anything—but I've done what you asked and I can't go on for ever…' She gave a little cry of fear as he grabbed her wrist, his fingers biting deep into her flesh. 'You are hurting me…'

'If you let me down over this you will discover that I can find ways of hurting you that will really make you scream,' the man said, his features twisted and angry. 'He has to pay for what he did! You told me that you had good reason to hate him. He was one of the men who kidnapped and murdered Richard

Palmer, wasn't he? Do you not want revenge for what he did to your lover?'

Ruth's gaze narrowed as she looked at him. She did not like him. He had given her money when she needed it, but he was not a good man.

'Richard Palmer was a gentleman. He wasn't my lover, but we had an arrangement. He knew the child was his and he gave me money for her. When he disappeared I was left with nothing. I thought he would come back, or send me money, but he didn't…and then I came in search of him and you told me that he had been kidnapped and murdered by some other gentlemen. You said Mr Elworthy was the ringleader, but I have only your word that—' She broke off as she saw the murderous look in his eyes. 'It wasn't him that killed his first wife…'

'What do you know of that?' The man's expression hardened in suspicion and his fingers dug into her flesh, making her wince with pain. 'Tell me what you know, girl! If you lie, it will be the worse for you.'

Ruth knew that she had gone too far. She threw her head back, looking into his eyes. 'I don't know anything,' she said. 'But I know John Elworthy and I've seen the way he has been haunted by what happened to his wife. He didn't kill her—' She gasped as he struck her across the face. 'No! Stop it…'

He let her go suddenly, thrusting her so hard that she stumbled and fell to her knees. 'Let me down and that child of yours will disappear, do you hear me? I want John Elworthy reduced to his knees for what he did to my Andrea. He drove her to her death and this is what I want you to do to that new wife of his…'

Ruth got slowly to her feet, her eyes opening wide in horror as he told her what he expected her to do next. 'I can't do that,' she whispered, her hand creeping to her throat. 'I won't…'

'You will either do as I tell you or face the consequences,' he growled. 'It's either her or the child…'

## Chapter Ten

Sarah spent the morning touring the house and examining its storerooms, of which there were several. Some of them were packed with furniture and ancient trunks containing old curtains, musty linens and tapestries that had fallen to pieces with the moth. It looked as if nothing had been thrown out for a century or more! However, amongst all the dross that had been uselessly stored, she discovered one or two pieces that she thought would be usable, and she asked that they be taken to the family rooms.

'I think everything in here should be taken out and burned,' Sarah told Mrs Raven when they left one of the rooms in the west wing. 'I intend to refurbish several of the rooms in the main section of the house and I think we should start by clearing out the things we don't need.'

'I'll ask Alfred to do it, ma'am,' Mrs Raven said. 'He's the under-footman—and he can detail a couple of the gardeners to help. We've three of them and a couple of lads.'

'How many servants do we have here, Mrs Raven? I've seen two maids besides Ruth, and two footmen, but that can hardly be enough to run a house like this?'

'It isn't, ma'am,' Mrs Raven said. 'Besides the nursery maid, and those you've named, we've the scullery maid, a bootboy and Jack, who is a man of all trades and chops the wood for me as well as a bit of silver cleaning. It has been too much for me running this huge house these past months, I can tell you. A lot of the servants left after Mrs Elworthy died, and then more ran off when Mr Elworthy was ill. Your own servants will be a help to us, and no mistake.'

'Ellie will be my personal maid, which means that Ruth will no longer be responsible for looking after me,' Sarah said. 'I also have a groom who wanted to come with me. And my husband has employed a valet, who is due to join us this week, but I can see that we need more help. I believe Ellie has a younger sister who would be happy to come to us, and I shall ask John to advertise for a cook. Your cooking is very well, Mrs Raven, but you have enough to do, taking charge of the house.'

'Yes, ma'am, I do,' Mrs Raven agreed and looked pleased. 'I'll send to the village. We might be able to find one or two girls willing to work here now that you're in charge. It was the late mistress that made them uneasy with her strange ways…'

There was something in her face that made Sarah hesitate before she asked, 'Why did the servants leave? Was it because of these wicked rumours concerning my husband, Mrs Raven?'

'This wasn't a happy house, ma'am,' the housekeeper said. 'It was unnatural, the way he treated her…like she was a child and no marriage at all. The servants were sorry for her. She used to wander all over the house at night in her night-robe…sleep walking she was and sometimes she would scream as if she had terrible dreams…' Mrs Raven shook her head. 'Some of the girls thought she was a little odd in the head, because she kept losing things and she would mutter to herself. It wasn't so surprising that she killed herself…only I know for a fact that she was terrified of the river. She told me once that she had a fear of drowning…'

'So it seems odd that she should have chosen that method to take her own life, doesn't it?' Sarah's gaze narrowed as she looked at the older woman.

'Yes, ma'am…' Mrs Raven hesitated. 'I don't think ill of Mr Elworthy. He has always been a good master to me, but some of the girls thought he was unkind to her. The child was born too soon for it to have been conceived after marriage, ma'am, and it was whispered that he believed she had been with another man and resented her for it…though I saw no sign of it. He was kind enough when I saw them together, but more like a father than a husband, if you know what I mean, ma'am—though it was only to be expected. If what they say is true…'

'What do you mean?' Sarah asked and looked her straight in the eyes. 'What are you suggesting?'

'I don't know if it is right or merely a tale, but I have heard it said that he had a mistress, ma'am… and that he made no secret of it. My late mistress told me once that he loved someone else…'

'I am sure she was mistaken,' Sarah replied. 'My husband is an honourable man. Any connection of that nature he may have had would have been ended when he married.'

'If you say so, ma'am,' Mrs Raven said. 'I was just telling you what I've heard.'

'Yes, I understand that,' Sarah said. 'My husband has done nothing wrong, Mrs Raven. I want it made quite clear to the others that he is not a murderer. Nor is he responsible for his wife's death. If need be, we shall bring in servants from outside the village. This house must be brought to life again, Mrs Raven— and I am determined to do it one way or the other.' Her head lifted and her face wore an expression of pride.

'Yes, ma'am.' Mrs Raven was looking at her with a new respect. 'I am glad we've had this little talk. Things have been far from right here and I am glad you've come. The master needed someone like you.'

It was a huge compliment from the housekeeper, for she was not given to praise. Sarah was glad that she had taken the trouble to clear the air. She smiled at Mrs Raven.

'Very well, I think we have come to understand each other a little better and that is good. Now I am going to the nursery to see how Nathaniel is getting on with his nurse.'

Sarah enjoyed an hour or so playing with the little boy and his nurse. June Harrington was a pleasant, friendly girl and it was clear that she liked being Nathaniel's nurse. He was certainly very happy in her company, a bright, intelligent little boy who laughed and crawled about the room as he played. June was pleased to see her mistress and made it clear that she was glad to work for Sarah.

'I'm very happy to see you home, Mrs Elworthy,' she said. 'Nathaniel has been good, but he does love his father—and you, I think. He has asked me several times when the nice lady was coming back to see him.'

'Well, I shall see him every day now,' Sarah said

and looked affectionately at the child as he played with his wooden soldiers and some skittles. 'I wanted to ask you if you are happy here, June? I shall try to engage another girl to help you as soon as I can.'

'I know someone who would like to come,' June told her, looking pleased. 'Mary is my cousin. She is only fifteen, but she is a good girl and willing. She would do anything I asked of her.'

'Will you ask her if she would like to work here please, June? I want as many servants as possible so that everything is easy and we have some life and noise in this big house. At the moment it is too empty and silent.'

'Yes, Mrs Elworthy,' June agreed with a smile. 'This house needs people to bring it to life, to make it a proper home, as it used to be years ago. For too long it has been left to gather dust and shadows. Mr Elworthy's father had other estates, which belong to Sir Philip now, of course. The family seldom came here, though it has been Mr Elworthy's home since he inherited it from his grandfather.'

'Well, I am going to blow away the dust and ignore the shadows,' Sarah said and laughed. 'Your cousin will be very welcome here, June.'

Sarah left the nursery and walked back towards her own apartments. It was as she was about to enter her rooms that she saw John come out into the hall. She hesitated for there was an air of anxiety about him, a stern look to his mouth as he met her gaze.

'You came in very late last night,' she said. 'I was beginning to worry about you, but then I fell asleep.'

'I put you to bed,' John said, his eyes moving over her face as if he were searching for something. 'I am sorry if you were worried, Sarah. I had business that kept me late.'

'You were not there when I woke. Why did you not sleep beside me, John? Why did you not wake me last night before you carried me to the bed? Have I done something to make you angry with me?'

'No! No, of course you haven't,' John said and a look of anguish passed across his face. 'Never think that, Sarah. You know I love you. I always shall— but I have so much to do. I have neglected the estate for a long time and I must work hard to set my affairs in order. My grandfather left this place to me, but it has not been refurbished for many years, as I am sure you have realised. I am a younger son and the bulk of the Elworthy estates were left to my brother, as is right and proper. However, I have made my own way in the world and am no worse off for it.'

'Yes, I understand that, my dearest,' Sarah said with a smile. She moved towards him, leaned up and kissed him lightly on the mouth. 'I have duties too and I have been very busy this morning. I have been touring the house, deciding what should go and what must stay.'

'Ah, yes, that is a good start,' John said. 'My grandfather ignored the house after his wife died, for it was her home and came to him through her family. He mourned her for more than twenty years, and I have always felt it was an empty, unhappy house. My father preferred the estate in Hampshire. I have thought of pulling both the wings and the tower down and extending on to the main section with a new wing.' He had meant to do it when he married the first time, but somehow he had not found the will to start, even though Andrea had hated the place, calling it dark and cold.

'The building is sound and not damp,' Sarah said, her eyes shining with enthusiasm. 'It is actually rather a wonderful old house, John. I like it now that I have been into most of the rooms, and I think all it needs is a woman's touch. I want to buy some new furniture, and we shall need fresh curtains in most of the rooms—but the house is very well made. Some restoration needs doing here and there, of course, but most of all it needs people to make it live. I have been talking to Mrs Raven. We must have several more servants so that she does not have so much to do, because when the house is finished we shall want to invite our friends to stay.'

'You are right, of course,' John said and looked relieved. 'You are the mistress here and you must do exactly as you please. You have my approval for anything you wish to order for the house, Sarah.'

'Thank you,' Sarah said. 'I did not bother with nuncheon for you were out and I was busy, but I think I shall ask for tea in the parlour downstairs—the one that looks out towards the park. I have decided that it will be my room when I am not entertaining and I have already made several changes. Will you join me for tea?'

John hesitated. He had meant to keep his distance so that his enemy would have no interest in harming Sarah, but he could not resist her when she looked at him and smiled as she was doing now.

'Yes, of course,' he said. 'But if I am not here another day, you must ask for something for yourself.'

Sarah slipped her arm through his as they walked to the head of the stairs together. She smiled at him, her eyes soft with love. 'I have promised Mrs Raven that you will advertise for a cook, John. She has more than enough to do. We should not expect her to produce meals as well.'

'That is an excellent idea,' he said. 'I shall place an advertisement in the *Yorkshire Gazette* and see who comes. My valet is due to arrive tomorrow and your maid was arriving just as I came home. I saw Mrs Raven taking her to her room.'

'I am pleased Ellie is here,' Sarah said, one of her doubts lifting instantly. She had said nothing to John about Ruth—she was determined that she would solve her problems for herself. Mrs Raven had come out of her sullen mood, and perhaps if Sarah spoke to the girl on her own she could find a way to break through Ruth's insolence. If that proved impossible, she would have to let Ruth go. But she would not be in a hurry to do so, for she suspected that it might be hard for the girl to find work elsewhere. 'We must make this house a home, John. So many of your servants left because the house is big and old and there were shadows here. I am determined to make them fade away, to let the light in and make the house live again.'

'If you can do that, you have more magic than I,' John said and smiled at her. They were alone and he had let down his guard, his love for her showing plainly in his eyes. 'But I think you will do it, Sarah, for you are brave and wise—and as lovely inside as out.'

Sarah smiled and hugged his arm. She paused at the head of the stairs, something making her turn her head to glance back. Ruth was standing at the far end of the hall, watching them, her eyes narrowed and hostile. Sarah felt a cold breeze at the back of her neck and shivered, but told herself it was nonsense to feel anxious.

Ruth was hostile and sulky, but she could not harm Sarah. If she continued to be unpleasant, she would be dismissed.

After tea, they talked for a while about the house and their plans for the future, and then John said he had some work to do in his library and left her. Sarah rang the bell and after a few moments Ruth came to clear the tea tray.

'I thought it was your day off?' Sarah asked as the girl began to stack the tray. 'You need not have come back this early. In future on your days off you may leave when you are ready and return before dark, that is all that is necessary. We shall have more than enough staff here to keep the house as it ought to be without you. However, when you are here, you will behave properly. I do not intend to stand for insolence.'

'Are you threatening to turn me off?' Ruth's dark eyes burned with a deep-seated anger. 'If you've heard anything, it is all lies…'

'What do you mean?' Sarah asked.

'About me and the master,' Ruth said. 'His first wife thought I was his mistress, but it wasn't true…' There was a gleam in Ruth's eyes, as though she wanted Sarah to believe otherwise, her head tilted proudly, challenging her. 'So am I to go, Mrs Elworthy?'

John and this girl lovers? No, she would not believe it! Ruth had made it up to distress her, but she would not fall for such a trick. Sarah's stomach churned, but she met the other's hard gaze determinedly.

'No, not for the moment. I believe Mrs Raven is your aunt?' Ruth nodded. 'If you are impertinent, it makes her life more difficult, Ruth. I know that we did not begin well, for I dismissed you from the nursery—but you might be a parlour maid and be happy here. It is up to you. All I want is for this to be a happy house, pleasant for us and for the people who work here. Do you understand me?'

'Yes, ma'am,' Ruth said and for a moment Sarah thought there were tears in her eyes. The woman stared through them, her expression clearly defiant. 'Was there anything else?'

'No, nothing more for the moment,' Sarah said. 'Unless you have something to say to me? I am not an unkind person, Ruth. I should like you to be happy in your work here if that is possible.'

Ruth looked at her in silence for a moment, then inclined her head. 'Thank you, Mrs Elworthy. I shall do my best to make myself satisfactory.'

'Then we shall say no more of this,' Sarah said.

'Would you ask Ellie to come up to my rooms, please? I am going to change before dinner and I want to speak to her about something.'

'Yes, ma'am,' Ruth said and went out carrying the tray.

Sarah got up and went over to the window, looking out at the gardens. Her thoughts were busy—she felt certain that Ruth had deliberately tried to put doubt into her mind. Now why would she do that? Why risk being dismissed if she wanted to stay here? It was a part of the mystery, which she was determined to solve. Ruth knew something she wasn't telling. She was hostile and insolent, and yet she was also vulnerable. If Sarah could find a way to gain her confidence, she might prove the key to whatever was wrong here.

Sarah woke and lay listening for a moment. She was in her own room for John had gone out that evening, apologising because he would once again be late back. She hoped that it would not be a regular occurrence, because she had not particularly enjoyed spending the evening alone, even though she had plenty of needlework to occupy her and her books. Accustomed to being in company with other ladies, she was finding it a little lonely—though not when John was at home. She knew he had his work, but she had expected that they would spend their evenings together, sharing their love of music and books.

Was there another reason why he had not attempted to share her bed since they had come home? The niggling doubt wormed its way into her mind as she recalled Ruth's sly look. Sarah had dismissed her insinuation as mere insolence, but she could not help wondering if there was more to it. Mrs Raven had told her that John was rumoured to have a mistress. If that mistress lived here in this house… something like that might drive any woman to such unhappiness that she took her own life.

Sarah sat up in bed, reflecting on her mother's warnings. Why had John spent every night away from her since their homecoming? Surely it was not to find his pleasure in the arms of Ruth? No, she would not believe that! It was ridiculous and she was being unfair to John even to consider it. But Andrea might have believed it… Sarah wondered again what had finally driven John's wife to take her own life. Andrea must have been desperately unhappy… Sarah's thoughts were distracted as she heard something.

There it was again, the sound that had woken her. It was the thin wail of a child, and yet it had not seemed to come from the nursery. She supposed that sound was often distorted in an old house like this.

It must have been Nathaniel crying. June would go to the boy if he were distressed. She slept in the room next to his and Sarah was certain that she would not neglect him. She waited, but there were no more cries and she turned over, drifting back to sleep.

In the morning she asked Ellie if she had slept well and the girl said she had, adding that she was settling down and thought that she would enjoy working here.

'I've been to the nursery this morning, ma'am,' Ellie said and smiled. 'I thought I would give June a hand until her cousin comes. That lad of Mr Elworthy's is such a cheerful little boy, always laughing and playing. June says he is never a bit of bother.'

'Yes, he is a happy little boy,' Sarah said, 'though I think he woke last night. I believe I heard him crying.'

'Well, that's odd, I never heard a thing,' Ellie said. 'My room is only two doors away from the nursery, ma'am, and I slept right through.'

'I am glad he did not disturb you,' Sarah said and looked thoughtful. 'I shall need my green walking gown this morning. It is a lovely day and I intend to walk in the gardens for a while.'

'Yes, ma'am. That gown suits you very well. You always look beautiful in green.'

'Thank you, Ellie.' Sarah smiled at her, thinking how nice it was to have her own maid to look after her. For even after her talk with Ruth, she sensed that something still simmered in the girl's mind, some secret resentment that she harboured inside.

After Sarah was dressed she went into John's room. There was no sign of him, though she could see that his bed had been slept in. He must have returned late and not wanted to disturb her.

Leaving her own rooms, she went along to the nursery to look in at June and Nathaniel. The little boy was eating his breakfast of soft rolls and honey, evidently enjoying them.

'He looks happy,' Sarah said as June filled a cup with milk for him. 'Did he wake and cry for a while last night?'

'No, Mrs Elworthy, I am sure he didn't,' June said. 'I looked in on him before I went to bed at eleven, and again when I woke at six this morning. He was sleeping soundly both times.'

'Oh, then I must have imagined it,' Sarah said, wrinkling her brow. 'I thought I heard a child's cry but it was probably the wind or something.'

'Wind can be terribly deceiving in a house like this,' June said. 'It makes the most awful wailing sound. I know because I stayed with my great-grand-mother a few times when I was small. Her house was very much like this and I often thought the wind sounded like someone crying when it got into the eaves.'

'Yes, I dare say you are right,' Sarah said. She smiled at Nathaniel and ruffled his hair in passing. 'I shall see you later on. I am going for a walk in the gardens now.'

Sarah took a light shawl with her when she went out, though she did not think she would need it, for it was very warm. She walked through the shrubbery towards an area of open grassland and large trees. As the house itself, the garden looked as if it needed some attention. The grass had been cut, but there was a general air of neglect, as if no one had bothered with it for a long time. She shaded her eyes, looking at some scrubby trees that seemed long past their usefulness. It would be best if they were to come down and a new avenue of beech or, better still, chestnut trees were planted in their place—and they might create a lake somewhere.

She decided that would talk to John about it, hopefully when he came back for luncheon that day, she decided. The landscaping should properly be his to order, but she had several ideas that might renew the park area and she hoped that he would agree to put the work in order. And she would like to have a new rose garden planted nearer to the house.

As she walked back to the house, her head buzzing with ideas, she glanced up at the roof and saw that some of the overhanging stone ornamentation looked as if it might be unstable in places. She must tell John about it, she thought, and then heard the rattle of wheels. She looked round and saw a carriage arrive and then a tall, attractive and distinguished man got down. He stood speaking to his groom for a moment, but then, as he was about to go up to the house, he turned and saw her. He stared at her for such a long time that Sarah was disturbed, but when she walked towards him he smiled.

'Good morning, Mrs Elworthy,' he said, offering his hand. 'I think you must be John's new wife?'

'Yes, I am,' Sarah said. 'And you are, sir?'

'I am Andrea's father,' he replied. 'I dare say John may have spoken of me?'

'Yes, of course,' Sarah said, though in truth he had not mentioned Andrea's father to her. Nor had he asked for him to be invited to their wedding, which he might have done had he chosen. 'I am sorry, but he did not tell me your name.'

'Sir Andrew Walton,' he replied, taking her hand. For a moment he held it, small and white against his own darker hand and then he raised it briefly to his lips. 'I am so pleased to meet you, Sarah—it is Sarah, isn't it? I hope we need not stand on ceremony?'

'Yes, my name is Sarah,' she said feeling oddly disturbed by something in his manner, though she did not know what it was. She was not sure she liked his familiar use of her name, but it might be seen as rude if she were to deny him. 'I am afraid I don't know if John is in at the moment. He went out early this morning. He has so much work to do and I have hardly seen him since we came home.'

'That is very remiss of John,' Sir Andrew said and frowned. 'He ought not to neglect you. This is such a dark, unfriendly house. I know that Andrea was often frightened of being alone at night here. She said it was full of sounds…noises that she felt were un-natural…ghosts, perhaps…'

'Oh, no, surely she could not have thought that?' Sarah said and laughed. She saw the spark of anger in his eyes and realised that she had offended. 'I did not mean to offend you, sir, or any disrespect to your daughter—but there are no ghosts here. If there were, I am sure they would be benign.'

'I would not be so sure,' Sir Andrew said. 'Do you know the history of this place, Sarah?'

'No, I do not,' she replied with a smile, 'but do come in and have a glass of wine with me, sir. I should like to hear if there are any stories concerning the house. I am sure there must be because it is so old.'

'I shall take a glass of wine with you,' he said, 'but

I am not sure that I should tell you the legends. You might have nightmares.'

'I am not so easily frightened,' Sarah said. Was he teasing or deliberately trying to frighten her? 'Please, you must tell me or I shall imagine all kinds of terrible things.'

She led the way inside. Once in the little parlour she had made her own by bringing some of the prettiest pieces down from the west wing, and changing the order to suit herself, she rang for Mrs Raven and ordered tea and wine for her guest. When the housekeeper had gone, she sat down in the chair opposite Sir Andrew and invited him to begin his tales. He sat down, his dark eyes intent on her face.

'You know that the house was once a monastery?'

'I know that the house was built from the ruins of a monastery,' she agreed, a hint of laughter in her voice. 'Do we have headless monks haunting us, Sir Andrew?'

His eyes narrowed as he saw her smiling face. 'You are much braver than my daughter, Sarah. She believed that an unquiet spirit—the spirit of a child that died here many years ago—was haunting her.'

'Oh, the poor little thing,' Sarah said the smile leaving her eyes. 'I hate to think of a child dying. It is so sad, isn't it? It must have upset Andrea to think of it, I am sure, especially when she was carrying her own babe. What happened to the child? Was it very ill?'

'There are many stories concerning the child,' he said and frowned. 'One of them says she was always weak and died of neglect. Others say that she was locked up in her room and died of starvation. It is said that her mother went mad when her husband was away at the wars. She dismissed the servants and locked the child in, then she went off and killed herself—in the river, as it happens.'

'Oh, no, what a dreadful story,' Sarah said, much shocked. She had not expected to hear anything so cruel. 'I do not like that story, Sir Andrew. If it is true, it would mean that the child must have suffered terribly.'

'They say her father found her skeleton when he came back from the wars and opened the house up again. He was so distressed that he hanged himself…in one of the rooms in the east wing, so they say. Some say that he walks the halls looking for his wife and child…'

There was a gleam in his eyes. Sarah looked at him for a moment and then she laughed. 'Oh, you are making it up,' she cried. 'You wicked man! I believe you were deliberately trying to frighten me?'

'Yes, of course I was,' he replied with a strange look. 'If that is what you prefer to believe.'

Sarah felt oddly chilled. He was certainly a gentleman and his manners were excellent, but there was something about him that made her uncomfortable. He smiled at her, but his eyes were remote, cold…as if he disliked seeing her in his daughter's place.

Mrs Raven entered with the tea tray at that moment and the conversation lapsed. Sarah concentrated on playing the hostess; when he had his wine and she her tea, she smiled at him.

'John and I plan to hold a large party for our friends once the house is ready,' she said. 'I do hope you will come, sir?'

'Yes, I shall be delighted,' he said and sipped his wine. 'I may visit you from time to time before that—if I am welcome? I grow lonely in my own house—and I shall think of you alone here in this huge mausoleum. I have told John many times that he ought to pull half of it down and build a new house.'

'Oh, please do not tell him that,' Sarah begged. 'I have fallen in love with it, sir. I know that it is big and a little dark as it is, but I shall soon get rid of the shadows and the cobwebs. We are to have a lot more servants and I am ordering new curtains for the windows, and some new furniture, though much of it only needs to be moved around to create a more comfortable home. If you return in a few weeks' time, sir, I shall have made so many changes that you will not know the house.'

'I shall be delighted to call on you then, but I hope that I do not need to stand on ceremony. I have been used to riding over when I please, for John was always a good neighbour, even before he married my daughter.'

'Oh, yes, of course,' Sarah assured him, though she hoped he would not come often, or at least not when John was from home. 'We shall always be pleased to see you, sir.'

Sir Andrew picked up his glass, draining it before putting it down. He stood up and walked to the door of the sitting room. Sarah accompanied him out into the hall. She was preparing to say goodbye to him when John walked into the hall. He stopped, clearly surprised and a little startled to see their visitor.

'Andrew—did you call to see me? I am sorry I was out. Perhaps Sarah has told you that I have been very busy since we returned home?'

'Yes, she has. You should not neglect her, John. I was sympathising with her for having to be the mistress of this awful old house, but she tells me that she loves it. She is not afraid of your ghosts, John. My poor Andrea was afraid of the dark and this house depressed her—but you are luckier in your new wife.' Something flashed in his eyes at that moment, but was gone so quickly Sarah could not tell what it meant.

'I have much to do, sir,' John said a little stiffly. 'It is not possible to be always in the house, even if one has a new bride.'

'Of course, my darling.' Sarah walked to John, putting her arms about him, smiling up at him. She turned her head to look at Sir Andrew. 'How could I be afraid of anything when I have John's love?' she asked quietly. She felt John's body stiffen, but kept her arms about him. 'I know that he would protect me with his life.'

Sir Andrew's gaze narrowed and she thought she saw a cold gleam in his eyes, but then in a moment he was smiling again. 'John is very fortunate in his choice of a wife this time. I shall see you both another day. My very best wishes for your continued happiness, Sarah. I must go…'

She watched as he walked to the door, which was opened for him by the footman. Sarah tucked her arm through John's as they walked through to her little parlour.

'How long had Sir Andrew been here?' John asked.

'Just long enough to drink a glass of wine with me,' Sarah said. 'He seemed to want me to think the house was full of ghosts, John, but I am afraid I laughed at him. He might have been a little bit cross with me.'

'Andrea heard a ghastly story about a child that died,' John told her. 'I shall not go into details, but I told Andrea that it wasn't true. She wouldn't believe me. She insisted that there was a child haunting the house…but I have already told you that I think her mind was playing tricks on her.'

'Poor Andrea,' Sarah said and looked thoughtful. 'I wonder who told her? It was very unkind, especially if she was prone to imagining things. Oh, it does not matter. Do not let us talk about it again. I am not sure that I really believe in ghosts. What I want to talk about is the park. I think we should cut down those old, scrubby trees and plant a beautiful avenue of chestnut trees. I wondered if you might consider creating a lake—and I should like some new rose beds near the house. Do you agree?'

'Yes, they are all excellent ideas,' John said and smiled at her. 'I have had some similar thoughts myself and shall speak to the gardeners about it in the morning. You make me feel so much better, my darling Sarah. I am glad to see you happy, for I have been so anxious for you…'

'For me—why?' Sarah was puzzled. She looked up at him, seeing the anxiety in his face.

'Because this is a big old house and full of

shadows, as it is bound to be when it has been so neglected. I thought you might find it hard to adjust—
and hard to order the servants…'

'I was not made particularly welcome the first night
we arrived,' Sarah said truthfully, 'but the problem has
sorted itself out. You should not be anxious for me,
John. As long as I have your love I can face anything.'

'Can you, my love?' he asked and looked at her.
'Yes, perhaps you can…' He sighed. 'I have tried to
put a distance between us since that afternoon at the
lake, Sarah. We know that someone intends me
harm, and I am able to cope with that. I have done
my best to protect us both, but I cannot be sure that
you will be completely safe, even in your own home.
So I thought that if I did not seem too wrapped up
in you I might fool my enemy into believing that you
were not important to me. I would rather he tried to
kill me than you, Sarah.'

'Oh, John,' Sarah cried, moving towards him, her
arms about his waist as she looked up at him. 'Pray
do not say things like that, my love. And do not
distance yourself from me. I can stand anything but
that…anything!'

'Then I shall not try,' John said because he could
not resist the look in her eyes. He bent his head and
kissed her. 'There, I shall not be foolish again. Are
you hungry, Sarah? I am starving…'

At that moment they heard the gong sounding in the hall. Sarah smiled as she saw the surprise in his face. 'It was my idea. It saves Mrs Raven having to find us to announce that a meal is ready. This is such a big house, John, and we might be anywhere. Besides, it establishes a routine to the house, and will be useful when we have guests.'

'You always think of everything,' he said. 'Let us go in, Sarah. I have done enough work for the time being. What would you like to do this afternoon?'

'I think I should like to go visiting,' she said. 'Perhaps we could drive over and see Elizabeth and Daniel for a while?'

'Why not?' he said. 'I think that is a very good idea, my love. Why do you not write to Miss Redmond and ask her if she would like to come and stay with you for a few weeks, Sarah? She could help you with refurbishing the house, and then you will not be lonely when I am out.'

'Yes, I think I might like that,' Sarah said. 'I shall write this evening, John. I have a great deal to do in the house and Tilda will help me decide what needs doing the most…'

Sarah hugged his arm and tried not to think about the moment she had felt his body go tense when she put her arms about him. There had been something in his manner when he saw Sir Andrew with her, a wariness in his eyes that bothered her. Why had he not wanted his former father-in-law to see that they were on good terms? Or perhaps she had imagined it, for the moment Sir Andrew had gone he had become her loving husband again.

Sarah put the doubt from her mind. She had sensed an undercurrent between the two men, and she had suspected that Sir Andrew was trying to frighten her—and yet why should he do that? Unless he was angry because of his daughter's death…if he blamed John for it…

'A penny for them?' John asked as she lapsed into silence.

Sarah shook her head and smiled. She would be foolish to let Sir Andrew's talk of hauntings upset her, even though she had woken in the night to hear a crying child.

John took her visiting that afternoon as he had promised. Elizabeth was at home, although Daniel had gone out somewhere.

'He has business to do with the estate, I expect,' Elizabeth told them. 'He will be disappointed to have missed you, John—and you, of course, Sarah.' She smiled at her and patted the sofa, inviting Sarah to sit with her. 'If you wish to see Daniel, a message can be sent.' She looked inquiringly at John.

'Oh, no,' he replied. 'This was just a social call for Sarah's sake, Elizabeth. I dare say we shall visit every week or so now that we are home. I believe Sarah wants to talk to you about some changes concerning the house.'

'Are you going to rebuild as you thought you might?'

'Oh, no,' Sarah told her. 'I love the house, Elizabeth. I shall order new curtains, some furniture and some restoration to the woodwork in places—but otherwise I think it is just a matter of changing the rooms we use. I have found a parlour at the back of the house that I like very much, and I have already had the furniture changed in there—but I plan to do a lot more…'

As she spoke Daniel came into the parlour. He walked to his wife's chair and bent to kiss her cheek. 'This is nice,' he said. 'It will be good for Elizabeth to have company nearer her own age, Sarah. Mama will be back from Bath soon, but she can be something of a trial.'

'Oh, no, dearest,' Elizabeth admonished. 'You know I love Dora—but it will be nice to have a friend living close by. Tell me, Sarah, do you think you shall like living at Elworthy Hall?'

'Oh, yes, I like it very much,' Sarah said. 'There is a great deal to do, of course, but when it is ready we shall hold a party and ask all our friends to come and stay.'

'It is exciting to change things and make them different, isn't it?' Elizabeth said. 'I began with Daniel's library when I first came here, but now I have made a few changes to the house. Not so very many, for Dora had already done most of what was needed—but our private rooms, you know.'

'I have been thinking about the best colours for the drawing room. I cannot decide between blues and greens…'

'I think that is our cue to leave the ladies alone for a while,' Daniel said, giving John a wicked grin. 'They can discuss styles and colours for hours at a time, you know, but do not make the mistake of offering an opinion—it is bound to be wrong. They will smile and agree and then do exactly as they please.'

'Daniel!' Elizabeth shook her head at him. 'You can be truly provoking, my dearest. Take John off and do what gentlemen do. We shall be quite happy together.' She smiled at Sarah as they went out. 'Now we can be really comfortable and abuse them all we wish.'

'I think you like to tease as much as the earl,' Sarah said. 'I have no need to abuse John, for he is truly kind and considerate—everything I could wish for in a husband.'

'Then what is worrying you, Sarah?' Elizabeth asked. 'I sense that something is on your mind— though you need not tell me unless you wish.'

'I am not sure,' Sarah said. 'But I think someone is trying to upset me and I am not quite sure what I ought to do about it.'

'Tell me,' Elizabeth said. 'Perhaps I can help.'

'Did you enjoy your visit?' John asked as they were driving home. 'I am glad that you get on so well with Elizabeth. It means that you will always have a friend, which Andrea did not. She was too much alone and I think the emptiness of the house unsettled her.'

'I shall not be alone, for I intend to make friends with all our neighbours,' Sarah said. 'I dare say we shall have more callers once people know we are at home.'

'Yes, perhaps...' John frowned. 'Andrea did not encourage our neighbours to call, and she did not care to go visiting often—and then only to her father's house. So it may be a while before people realise that you are willing to be friendly. But we could give a small dinner party quite soon, if you wish?'

'Yes, I should like that as soon as we are ready to receive guests. Elizabeth said that she would give a picnic in her gardens quite soon. It will be an opportunity for us to meet people, John, and then I can call on them if I wish. She was telling me about some people she likes and I am sure that I shall like them too.'

'Yes, of course,' he said but looked thoughtful. 'In

time you will make friends here, Sarah. At least I hope that you will…'

He looked so anxious that she wanted to ask him what was on his mind, but he seemed to be lost in his own thoughts. They spoke very little on the way home and it was time to change for dinner when they arrived.

As soon as dinner was over, John apologised. 'I am afraid I have something important to do tonight, Sarah. Will you be all right on your own?'

'Yes, of course—but it would be much nicer if you were here in the evenings, John. I am not frightened and I can amuse myself with books or my sewing, but I miss you.'

'I am sorry, Sarah. It has to be like this for a while. Please try to understand. When things are settled I shall be with you all the time, I promise.'

'You must do what you have to do,' Sarah said. 'Do not look so anxious, John. I am not afraid of shadows.'

He smiled and bent his head to kiss her briefly on the lips. Sarah watched him walk from the room, feeling a sense of loss. John loved her, she knew he loved her—so why was he leaving her alone so often? For one second she wondered if Mrs Raven's tale of his having a mistress could be true, but then she dismissed it, crushing it ruthlessly, before it could take root in her mind. Despite the insinuations, the malicious gossip and Sir Andrew's odd tales, she would not let her mind be poisoned against John.

Sarah thought about John's first wife, recalling what he had told her and the things that Sir Andrew had hinted at, but not said in so many words. Just what kind of a man would tell a new bride such a chilling tale about her new home? It was almost as if he had wanted to frighten her…

There was no use in dwelling on it! Sarah did not feel like sitting alone in the large, formal drawing room. She decided that she would go to her own apartments and read until she felt ready for bed.

She sat down in a chair by the window, looking out at the garden for a few minutes before she began to read. She had just picked up her book when she heard a sound…the thin wail of a terrified child! This time she was quite certain of what she had heard. It was not in the least windy out and she was wide awake.

Now was her opportunity to see if she was imagining things. She walked to the nursery, meeting June as she reached the door.

'Is the boy crying?' she asked.

'No, ma'am, he is fast asleep,' June said. 'Come in and look for yourself.'

Sarah followed her into the nursery, which was lit by one small candleglass, which shed a pale golden light over the room. Nathaniel was lying on his back, one chubby fist against his cheek, his eyes closed.

Sarah glanced at the boy's nurse and nodded. They crept out of the room again. Seeing that June was curious, Sarah hesitated and then told her that she had heard a child's cry.

'Where did it come from, ma'am?' she asked. 'Was it above your head—or in the main section…or perhaps the East Wing?'

'I'm not sure,' Sarah said, 'but I do know that it was not a ghost, June. I do not believe that an unquiet spirit walks this house. I believe there is child here somewhere.'

'I have not heard it,' June said, 'but I am in the nursery most of the time. There are attics above you, Mrs Elworthy. I think once they were used for some of the servants, though they have been disused for years. We are housed in the east wing for the main part these days, as you know.'

'I shall speak to Mrs Raven,' Sarah said. 'But I have heard the child at least twice now, June—and I am not imagining things.'

'I would never think it, Mrs Elworthy,' June said and smiled. 'I wondered if it might have been the wind last night; one often hears strange noises when it is dark—but it is still light out. If you heard something then I think there must be a child other than Nathaniel in the house.'

'Yes, so do I,' Sarah said. 'I shall speak to Mrs Raven about it at once.'

She went downstairs, knocking at the housekeeper's door. It was a moment or two before the housekeeper opened it to her.

'Yes, ma'am? Did you ring? I am sorry I did not hear.'

'I did not wish to drag you upstairs,' Sarah said. 'A few minutes ago I heard a baby crying. Nathaniel is sound asleep—do any of the maids have a child in the house?'

'No, I should not allow that,' Mrs Raven said. 'At least, I might in certain circumstances—but the girl would have to ask permission before she brought the child here.'

'And no one has?'

'No one has even suggested it, ma'am.' Mrs Raven's gaze narrowed. 'Are you sure it wasn't just the wind? These old house make strange noises at times. The late mistress…'

'Yes, I know Andrea thought an unquiet spirit haunted the house,' Sarah said, a sharp note in her voice, 'but I do not believe in such nonsense, Mrs

Raven. I know what I heard. It was a child—not the wind and not a ghost.'

Mrs Raven gave her an odd look. 'I'm sorry, ma'am, I do not know of a child other than Mr Elworthy's boy. If you are sure you heard it, I shall make inquiries.'

'No, in this instance that will not do,' Sarah said. 'I understand there are attics above me that were once used for servants?' Mrs Raven nodded, a wary expression in her eyes. 'Then I shall ask Alfie to accompany me while I make a search.'

'Are you sure that is wise, ma'am?' the house-keeper asked and looked nervous. 'Perhaps you should leave it until the morning?'

'Oh, no, Mrs Raven. I am not frightened easily,' Sarah said. 'Someone is trying to make me think this house is haunted, but I am not going to have night-mares or start wandering in my sleep. I intend to discover the truth.'

She went back to the hall, where Alfie was sitting in his porter's chair as he did until late every evening. He got to his feet as she told him what she wanted, picking up a branch of candles in his left hand.

'I am with you, Mrs Elworthy,' he said. 'Lucy—she's the parlour maid—well, told me she thought she heard crying the other night, proper upset she was. I told her she was dreaming or imagining things—but if you heard it too, then it sounds as if there is more than one child in the house…'

'Can you show me where the attic rooms are, Alfie?'

'Yes, Mrs Elworthy. It is easy enough to get to them, for there is a stairway. When the house had thirty or more servants they were in regular use, but as you know these days the maids use the rooms on the top floor of the east wing.'

'Let us go and see what we can find,' Sarah said. She followed him up to the west wing and to the end of the landing, discovering a set of stairs behind a door, which she had not known was there. It was dark on the stairway, which was why Alfie had come prepared with his candles. When they reached the top, Sarah saw that the attic had been divided into what looked like small cubicles, divided by wooden partitions with, in most cases, just a curtain to provide some privacy. The air was musty, hot and stifling. 'How awful this is,' she said to the footman. 'I think it was most unfair to expect girls to live in these conditions. It must have been terribly hot in summer and bitterly cold in winter.'

'Servants had to sleep where they could in the old days,' Alfie told her. 'Some of them had nowhere but the kitchen floor in the times these houses were first built. There was no privacy nor comfort for a servant then, Mrs Elworthy.'

'I am very sorry for it,' Sarah said, making a mental note to discover the state of the rooms their servants occupied now and do what she could to improve them. 'Listen…' Alfie had turned to her and she knew he had heard the murmuring noise that she had heard coming from a room at the far end.

Alfie held his candles aloft, a grim look on his face. He walked to the end of the row of cubicles, pulling back the flimsy curtain to reveal a woman holding a child of perhaps three years. She looked up with a startled expression on her face, fear coming to her eyes as she saw Sarah. She got to her feet, her head raised as she looked at her.

'I know I shouldn't have done it,' she said. 'My aunt will be furious when she finds out. I didn't tell her, Mrs Elworthy. She wouldn't have let me bring her here, but there was nowhere else. He said he would take her away. I was afraid that he would hurt her if I didn't do what he wanted and—' She broke off on a sob. 'I know I've done things I shouldn't. I put that shift in the armoire and sprinkled the late mistress's perfume all over the room, and I've done other things, things I'm ashamed of—but *he* gave me money when she needed the doctor and he made me do it…'

'You certainly shouldn't have brought the child up to this awful place,' Sarah agreed, looking round her in disgust. It was thick with dust and smelled of mice. 'I am not surprised she has been crying. Why didn't you take her to your own room?'

'I thought I should be dismissed…' Ruth stared at her, her eyes wet with tears. 'I've nowhere to go but the road. People won't employ a woman with a child. She was so ill as a baby and I thought I could settle here.'

'You shouldn't have done what you did, Ruth,' Sarah said and gave her a straight look. 'But I am certainly not going to dismiss you for having a child. You need at least two rooms to call your own. I believe there are plenty of spare rooms in the nursery wing. Ask Mrs Raven to sort it out for you. I am sure that June and Mary would be willing to keep an eye on your daughter while you are working. What do you call her?'

'Her name is Deborah,' Ruth said. She looked at Sarah uncertainly, not quite sure whether she had heard right. 'Are you saying I can stay here? You are not turning me off?'

'Yes, of course you may stay. Why not? All I ask is that you do your work properly and willingly.' Sarah smiled at her. 'I am very glad to have cleared that little mystery up. Tell me, when did you bring Deborah here?'

'Only two days ago. I had lodged her with an old woman who takes care of children for working girls, but I was afraid that something might happen to her.'

'Yes, I see, that explains something,' Sarah said, but it did not explain why Andrea had thought she'd heard a child crying. But perhaps John's first wife had been a vulnerable girl with darker things on her mind. 'Take Deborah with you and go to your aunt, Ruth. Tell her that I have given permission for the child to stay here. I shall want to talk to you again about this, but it will do tomorrow. You will be busy settling into your new rooms this evening.' She turned and nodded to Alfie. 'You can see me down the stairs and then come back and help Ruth if you will.'

'Yes, Mrs Elworthy.'

Alfie went ahead of her down the stairs. When she reached the main landing it was much lighter and she was able to make her way along the hall to her own rooms.

Sarah was thoughtful as she went to bed that night. She was glad to have sorted Ruth's problems out, but who had threatened to harm her child if she did not do as he asked? She thought that she might have taken a step towards discovering the identity of John's enemy—and she had her suspicions concerning Andrea's death.

## Chapter Eleven

When Sarah rose she discovered that John had been home for a while during the night, for his bed had been slept in, though he was not there and his things had been left on the floor. His valet came in just as she bent to pick up a shirt he had discarded. It was only the second time they had met, for Harris had arrived the previous day.

He frowned as he saw what she was doing. 'Leave that to me, Mrs Elworthy. I shall soon have this right. I have been down to the boot-boy's room, to complain about the state of the master's boots. I wished to make it clear that I shall be looking after them in future. They have been sadly neglected.'

'Yes, I am sure they have, Harris,' Sarah said with a smile and placed the shirt over a chair. John's man-servant was already a presence in the house, and she had noticed that Mrs Raven seemed to have pulled herself up since he arrived, suspecting that there was a gentle rivalry between the two. 'Have you seen my husband this morning?'

'No, ma'am. I placed hot water in his bedchamber last evening, and it had been used when I came to wake him this morning. He was clearly in a hurry to leave. I believe someone came with a message for him. I think he must have dressed in a hurry, for he did not ring for me.'

'Yes, so I see. It must have been important for him to go off so suddenly,' Sarah said and smiled. 'I think it is a good thing that you have come, Harris. My husband needs a man to take care of him.'

'Yes, just so, Mrs Elworthy. We shall soon have his wardrobe in better shape.'

'I am sure that I may rely on you,' Sarah said and returned to her own room. She found Ruth there and frowned as she saw the girl lay something on the bed. 'Is that for me, Ruth?'

'I wanted you to see these, Mrs Elworthy,' Ruth said. 'They are letters from the late Mrs Elworthy to her father. I was asked to leave them in your room, hide them in drawers so that you came upon them by accident—but I didn't want to do that, because they are horrible. I thought that if I gave them to you and told you why, it would be best, but you weren't here and I wasn't sure what to do…'

'Have you read them?'

'I read one,' Ruth said hesitantly. 'It would be best if I destroyed them for they are wicked, slanderous things and no one should see them—but perhaps you ought to see them, Mrs Elworthy.'

'What did the letter you read say?' Sarah asked, picking up the little bundle. 'What is so terrible that you think they should be destroyed?'

'The one I read accused Mr Elworthy of hating her,' Ruth said. 'She can't have been right in the head, Mrs Elworthy. She writes that he wants her dead so that he can be free…that he is unkind to her…'

'I am sure that is not true,' Sarah said. 'My husband would never have been deliberately unkind.'

'I didn't know what to do,' Ruth told her. '*He* made me bring them, said that he would take Deborah away from me and that I would never see her again. He told me that I must make you think that the master had a secret mistress and that it was me. I said things to you, ma'am, and I regret it if I distressed you. Deborah is all I have, Mrs Elworthy. I had to bring the letters, and I had to hide her in the attics.'

'No, your insinuations did not upset me, for I did not believe them.' Sarah looked thoughtful. 'I do not believe that my husband would betray me. Nor do I think he betrayed Andrea. He is too fine a man for that.' Sarah smiled at her. 'But tell me, is your daughter settling down in your new rooms?'

'Oh, they're lovely, Mrs Elworthy. I've never had such a nice place to put her since her father disappeared. Mr Palmer always used to look after me...' She hesitated, and then, '*He* told me that Mr Elworthy murdered Richard, but I think he was lying to get me to do what he wanted. He wanted Mr Elworthy punished, and he made me hide her things in his room so that he would find them and think she was haunting him. When you came here he said I was to do the same to you, and I did the first night, but I knew you would dismiss me if I did it again, and I wanted to stay.'

'Mr Palmer...' Sarah frowned—she vaguely recalled hearing that the Earl of Cavendish, her brother and some others had kidnapped a Mr Palmer and made him confess to his part in her abduction. 'When did your lover go missing, Ruth?'

'It was more than two years ago now,' Ruth said and sighed. 'I think he must be dead, Mrs Elworthy, for he would not have left us to starve. I think he was mixed up in some kind of trouble. He wasn't my lover, more my protector, ma'am. We had an arrangement and when I had the child he promised me that he would look after us. He used to visit with presents for her and money for me even after the rest of it was over. He was a real gentleman.' Her eyes held regret and wistful memories.

'I know that a Mr Palmer was sent to the West Indies at about that time,' Sarah said. 'I think John may have known about it, my brother certainly did—but it wasn't a case of murder. Mr Palmer helped them solve a mystery and in return they sent him overseas to escape an enemy.'

'You think that he may still be alive?' Ruth looked at her hopefully. 'I am sure he wouldn't have forgotten us…but I moved away. I couldn't afford the rent of the house. If he sent money later, I wouldn't have been there to receive it.' She narrowed her gaze. 'I didn't think to go back and see if anything had come for me, because *he* said that Richard had been murdered by Mr Elworthy and his friends.'

'I assure you that my brother and his friends did not murder anyone, Ruth. I shall ask John for more information—but you keep speaking of someone making you do these things, of someone who clearly hates my husband. Who is this person?' Sarah had her suspicions, but she wanted to hear it from Ruth.

Ruth looked at her uncertainly, fear in her face. 'If he finds out I've told you, he will kill me.'

'No, he will not,' Sarah said, 'for he will be in prison. Someone has tried to kill John…when we were in Scotland he was fired at, but from such a distance that we could not see who it was.'

'I don't know anything about that,' Ruth said. 'But the person who gave me the letters was her father. Sir Andrew. He was the one who made me hide those things in Mr Elworthy's room—and he wanted me to do the same to you. I didn't want to do it, Mrs Elworthy, and that was when he threatened me.'

'I see…' A little shiver ran down Sarah's spine. She could easily believe Andrea's father capable of sending the spiteful letters and forcing Ruth to hide his daughter's correspondence in order that Sarah would find them and read them. Yes, that made perfect sense. It was the reason he had tried to plant his stories of a ghost in her mind. 'Thank you, Ruth. I shall think about what you have said. In the meantime I hope you will be happy working for us, but if you want to discover if money has been left for you somewhere, perhaps my husband can help you.'

'I could give you the address of the house he used to rent for me in York, Mrs Elworthy.'

'Do that and we shall make inquiries for you,' Sarah said. She smiled at Ruth. 'Run along now and do whatever you have to. Mr Elworthy will be shown the letters and told of what you have said, and perhaps he will be able to sort out this mess.'

She sat down on the edge of the bed after Ruth had left, beginning to read through the letters. The sweet perfume that Andrea had used still clung to them, slightly overpowering in itself. As she began to see what was written, she realised that they were clearly the product of a deluded mind, for they rambled and did not make sense. In one letter Andrea went from telling her father how kind John had been to her that morning, changing suddenly into dark, meaningless scribble that accused him of torturing her with a crying child and wanting her to die. But the others made wicked accusations concerning John that made Sarah feel upset and angry. She did not believe any of it was true. John could never do these things!

Sarah stared at the handwriting. Something struck her as odd, because they had gradually grown less and less legible, as if the person who had written them was ill…or was it possible that they had not all been written by the same hand?

After re-reading three of them, Sarah retied the bundle and slipped them into the drawer of her desk. She would speak to John when he came home, tell him about the letters and Ruth's revelations. She had sensed from the very beginning that Sir Andrew's friendly manner was hiding his true feelings when he had called earlier that week. His tales about the house being haunted by a child's ghost had obviously been meant to disturb Sarah, to make her frightened and unhappy, as his daughter had been.

Did he truly believe that John had driven his wife to take her own life? Sarah thought that she had discovered the source of the gossip and the slanderous letters that had been sent to her. Sir Andrew had obviously wanted to drive a wedge between her and John, to cause as much pain and unhappiness as he could—while pretending to be John's friend.

Was he also the hidden assassin who had shot at Sarah and John from the woods? It seemed likely, and yet she had a feeling that the puzzle was not yet solved. But why would someone else want to kill John?

She frowned over it as she left the bedchamber. It was too nice a day to spend indoors brooding over those letters. She would ask for her mare to be saddled and go for a good gallop across the moors.

'You were caught snooping about the grounds,' John said as he looked at the other man. He was a few years younger, a tall, attractive man with dark eyes and hair, and the bearing of a soldier. 'What were you doing on my estate—and why? If you tell me the truth, it will be better for you than if you lie, sir. The letters and the whispers—and the shot someone took at my wife, and again at me when we were in Scotland. I am determined to get to the bottom of this, because it has gone on long enough. I would know your name, sir, and what part you have played in this business.' John spoke quietly, but from the look on his face, it was clear that he was in no mood for being denied.

The other man gave him a hard look, his dark eyes proud and angry. 'My name is George Rathbone, and I am a sergeant in his Majesty's army. I know nothing of any letters. I've heard the scandal and I know Andrea was desperately unhappy. I begged her to leave you and bring the child. I would have taken them away and cared for them, even though I couldn't give her a big house and fine clothes the way you did, but I loved her and I would have made her happy.'

'You were Andrea's lover?' John stared at him, his eyes narrowing. 'She told me that she was forced…'

'I never forced her,' George Rathbone cried, his dark eyes flashing angrily. 'That is a damned lie! She came to me willingly. I loved her and she loved me. I wanted to marry her, but when I asked for her, her father told me that he would never allow it. He sent word to my father that if I continued to see her he would turn my family out of their home. We were his tenants and that meant our ruin; my father took a horsewhip to me in a rage for our family has farmed the land for three generations. He told me that if I saw her again he would kill me. I met Andrea again the next day. I told her that I was going away and would come back for her when I had enough money to marry her—and I did. I've been in the army and I've earned my share of prize money. I could have given her a home and food to eat, though not the luxuries she was used to.'

'You say you saw her after we were married—when exactly?'

'It was after the child was born,' George said and his face creased with grief. 'I was shocked when I saw her, for she had changed so much—seemed almost wild, strange, as if her mind wandered. She knew me and I think she still loved me, but she was frightened. I begged her to come away with me, promised that I would take care of her… I believed that she still loved me, that she would come to me in the end. And then I heard that she had drowned herself in the river. I was devastated when they wouldn't let her be buried in church ground. I watched her being buried and I cursed you. I hated you for taking her from me and I wanted to punish you.' He paused, his eyes narrowing as he looked at John. 'Yes, I fired at you when you were in Scotland—and I fired into the air when I saw the girl you were to marry out riding, but I did not try to kill either you or her. Had I done so, you would be dead. I wanted to frighten you, to punish you—and sometimes I thought of taking your life or that of the woman you loved, but I could never have done it. I am no murderer—but I believed that you were.'

John's eyes narrowed with anger. 'You are grievously at fault, sir. Sarah might have died if she had fallen from her horse. It was only good fortunate that prevented her from being injured.'

'Yes, I know,' George Rathbone said and a look of shame came into his eyes. 'That was wrong and I have since regretted it. I fired on impulse because I was angry when I heard that you were to marry again. It was you I hated, not her. Why should you be happy when I have lost everything I loved?'

'I am sorry that Andrea died, and that you were forced to leave her by your father and hers,' John said, looking thoughtful. All this was much as Charles had predicted, but it was not the end of the story. He suspected much more, much darker mischief than this. 'I ought never to have married her, but she came to me and told me that she had been forced and was with child. She did not dare to tell her father, and I wanted to protect her, to help her. After we married, she seemed to withdraw from me. Perhaps a part of that was my fault. I am not blameless. I never loved Andrea—my heart was given elsewhere. At the time I thought my case was hopeless and that being married to a woman I did not love would not matter—but perhaps I shut Andrea out. I cannot say for sure. If I made her unhappy, I am sorry for it, and I suffered terrible guilt for months after she died. But I think the darkness was in her own mind… I think she lied to me about being forced, perhaps because she was afraid that I would not have married her if I had known the truth. Yet she was in such distress that I believe I could not have done otherwise, whatever her story.'

'She was terrified of her father's anger.' George's face was anguished. 'She told me once that he treated her as if she were an angel, more fragile and precious than the Sèvres porcelain he treasures… It may be that she made up the story for his benefit, because he might have harmed her had he known that she came to me willingly.'

'Yes, I have thought that she was afraid of something…but her own father…' John met his eyes uncertainly. 'I have blamed myself for her unhappiness…but something happened recently that makes me wonder if he told Andrea things to distress her as a punishment for what she had done. He may even have guessed that she lied because she had lain with you of your own free will.'

George nodded, his dark eyes thoughtful as he

looked at John. 'I've hated you,' he said. 'Sometimes I wanted to kill you, but even though I've had the chance I didn't take it…perhaps because I suspected there was more. The man I want to kill is the man who destroyed her.'

'Yes, I believe he did destroy her,' John said. 'I don't know for certain that it was Sir Andrew—but I have suspected it for a while. I think he forced her to come to me and beg for my help. And then I think he continued to punish her for disappointing him. Someone had told her a wicked story about a child being left to die in the house, locked up and deserted by its mother so that it died of starvation. I know the story haunted Andrea, and that in her black moods she believed she could hear the child crying out for its mother. Recently, Sir Andrew told my wife the same story…'

'Then it was he! He deliberately set out to punish her…to ruin the happiness she might have found with you…it may have been he who murdered her, for I have never believed that she killed herself.'

'Yes,' John agreed, a grim set to his mouth. 'I have been thinking on the same lines for a while now.' He raised his head to meet the other's angry gaze. 'If I let you go—if I agree to forget the shot you fired at Sarah—what will you do?'

'Watch him,' George said. 'Wait my chance and make him confess if I have to thrash it out of him.'

'Then I am afraid I shall have to keep you confined for a few days,' John said and nodded at his men, who had been standing at a discreet distance. 'You will be made as comfortable as possible, Sergeant Rathbone, and when this business is finally finished you shall have your freedom. However, for the moment I cannot let you go. I must have this done properly—an unexplained death might reflect badly on both me and my wife. I want this out in the open and done with.'

George looked at the four burly men waiting to grab him if he tried to escape. 'I haven't much choice, sir. But I shall warn you to be careful. If he has done all we think he has, he wouldn't hesitate to take your life if it came to a case of him or you.'

'It is a pity we did not meet face to face much sooner, Sergeant Rathbone. We might have thrashed this out as we have today.'

'I was too bitter, sir,' George said. 'It was foolish of me, no doubt—but I believed that Andrea was beginning to trust me. I thought that she might run away with me—and when she died…I hated you.'

John inclined his head. 'I do not blame you for hating me. In your shoes I would have felt the same. We shall talk again when this is over, Sergeant Rathbone.'

John nodded to his men, who took hold of George by his arms and led him from the room. His hands were bound behind his back and he went easily, not trying to resist.

'You were lenient,' Daniel observed as the door closed and they were left alone together. 'I am not sure that I should have been as forgiving.'

'He had a right to be bitter,' John said. 'If someone hurt Sarah, I should have felt much the same, though I hope I would not have taken to lurking in the woods and firing at people.'

'Do you think he was right—is it Sir Andrew?'

'I can only guess at much of it,' John said, 'but I have suspected him of writing the letters almost from the beginning, though I tried to tell myself I was wrong. He may have paid someone to leave Andrea's things in my room—one of the maids, perhaps. I thought he might be trying to punish me for making Andrea unhappy, and I believed that if I gave him enough time his grief would ease and it would all fade away. But when he came to see Sarah, told her the stories that had frightened Andrea, made her terrified to be alone in the dark, then I began to wonder. Why did he tell his own daughter that story? I could understand why he told Sarah, because he might want to punish us for being happy—but he must have told Andrea first. Why?'

'Because he wanted to hurt her?'

John nodded. 'When I first told him that I was to

marry Andrea, he seemed to accept it. I know she had confessed to him that she was having a child, and that the child was not mine…' John shook his head. 'I have hardly dared to think it, Daniel—but I think he may have killed Andrea in a fit of temper.'

'But why would he murder his own daughter?'

'I think it may not have been his intention. He was angry with her for letting him down. He cherished her as a delicate flower,' John said. 'She was his angel, his perfect flower—and then she took a lover, a man that he would think not fit to kiss her feet. Can you imagine his anger, his hatred of the man that had dared to touch his little girl? If he thought that she might shame him by leaving her husband and running off with her lover…'

'They quarrelled. Perhaps she stood up to him, told him that she was no longer prepared to do his bidding…that she meant to leave you…'

'Yes, I think that may have been what happened. She had seen the man she loved again and she wanted to be with him. Her father saw her with him, and later he found her alone wandering near the river—and in his anger he killed her.' A look of anguish came to John's face. 'If only she had come to me, told me the truth, I would have helped them. And yet I think she may have made an attempt at reconciliation, but in my ignorance I rejected her. After that she may have decided that she would go with her lover. If I had guessed the truth, she might still be alive. I blame myself for not asking her why she was so unhappy…'

'You are not responsible for any of this,' Daniel said, looking grim. 'If what you believe is true, there is only one person to blame for what happened to Andrea.'

'And he must be punished,' John agreed. 'At first I thought his own grief and guilt sufficient, but that was before he came to the house and said those things to Sarah. She laughed at him, Daniel. She didn't like the story of the child being left to die, no woman would—but she didn't believe in his ghost. I am afraid that if he cannot frighten her, he may try to harm her in some other way.'

'What are you going to do about it?'

'I am going home to see Sarah,' John said. 'I want to warn her that she must never be alone with him. I think he has gone beyond recall, Daniel. His obsession has made him a dangerous man. And then I shall go to see Sir Andrew. This has to be sorted out once and for all.'

'Then I shall come with you,' Daniel said. 'You need a witness and you need a friend for your own protection.'

'Thank you,' John said. 'I thought you would want to hear me question Rathbone—that is why I waited until you came. However, I have hardly seen Sarah since we visited you yesterday, and she will be thinking that I have deserted her. We shall have nuncheon together and then we'll ride over to see Sir Andrew…'

George Rathbone allowed the men to lock him up in the barn, where he had been kept since his capture. He made no show of resistance, for he knew that his best chance of escaping was to wait until they had left him alone. His hands had been carelessly tied behind him. Twenty minutes or so alone would be sufficient to free them, and then he would work out a way to evade his captors. He already knew exactly what he was going to do after that.

John Elworthy meant well by locking him up, but George knew now who had killed his love and he was going to make sure the devil was punished as he deserved.

On entering the house, John went straight up to Sarah's rooms. As he walked in he could distinguish the strong smell of Andrea's perfume, and, as he looked at the dressing table, he saw that the top drawer was slightly open. The smell of perfume was coming from there. Pulling it open, he saw the letters and recognised the hand. He ripped the ribbon off and began to read a few lines of the first two or three, realising at once what they were and why they had been placed there for Sarah to find and read.

As the door opened, he turned on the maid who entered in a fury. 'Where is my wife?'

'She went out riding sometime ago, sir. Is something wrong?' Ellie looked at him anxiously.

'These letters—did you put them here?' John gestured to the open drawer.

'No, sir. Is something the matter?'

'I pray not,' John said, his expression like thunder. 'I shall have something to say to whoever put these here when I return.'

Running back down the stairs to where Daniel waited, talking to one of the footmen, John called to him.

'Sarah has gone riding,' he said. 'I am not sure, but I think she may have gone to visit Sir Andrew…'

'In that case there is no time to lose…'

Sarah had ridden further than she intended and now her horse was lamed. She dismounted and looked at the animal ruefully.

'I think the poor thing has a stone in its hoof, Joshua,' she said to her groom. 'We shall have to walk her home…' She looked about her and saw a house through the trees. 'Do you think it would be best to go there? Do you know who lives there?'

'No, Mrs Elworthy. I am as new to the district as you. I haven't got my bearings yet.'

'No, of course you haven't,' she said. 'But I think it would be cruel to walk my poor mare all the way home. If my neighbour is kind, he might allow me to leave her there and perhaps lend me another to get me home.'

'You could ride my horse, ma'am,' the groom said. 'I could go up to the house and ask where the nearest blacksmith is if you like.'

'We shall both go,' Sarah said. 'If I am not offered the loan of a horse, I may take your offer and let you lead the mare to a blacksmith while I ride home— but we may be lucky.'

The groom nodded. 'I dare say they will lend you a horse, ma'am. It may be an old nag, but it looks a decent place—a gentleman's house.'

'Yes, it does,' Sarah agreed. 'I am not sure who our nearest neighbours are yet. Elizabeth is about ten miles in that direction…' She pointed to her right. 'It is a pity I did not ride that way, for I should have been sure of a welcome there, but I wanted to explore a little…'

She led her horse as far as the end of the drive, then gave the reins to Joshua, leaving him to hold both horses while she went up to the house to inquire if the owner was at home. She knocked at the door, which was opened after a few minutes' delay by an elderly man in a rusty black coat and breeches. He squinted at her, holding a hand to his ear.

'You'll have to speak up, ma'am, I'm a bit hard of hearing these days.'

'Is your master or mistress in please?' Sarah asked. 'My horse has gone lame and I wondered if I could leave her here and borrow another to ride home.'

'What was that…something about borrowing a horse?' The old man asked. 'Can't quite hear you, ma'am.'

'I said my horse is lame…' Sarah began, but just then a man came into the hall. Seeing her at the door, he looked surprised and then smiled, coming forward to greet her.

'Sarah, my dear lady, how nice of you to come and visit me. Please come in. You may go, Hoskins. I shall deal with Mrs Elworthy.' He smiled at Sarah as the elderly man walked off. 'It is such a shame, don't you think. Hoskins has been so loyal that I don't like to turn him off, but he is as deaf as a post.'

'Sir Andrew,' Sarah said, stepping inside the hallway. It was a pleasant house, light and airy and built no more than fifty years earlier. 'I am sorry to call on you so unexpectedly, but I have been out riding and my poor mare has gone lame. I think she has a stone in her hoof. I came to ask if I could leave her here and borrow another mount to ride home.'

'I am sure my grooms will be glad to help,' Sir Andrew said. 'But come into the parlour. I shall offer you some refreshment while the arrangements are being made.' He led the way into a small sunny parlour to the left of the hall. 'Please be seated, Mrs Elworthy. I shall ask one of the maids to bring refreshment and then speak to your groom myself.'

'Thank you.' Sarah took a seat by the window and looked out. After a moment or two she saw Sir Andrew speaking to Joshua, who turned his horse and led her mare towards the right, obviously going to the stables.

Sir Andrew came back to the house, but did not immediately return to her. She got up and began to look about the room. It was a pretty parlour furnished in soft shades of blues, greens and cream. In one cabinet she saw a collection of beautiful figurines that she thought might be Sèvres porcelain, and in another display table there were several miniature paintings, including one of a rather pretty girl. Sarah lifted the lid and took out the oval porcelain plaque, looking at the girl more closely. She could have been no more than ten when it was painted and it was so charming that Sarah smiled.

She was unaware of the man at her shoulder until he spoke. 'I see you like pretty things, Sarah.'

'This is exquisite,' Sarah said. 'Forgive me for

touching it, but it was so appealing that I could not resist.'

'I often take it out to admire and hold it,' he said, an odd expression on his face. 'It is one of the few things that gives me comfort in my lonely life, Sarah. You see, it is a picture of my angel when she was at her perfect best.'

'This is Andrea as a child?' Sarah laid the miniature back with gentle reverence. 'You must treasure it, sir.'

'Yes, I do,' he agreed. 'I have other pictures of her that I had drawn as she grew older, but she changed…as everything does. Have you noticed, Sarah, that all things have their moment of perfection? A rose when it is just opening from a bud, not quite full but deeply scented and fresh…a kitten before it becomes too old to play…a lamb in spring…' His eyes had become distant as if he were looking into the past 'But the lamb becomes mutton and we eat it, the rose fades and is so much compost to be thrown on a heap…and a thing that is broken or tarnished can never be as lovely again.'

He brought his gaze back to Sarah and she was disturbed by the expression in his eyes. She moved away from him, intending to escape through the door, but then it opened and a maid carried in a tray, which she set down on a table by the window. In that instant, Sir Andrew seemed to recover himself. He smiled at her, that strange look gone from his face.

'Will you pour, Sarah? It is so pleasant for me to have a guest—such a young and lovely guest too. Did you know that you are not as I had expected you to be, Sarah? There is something serene about you…restful. At first I thought you were older, but it isn't that, is it? You have experienced life. You are not afraid of things that my poor child feared…' He sighed. 'My poor Andrea. She was perfect and I loved her…' He shook his head and sighed as she indicated his cup. 'A little milk, but no sugar, thank you.'

She poured the tea and took it to him as he sat on an elegant little sofa. He took it and placed it on the wine table beside him, but did not drink. Sarah poured herself tea with milk and sugar but made no attempt to drink it either. She felt tense, ill at ease, waiting for something, though she knew not what. However, Sir Andrew seemed to have drifted away in his own thoughts, almost as though he had forgotten that she was there.

She waited for a moment or two and then stood up. 'I really think I should be going, sir. My groom will have a horse ready for me now, I dare say.'

'Oh, no, I sent him home,' Sir Andrew said, smiling at her in that strange way again. 'Your mare will be cared for, Sarah. You need not fear for her—

but you shall not leave this house until I am ready to let you go.'

Sarah's hand crept to her throat. What was he talking about?

'I do not understand you, sir. I must go home. My husband will be waiting for me.'

'So that you can tell him what you have discovered?' Sir Andrew's eyes narrowed. 'Did that stupid girl tell you it all? I know she suspected me…Andrea must have told her that I had threatened I would kill her if she shamed me again. She was going to leave her husband…she would have shamed us both by going to *him!* I warned her that I would not stand for it, but she refused to listen. She told me that she had made up her mind and that nothing I said or did would stop her…so I had to do it.' His eyes took on a haunted look, as if he were reliving that moment by the river.

'You grabbed hold of her,' Sarah said, for his confession had not surprised her. 'She struggled and then she slipped, falling into the river.' She raised her eyes to his. 'Why did you not try to save her? You must have known that she had a fear of water.'

'Yes, that is how it was,' he said and a shudder ran through him. 'I never intended that she should die…just that she should behave, be my little girl again…'

'But why did you start those wicked lies?' Sarah asked. 'If you knew the truth, why did you try to make others believe that John had driven Andrea to take her own life?'

'It was his fault!' Sir Andrew said, his eyes glittering with hatred. 'If he had cared for her as he ought, made her happy, she would not have thought of leaving him for that worthless rogue…'

'But it was you that made her unhappy,' Sarah said—it had suddenly become very clear in her mind. 'You sent her to John to ask for his help, because he was your friend and you knew that he would do the decent thing as he saw it. Andrea didn't want to do it, but you made her. You were angry with her and you continued to punish her after she was married. You made her hate her home, and you were angry with her, because she had seen her lover again. And then, when she would not listen to you, you killed her. You stood by and watched her drown. And now you are haunted by your guilt…you cannot forgive yourself for what you did…'

'You think yourself so clever…' Sir Andrew's eyes narrowed with a mixture of anger and hatred. His guilt and pain had driven him to the edge of despair over the past months, and now it had all boiled up into a black rage. 'Why should he have you when I have nothing?'

Suddenly, his hands were at her throat, pressing so tightly that she could not breathe. She was choking as everything went black around her. And then just as she thought that she was dying, there was a shot and his hands fell away from her throat. She stumbled backward as he let her go, collapsing on the floor as he crashed down, pinning her body to the rich Persian carpet, his blood seeping from the wound to his head.

She lay unmoving, barely conscious for a few moments, then the door to the parlour was thrust opened as two men rushed in. One of them knelt beside her, his hands running over her face as the other hauled Sir Andrew's crushing weight from her.

'Oh, my God,' John cried. 'Are we too late? Sarah? Sarah, my love, speak to me.'

'It's his blood, not hers,' Daniel said. 'Someone must have shot him—through the window by the look of it, for there is glass on the floor.'

'John…' Sarah opened her eyes, looking up at him. Her voice was a hoarse whisper as she tried to tell him what had happened. 'He killed Andrea. When he realised that I knew, he tried to strangle me…and then…' She gave a cry of fear as she saw Sir Andrew's body lying near her. 'Someone shot him and he fell on me…'

'It is all right, my darling,' John told her. 'He is

dead. He won't harm you ever again. I promise you are safe now.' He helped her up, leading her to a chair and easing her into it. Sarah was aware of other people in the room now, but her throat was sore and all she could think of was the look in Sir Andrew's eyes as he tried to kill her.

Someone handed Sarah a glass of brandy and water. She took a few sips but it stung her throat and made her choke. 'Just water, please…' she rasped.

The glass was replaced, she drank a little and the room steadied. She became aware of John and Daniel, of the elderly man who had opened the door to her, a maid and another man.

'I shot him,' the man was saying. 'I escaped from those fools you set to guard me, Elworthy, and I came straight here. He killed Andrea, because she would have shamed him by leaving you for me, and I wanted my revenge. I don't care if they hang me. I haven't much to live for. But he was trying to kill your wife. If I hadn't shot him when I did, you would have been too late. I saved her life.'

'It would have been better if we could have given him over to the law,' John said, a grim line to his mouth, 'but I thank you for what you did, Sergeant Rathbone. Sarah is alive thanks to you.' He placed his hand on her shoulder. 'I am so sorry, my darling. I should have warned you never to come here—why did you? Was it because of the letters that I found in your drawer?'

'Letters?' Sarah was puzzled. 'Oh, those letters. Ruth gave them to me this morning, because *he* made her. No, I did not mean to come here, John. My mare lost a shoe. I did not know that he lived here or I might not have come. I did not expect him to attack me, but I knew he did not like me.' Her voice was no more than a croak and she put a hand to her throat. 'Forgive me, I cannot talk more for the moment.'

'Take her home, John,' Daniel said. 'You can leave this to me, my friend. I shall sort it out and I'll come to your house when I've finished here.'

'Yes, thank you,' John said, helping Sarah to rise, his arm about her waist. 'I have a carriage waiting outside, my love. Do not try to talk. You must rest and let your throat ease. We shall talk when you are feeling better.'

Sarah leaned her head against his shoulder. Seeing that she was nearly exhausted by her ordeal, John swept her up into his arms and carried her out to the carriage. He placed her on the seat and then climbed in beside her, pulling her to him so that she rested against him as the carriage moved off.

'Sleep now, my dearest one,' he told her. 'When you are better we shall talk of all the things I ought to have said and did not…'

'I never believed the letters,' Sarah said. 'I love you, John…'

'Rest, my love,' John said. 'We have all the time in the world to talk.'

'How is Sarah now?' Daniel asked when he arrived three hours later. 'I have spoken to the magistrate, John, and I don't think we shall have too much trouble. Rathbone told him that he had shot Sir Andrew because he was trying to strangle Sarah. I explained the whole to him, and he told me that he had known something wasn't quite right with Walton for a while. They meet now and then in York apparently, and he believes that Sir Andrew has been going downhill since his daughter's death. Rathbone has been told to hold himself available in case he is wanted for further questioning, but that seems to be an end to it.'

'Sarah is sleeping,' John said. 'Mrs Raven made her a soothing tisane for her throat and she drifted off almost immediately. I was sitting with her, but I saw you arrive and came down at once. It is a relief to me to know that it is all over. I was afraid that he would try to harm Sarah, as I told you earlier. Now at last I can relax my vigil. I owe Rathbone a debt I can never repay—and should he need it, I shall hire the very best lawyers to defend him.'

'I doubt it will be needed,' Daniel said and smiled at him. 'We have all the evidence Tobbold gathered, Rathbone's story—and I think Sarah will probably provide all the missing links when she is able to talk again. When the truth comes out everyone will say that they always knew you were innocent, and your friends will mean it.'

'Thank you,' John said. 'You have been a good friend in this, Daniel.'

'You, Charles and I stand together in these things,' Daniel said. 'I think we can genuinely say that all three of us have had to walk through hell and fire these past few years, but with good fortune it is over now and we may put it all behind us.'

'I truly hope so,' John said. 'I hope that this will not have been too much for Sarah. She has been though such a lot one way and another.'

'Sarah is a very brave lady,' Daniel said. 'And now I must go home to another brave lady, John. Elizabeth awaits me—and you are needed upstairs. You should be there when Sarah wakes, my friend. She will need to have you with her and to know that she is loved. As for the rest, only time will tell.'

Sarah woke to see the sun filtering in through half-drawn curtains. She stretched and yawned, wondering why she was in John's bed, and then she saw him enter from his dressing room, clad only in a shirt and riding breeches and she smiled.

'Are you going riding, John?'

'Perhaps later,' he said. 'There are a few things I need to do, but only if you are feeling well enough for me to leave you.'

'I am quite well,' Sarah said. She sounded slightly husky and she could feel a little soreness in her throat, but it was bearable. 'You will not stay away too long? I need to talk to you.'

'We shall talk first if you wish,' John said. 'I shall not be long in any case. I have been busy since we came home, but most of that was because I had to protect you, Sarah. I had always suspected Sir Andrew of writing those letters, and of paying someone to leave Andrea's things in my rooms—but I did not think it was he who shot at me in Scotland, and I was right.'

'Sit here and tell me,' Sarah said patting the bed. 'I have sensed things, pieced them together in my mind, but I do not know it all.'

'Andrea had a lover—the man who shot Sir Andrew and saved your life,' John said and Sarah nodded in understanding. 'It took us a while to catch him, but finally we did and I questioned him. He knew nothing of the letters, but he did fire a shot at you and then at me in Scotland.'

'Because he suspected that you had killed Andrea,' Sarah said. 'Yes, I understand why he would hate us—but why was he at Sir Andrew's house?'

'Because after we talked, we both knew that it must have been Sir Andrew,' John said. 'Rathbone was determined to kill him and he gave Tobbold's men the slip somehow…and I am very glad he did, my darling. Daniel and I came here first. I wanted to warn you about Sir Andrew, and then I found those letters…'

'Ruth gave them to me this morning.' Sarah explained Ruth's story and her reasons for doing what Andrea's father demanded. 'I believe she had some idea that Andrea's father might have had something to do with her death, though she did not say it in so many words. I have promised that we will discover if any letters have come for her from Richard Palmer. You will do it, John?'

'By rights she should be dismissed for what she has done,' John said, looking angry, 'but, yes, I shall do it because you ask if of me, my darling. I would do anything you asked, Sarah. When I thought he had killed you I was desperate. I should have had nothing to live for if you were dead, my love.'

'Yes, I know, John.' Any lingering doubt that he had married her because she had compromised herself dissolved like the morning mist. She reached out to touch his cheek. The scars left by his illness were still there, but not quite as livid as they had been at the start. They might fade a little in time, but, like the mental scars she still carried from the past, they did not matter. 'I love you so much, John, and we are so lucky. We must be kind to others less fortunate.'

'You are always so generous,' John told her. 'But Palmer is alive and he may have written to her. Ruth has a right to any letters he sent her and I shall investigate.'

'Thank you,' Sarah said and frowned. 'I looked at some of the correspondence Ruth brought me, John, and then put it away. I was shocked, but also a little puzzled by something. I intended to give them to you when you returned. What made you look for them?'

'The drawer was slightly open and I could smell Andrea's perfume,' he said. 'I thought someone was playing a trick on you—and in a way I was right. Andrea wrote only one of those letters. The rest were forged and meant to distress you.'

'Ah, yes, I thought the hand was slightly different, though it could have been illness that made it less legible. I suppose they were written by her father,' Sarah said. 'I think his grief and his guilt drove him near mad in the end, John. I was looking at a miniature of her at his house, and I think it was talking of her that finally caused him to crack.'

John nodded, 'May God forgive him for what he did to her—and what he almost did to you.' John's voice broke. 'If it had not been for Rathbone…'

'Hush, my love,' Sarah comforted him. 'I am safe and you are with me. As long as I have your love I can face anything.'

'You truly mean that?' John asked. 'All the whispers and the lies—that devil's attack on you—you can forgive and love me still?'

'You were not to blame for any of those things,' Sarah said and laughed softly. 'I blame you for only one thing, John.'

'And that is?' His eyes were anxious as he looked at her, but she was smiling, teasing him.

'For leaving me to sleep alone since we came home,' she said and caught his hand. 'Promise me that you will not continue to neglect me.'

'I promise willingly,' John said. 'I tried to keep my distance, thinking that if Sir Andrew's spy told him that I neglected you he might stay his hand as far as you were concerned. But then you came to me and put your arms about me, and I knew that it was useless to try and deceive him. But it also meant that I was forced to redouble my efforts to discover who had been shooting at us. I suspected that there were two different men involved in this business and I had to find out who was the more dangerous of the pair.'

'Then you are forgiven,' Sarah said, 'but I shall expect a visit this night, my husband.'

'And you shall receive it,' John promised, bending to kiss her on the mouth. 'But now I really do have to go…'

Sarah turned in her husband's arms. They had made love again and again the previous night, released at last from the doubts and fears that had hung over them all these weeks.

'Are you awake, Sarah?' John whispered close to her ear. 'I have been watching you sleep. You are so beautiful when you sleep…'

'I was dreaming,' Sarah said and snuggled up to him, inhaling the slightly salty scent of his skin. 'We were together in a garden bright with flowers and there were children playing nearby. I think they were our children, John.'

'Did that make you happy, my love?'

'Yes.' She looked up at him as he pushed himself up on his elbow, gazing down at her face, looking into her eyes. 'Yes, it made me very happy. I think that we have a wonderful future waiting for us, John. I have been thinking about the house, the changes I want to make—and the gardens too. We should plan those together, have them landscaped properly. This is a wonderful old house, and it should be cherished and lavished with care and love. It will become a home that we can be proud of—a home that our children will grow up in and be proud to bring their own children to one day.'

'Then that is what we shall do,' John said and touched her cheek with one fingertip. 'Whenever I went to Daniel's home, or to others of my friends, I used to envy them. Their houses seemed so full of light and warmth and happiness. When I came back here I was aware that it was dark and full of shadows, but I did not know what to do to change it. I married Andrea because she needed help, but also because I was lonely and empty. I thought that she would help, but she withdrew from me more and more, especially after the child was born. It may have been my fault or perhaps…' He shook his head. 'That is over. I have you now, the woman I truly love—and between us we shall make a family.'

'Yes, we shall, my love,' Sarah said and drew her down to him. He began to kiss her, softly at first, gently, but then the hunger flared between them and their passion swept them away to another place where there was nothing but the beating of two hearts and the sweet rhythm of bodies perfectly attuned. 'I love you so much, John…always with all my heart.'

'And I love you, my dearest Sarah,' he murmured. 'My soulmate, my lovely wife…'

Sarah gave herself up to the pleasure of loving. All the doubts and fears of the past years were swept away by the white heat of their passion as they moved together, holding each other close.

## Chapter Twelve

Sarah took a last look at the dining table before going to change for the evening. It was their first real party and she wanted everything to be perfect. The long mahogany table was set with gleaming silver, crystal glass, beautiful porcelain and garlands of flowers that twined along the centre. She moved one glass a tiny fraction, and then stepped back, well pleased that it was all as she had ordered it.

'May I have a word with you, Mrs Elworthy?'

Sarah turned to see Ruth standing a little way off and smiled. The girl was perfectly amenable these days, though she sometimes thought she wasn't quite happy.

'Yes, of course you may, Ruth. What was it you wanted to say?'

'I have had another letter from Mr Palmer, Mrs Elworthy. After I had the first of his letters, which Mr Elworthy found for me, I wrote to Richard, telling him that I had a job here and that you had been kind to me—but also that we had almost starved after he left us. He has sent me money and asked me to go out to him. He says that we shall be married.'

'Ruth!' Sarah stared at her in surprise. 'That is news indeed. Do you wish to leave us and go to the West Indies?'

'Yes, I think so, ma'am,' Ruth said. 'Richard says that he has a good house—not a big beautiful house like this, but adequate. I think it would be better for my daughter to know her father.'

'Yes, of course,' Sarah agreed. 'If it is what you want, you must go.'

'Thank you, ma'am. I shall leave after your house-guests have gone next week. I wouldn't let you down while you are entertaining, though you have more than enough servants here now. Mrs Raven says that she had to turn two girls away this morning.'

'Yes, we have all we need these days,' Sarah said. 'But I shall miss you, Ruth. I think we have come to like each other now, don't you?'

'Yes, Mrs Elworthy,' Ruth said, her face glowing. 'I wouldn't leave you for another employer—but to be Richard's wife, that is something I have dreamed of.'

'Yes, I am sure it is,' Sarah said, smiling at her. 'It is a good opportunity for you, Ruth, and I wish you every happiness.'

'If I could be half as happy as you, I should think

myself lucky,' Ruth told her. 'Mr Palmer isn't Mr Elworthy. I think he may not always treat me as he ought—but I am willing to take the risk for my daughter's sake.'

'Then I wish you good fortune,' Sarah said. 'Come to me before you leave and I shall give you a present.'

'Thank you, ma'am. You have been very kind.'

Sarah nodded to her and Ruth went her way. She looked at the table again, and then went out into the hall and made her way along the landing to her own apartments. Ellie was there laying out her gown for the evening. It was a midnight blue silk and trimmed with exquisite Brussels lace at the neck. Ellie smiled as Sarah walked in, two King Charles spaniels at her heels. John had asked her what she wanted as a birthday gift. Sarah had asked for the dogs, and the sound of their scampering feet meant that these days the house was never silent.

'This is a lovely dress, ma'am,' Ellie said as her mistress came to look at it. 'I think it becomes you as well as anything you have.'

'But will it fit me?' Sarah said. 'Were you able to make those adjustments that I asked?'

'Yes, quite easily,' Ellie said and smiled at her. 'I have added a ribbon band here and there, but it does not look out of place. Try it on and see what you think.'

'If it does not fit, I am in trouble,' Sarah said with

a rueful laugh. 'Most of my dresses are a little tight. I think I must have some more made soon.'

'Yes, ma'am, for you are bound to expand a great deal over the next few months…'

'Yes, I am,' Sarah agreed and laughed. The excitement was in her eyes, because she was sure enough of her secret now to share it with her friends. She had told John as soon as she suspected that she was with child, but he had already guessed. She wondered if Elizabeth might also have guessed, but she had not seen many of her friends for some months, though Tilda had come to stay with her for a few weeks late in the summer, before returning to town. 'It is exciting, Ellie, but also a little frightening. I know Arabella has her little girl and is perfectly well again, but the first time is a little unnerving.'

'Oh, you should not be frightened,' Ellie said. 'There were nine of us at home before my mother stopped having babies. She said there was nothing in the world easier, though she made enough fuss for an hour or two—but afterwards, when the babe is in your arms…well, Ma says you forget all the rest.'

'Yes, I am certain of it,' Sarah said. 'I do not truly mind, Ellie. I am looking forward to a big family. We want at least two boys and two girls.'

'Well, you'll have to see what God sends you,' Ellie said, laughing as she lifted the gown over

Sarah's head and smoothed the full skirts down on her hips. The buttons at the back of the bodice did up easily, and because of the style she did not look in the least fat, though her face had a certain bloom that advertised her feeling of contentment.

'Yes, that is well done, Ellie,' Sarah said approvingly. 'I cannot see what you have altered so I am sure that no one else will. I am very pleased with it.'

'Thank you, ma'am,' the girl said. 'It is a pleasure to do things for you, Mrs Elworthy.'

'Thank you, Ellie.'

Sarah sat while her maid arranged her hair in a becoming style that left one fair ringlet hanging over her shoulder, the bulk of her hair piled high in curls on her head. She had just finished the task when the door leading through to John's dressing room opened and he came in.

'Am I too early?' he asked. 'I can come back if you are not ready, my love.'

'Mrs Elworthy is ready apart from her jewels, sir,' Ellie said. 'I can return later if I am needed.'

'You will not be needed until later tonight,' Sarah said, and the girl bobbed a curtsy before going out. John came to stand behind Sarah, placing one hand on her shoulder as he looked at her in the small dressing mirror.

'Have I told you recently that you are beautiful?'

Sarah twisted her head on one side. 'I am not sure if it was this morning or yesterday—but much too long anyway.'

John laughed and bent to kiss the back of her neck, which made her tingle. 'I have a gift for you, Sarah. Shall I put it on for you?'

'Yes, please,' she said, smiling as he placed a diamond-and-sapphire choker around her throat. She touched the magnificent necklace, thinking how well it set off her gown. 'Are these the Elworthy sapphires, John?'

'Yes. I inherited them from my grandmother. My brother has the bulk of the family jewels, of course, but my grandmother left all her personal estate to me. I had them reset for you, Sarah. They came back from the jeweller today. They are more attractive now, I think. Do you like them?'

She touched a hand to the glittering jewels. 'They are exquisite, John. Thank you for having them done for me. They are exactly what I need tonight with this gown. I was wondering whether to wear the pearls or diamonds, but these are very grand.'

'They are my gift to say thank you for transforming this house into a home,' John said, giving her a loving smile. 'I still walk into rooms that used to be dull and dark and wonder how you did it—but you have and I am very grateful.'

'I learned about design and elegance in Italy,' Sarah said. 'Some of the houses there were very grand, but also tasteful…and that is what I wanted for our home, a mixture of elegance and warmth. Guests must be able to sit down and feel comfortable, but it is nice to have elegance in some of the rooms—to create light and air.'

'Yes, and that is what you have done,' John told her. 'You have brought light to this house that was filled with shadows.'

'We have blown them all away,' Sarah said and stood up, moving into his arms and leaning up to kiss him on the lips. 'Soon we shall have our child, John—a playmate for our darling Nathaniel.'

'You don't mind that he is thought by most people to be my first-born? I shall of course divide my estate when our children are older. And naturally Sir Andrew's land has come to Nathaniel. He will grow up to expect that he inherits that, but everything else must be shared between all our children for there is no entail on my inheritance.'

'Shall you tell him the truth one day?'

'Perhaps, if I think he is able to understand it without being distressed. But whatever the future brings, he will know that he is loved—our child in all but blood.'

'We must pray that it is enough for him. I have some

money of my own,' Sarah said. 'As you know, Arabella settled ten thousand pounds on me when she married, and I have what my father left in trust for me, which is a similar amount. I want you to use some of it to buy more land, John. Something close by us that you can manage with the help of your bailiff.'

'Yes, you would,' he said, understanding her mind. 'We must protect all our children.'

'I do not want there to be quarrels one day,' she said and looked up at him. 'But our guests will be waiting, John. Arabella could not stop praising the house when she saw it, and even Mama was impressed. I think she may finally be won over when I tell her my news.'

'Are you going to tell her this evening?'

'Yes, I think so,' Sarah said. 'You don't mind?'

'Of course not,' he said and looked at her indulgently. 'I am hoping that this visit will bring me Mrs Hunter's approval at last.'

'Oh, I am sure it will,' Sarah replied, laughing at him. Her happiness was so great that nothing could mar it, and besides, she knew that her mother had already mellowed towards John, was beginning to approve of his quiet ways and gentle manners that hid nerves of steel. She slipped her arm through his and looked up at him. 'Come, my dearest, let us go and greet our guests…'

* * *

Sarah glanced around her long dining table, looking at the happy faces of her guests. They had all suffered. Elizabeth had been kidnapped and might have died had her beloved Daniel not arrived to save her at the right moment. Arabella had been alone and lonely until Charles came into her life. She too had been at risk from the spite of evil men, but Charles, John and Captain Hernshaw had saved her. Sarah had escaped a fearful kidnap only to wander friendless, her memory gone, until Arabella and dear Nana had taken her in. She had had to wait some years before finding happiness, but now, despite all that had gone before, she and John had found the life of peace and content that both had wanted.

Getting to her feet, Sarah lifted her glass. 'It is such a happy day, to see all my friends and loved ones gathered about this table,' she said. 'Arabella, I owe you so much. Without you and Nana I might have died. Charles is my dearly loved brother, who has done so much for me. Elizabeth and Daniel have been such good friends that I do not know how we should go on without them. And my dearest Mama…who has, I believe, forgiven me at last. Tilda, and everyone else. I want to thank you all for coming to stay and I should like to tell you our news, which I think Elizabeth has already guessed. John and I are to have our first child. So now I should like you all to toast the future…happiness and love to us all…'

John stood and raised his glass to her from the other end of the table, her friends getting to their feet to raise their glasses aloft.

'To love and happiness,' Elizabeth said. 'Your news has given us all great pleasure, Sarah.'

'To Sarah…and John,' Mrs Hunter said. 'May you always be as joyful as you are today.'

Charles, Daniel and John raised their glasses.

'To friendship and the ladies we love,' they said as one. 'May we all live in love and peace together…'

# HISTORICAL ROMANCE™

LARGE PRINT

## THE WICKED EARL
### *Margaret McPhee*

The very proper Miss Langley does not know what she has done to encourage the attentions of a lord, only that they are most unwanted and very improper! So when a handsome stranger saves her from his clutches, Madeline is too relieved to suspect that her tall, dark defender may have a less than reputable reputation…

## WORKING MAN, SOCIETY BRIDE
### *Mary Nichols*

Well over six feet tall, with broad shoulders, he was the most good-looking man Lady Lucinda Vernley had ever seen. But with her family expecting her to make a good marriage, it wouldn't do to be fantasising about a man she had seen working on her father's estate… Myles Moorcroft certainly didn't dress like a gentleman, but by his manner there was something about him that had Lucy intrigued…

## TRAITOR OR TEMPTRESS
### *Helen Dickson*

Lorne McBryde can't abide the savage violence of the Highlands, and desperately seeks a means to escape. Her wilful streak is countered by her instinctive kindness – yet for Iain Monroe, Earl of Norwood, she will be marked forever by her family's betrayal. Kidnapped in the dead of night, Lorne is now in Iain's hands. She protests her innocence – but does her tempting beauty hide a treacherous spirit?

MILLS & BOON®

*Live the emotion*